#tractor4

1608

A diary highlighting the plight of Mr H and his desire to own a tractor

Joanne 'New-Shoes' Hughes

Copyright © 2016

Book cover designed by: Nick White Writing

For Hug-Bug...

I know that I take the piss out of you but there is no one else that I would rather have spent the last 25 years with and the next 25 years.

Love you today xxx

Introduction

Let me set the scene... (and don't think about skipping this bit. It is important background for the rest of the book and if you don't read it you will have no idea about what's going on).

I am 42 years old and live with Graham (or Mr H as I often call him) in an old farmhouse in Staffordshire. We have a Wolverhampton postcode and Mr H insists on telling everyone that we meet that we do not live in Wolverhampton. I do the opposite, mostly just to rile him. It might be helpful when reading this book if you try and do it in a 'faint Brummie' accent. I'm not a Brummie but all my Southern friends think that I have a Brummie accent.

We have about two acres of land on which Scooby the cockerel, chicks and ducks live. And we are just about to buy another two acres so that George and William the Alpacas can come and live with us. We started naming our chicks and ducks after our friends but we have stopped doing that as it's a bit depressing when they die and we have to tell their namesake.

The Farmer still lives next door to us in his converted pig barn and is 93 years old. The glint in his eye tells us that he's 33. He will often happen to be wandering through the farm when the girls with their horses are in their tight jodhpurs. The farmer was 83 when we bought the house from him. I think that he saw Mr H as a new apprentice as he decided to get some sheep shortly after we moved in. He had always had pigs and turkeys and fancied giving sheep a try. What he meant by that was that he would buy the sheep and Mr H could be the shepherd and look after them.

Mr H and I have been together 25 years (for those of you good at maths, we met when I was 17) and have been doing up the house for the last 11 years. In Mr H's words, "You can't rush these things." I'm much more organised and a 'strike while the iron is hot' kind of a girl. Although, I do think that we need to come up with more modern phrases these days, so maybe 'write while the Wi-Fi is working' would be more appropriate?

I think though that the 25 years has taken its toll as I have become suspicious lately that Mr H is trying to kill me… really it should be me wanting to kill him. 25 years of putting up with 'man-logic' and 'man-nonsense' is enough for any woman.

Mr H has a son from his previous marriage who got married in our paddock last year. I am the youngest of three children. My sister is four years older than me and my brother is the middle child. Mr H is also the middle child in his family... I'll just leave a pregnant pause there. I am lucky that I still have my Mum and Dad in my life. I call Mum 'Mummykins' and she has been a star as she has read through each bit as I've written it.

I also have two quasi-little sisters. We used to live next door to Nicky* and have known her since she was seven. She moved to Wolverhampton as an adult, so luckily I got to see her again regularly for a good number of years. My other sort-of-little sister is 'Little Wren'. I met her belly dancing (before we got kicked out of class for being too loud) and we often go away together. You'll find that she is in a number of these tales.

* The only real names in this book are mine and Mr H's — oh and the pets as well. Everyone else's names have been changed to protect the innocent.

We have two black and white rescue border collies. Lucy is 15 and a half years old and has tablets for her legs to keep her upright, syrup for her wee-valve so that she doesn't wet herself (I don't think it is called a wee-valve but I don't know the technical name) and sprinkles to keep her poo firm (apologies to the squeamish). In the vet's words she is a walking pharmacy. Personally, I think she is a walking money pit... but I love her to bits and if it means that I have to dock Mr H's pocket money to pay for her meds then it's a sacrifice I'm willing to make. Bonnie is 11 and a half years old and is also known as 'my furry psycho' as she was abused by a previous owner and has issues. On the plus side she does not rattle like Lucy as she takes no medicine.

Lucy is a typical Border Collie. She likes to round up other animals, will drop into the 'stalking' pose and once went head to head with a ram and won. Lucy will lie outside in all weathers and loves to watch the geese on the moat. Oh yes, that reminds me, I forgot to tell you that our farmhouse is so old that it has a moat that runs three quarters of the way around the house. I'm not sure what happened to the other quarter. They're quite tight around here so maybe they couldn't be bothered to shell out for the other quarter to be done?

Bonnie is not a typical Border Collie. She doesn't like to round up other animals, will not drop into the stalking pose and was traumatised when we showed her the sheep. She is a typical pampered pet and that is all she aspires to be. She likes to be with us at all times and does not like lying outside. She hates the rain. Occasionally though she does like to remind the local foxes that this is her land and will chase them if she sees them.

Casper the black and white cat joined our family about four years ago (we like to colour code our pets) and is also known as 'TSK', which stands for 'The Serial Killer'. His most prized victims to date have been two squirrels. He has a white moustache on his all-black face and we think that he should have been named 'Monsieur Poirot'. Like the Belgian detective, he is a sneaky little devil. He steals any food that he can get his paws on.

I remember once calling to Mr H from the kitchen, "Casper's been licking the gravy".

Mr H called back, "How do you know? Is his face brown?"

"No, his head is stuck in the gravy jug."

Dad made me a big kennel for Lucy and Bonnie two years ago. Unfortunately for them they rarely get a look in now as Casper has firmly decided that the kennel belongs to him.

It is well known on Facebook and in our circle of friends that Mr H wants a tractor. I've told him that if I become an international bestseller then he can have one (I think it's safe to say that he's not getting one). Tractors are ridiculously expensive things and even if they are 40 years old they still cost a fortune. This is why he isn't having one unless this book sells. #tractor4graham has become a well-used tag line by our friends.

So why am I writing this book (apart from the tractor-thing)? I started to write 'tales from...' as my status updates on Facebook and around 11 of my friends said,

'You should write a book'. (The rest of them really couldn't give a s**t.)

The tales are me recounting funny things that have happened to me when out and about and at home too. One of my favourite pastimes is 'people watching', or as my mum would say I am genetically nosy. I happily remind her that it comes from her side of the family, as well as the alcoholism (more on that later). What I inherited from Dad's side of the family is my work ethic and my double chin. I look nothing like Mum but have inherited her ability to sleep well. This is something for which I am extremely grateful.

The friends that told me to write a book got me thinking as to how I could combine my love of writing with raising money for the elusive tractor. If these 11 friends buy my book then Mr H can at least have a toy tractor and if by some miracle I become an international bestseller then I promise to buy him a real one (no pressure people).

Now for the boring part... what do I actually do for a 'proper' job? I work for myself and I provide training for adults. This involves me travelling to 'smelly'* London, amongst other places and the rest of the time I get to work from home writing my training materials. Mr H seems to like it when I go away, although I like to think that he secretly misses me. It's just such a deep secret that he's forgotten to share it with himself.

* Just to be clear as to why I call it 'smelly' London. I have been travelling there for most of my working life and I have always noticed how different the air is there compared with rural Staffordshire. When I am in London, I have to wash my hair every day and when I blow my nose what comes out is a very strange colour which I can only conclude is from a concoction of vehicle fumes and pollution. According to the Evening Standard, 100 people a week die from pollution in London. Personally, I am more likely to be killed crossing the road, as I am very accident prone. You will read about my accident-proneness later in the book.

When I am in 'smelly' London I sometimes have the company of my work wife, Alexandra*.

* Remember – that's not her real name. I call her my 'work wife' because she often works in London and when we coincide we stay in the same hotel together.

Alexandra shares the same sense of humour as me and love of skiing and shopping for skiing equipment and clothes. I think everyone should have a work spouse and she is the finest. We often go on holiday with her and her husband. It gets very confusing when we are on holiday and try and explain to people the spouse and work-spouse relationships.

You also need to know that I'm not naturally bright. I don't understand Physics and although I got an 'A' in my GCSE, I just learned what to write in order to do well. It just goes to show how useful our education system is. Conversely, Mr H is very good at Science, so he teaches me what I need to know about Physics and *MacGyver* on CBS Action teaches me what I need to know about Chemistry. I generally update my general knowledge by watching *Pointless* on BBC1. I, conversely, teach Mr H about English and why you need punctuation in a page full of words. We complement each other well.

We also have very defined roles in life. I cannot make a nice cup of tea for love nor money. Although to be truthful if someone did offer me a million pounds then I would probably try harder (or subcontract to someone that can make one). Making tea shouldn't be a tricky concept but it appears to have bypassed my capabilities. As a consequence Mr H makes all the tea in this house. Conversely, Mr H can never get served at a bar in a pub. He stands at the end of the bar doing some sort of 'winking, moving of the head' manoeuvre which results in the female bar staff avoiding him like the plague and whispering to each other, "Perv at the end of the bar".

Mr H isn't a big drinker. This is one of the main reasons that I married him. The rule that I have when going out is 'If it's dinner with my family, then I'm allowed to drink and if we go out with your family, then I'm allowed to drink.' It's a good rule to live by and if Mr H deviates from it, I remind him that it was in our vows.

When I go shopping I reference everything to the cost of a Starbucks latte (now that I'm a Costa* girl, I should really change it, but given that Starbucks is more expensive for coffees, the analogy works better to keep it as it is). What I mean by this is if I see a top in Primark for three quid then I will justify buying it by saying, "Well, it's only one Starbucks latte," and if it's six quid then it will be, "Well, it's only two Starbucks lattes." I think you get the gist.

* As Costa generally have toilet paper in their loos when I go in, I now prefer to buy coffee from them. (You'll see more on my 'toilet issues' later.)

Doing maths in my head is also something that seems to have escaped me. This is something that my work wife and I definitely have in common. She will swear blind that 1/5 is 25%. Thank goodness we only have to split a bill in half when we are together in London. I'm kidding of course. We take alternate turns to pay...

Mr H and I are quite similar in some respects, which makes for a harmonious marriage. We both love watching *The Big Bang Theory* (Sheldon Cooper is a guilty pleasure) and *8 Simple Rules* and we love *Criminal Minds*. Let's face it, *Criminal Minds* has something for everyone; Derek

Morgan for the girls and JJ for the boys. There is also a rule in our house that Mr H can criticise any programme that he likes on TV but he is not allowed to criticise *Criminal Minds*, ever.

What does drive me insane though is that Mr H's bedtime choice of TV is watching *UK Parliament*. Once, I lost to 'Rock, Paper, Scissors, Lizard, Spock' and we ended up watching some politics show on Channel 4 and Mr H spent most of it explaining 'socialism' to me. I find this wrist-slitting telly.

I'm ashamed to say that I have little interest in politics and I get my daily fix of current events from Facebook. The most uplifting thing to have happened when I started writing this book was the vote for the research ship with 'Boaty McBoatface' being the favourite in the running. I do also like to keep abreast of what is happening on Facebook. Once Facebook sent me an email to say that I had been inactive for 11 hours and was I ok? It's like having a second mum really.

I am most definitely not a 'morning person'. I need at least two hours on the settee after I wake up along with two large lattes before I can function for the day. I think that our Postman is convinced that a) I don't work, b) have some awful incurable illness or c) am just totally lazy. I generally don't get dressed until after 10am. I don't think that he has ever seen me in daytime clothes.

What you also need to know before reading any further is that these tales are what I call 'fact-ion'. They are based on true events but given that a lot of what happens is how I see or perceive a situation then there is the element of poetic licence (OK.... a LOT of poetic licence). And to be frank, if I didn't add the embellishments, then this book would also be wrist-slitting to read...

Note for the professionally offended: The book is not meant to offend but is meant to make you chuckle. A lot of what I see and describe is meant as tongue in cheek. I just hope that at times I make you chuckle and if not then Mr H won't get his tractor. So not to lay blame but it is totally all your fault!

Seriously though (as I can be occasionally), I hope you enjoy my tales and if you do then my mission is complete.

Monday 14th March – the day after my birthday

Mission for today:

- *Get Bonnie booked in at the vets*

I promised the 11 people that have encouraged me to write this book that I would start writing as soon as we came back from holiday. This is that day. Not much has actually happened today but on my to-do list I need to get Bonnie booked in at the vets for some dental work. I'm a bit surprised that it isn't Lucy that needs the work as her breath is disgusting. But then she does eat Bonnie's poo and horse manure, so that could be why. Whilst I was looking at dates to get her booked in it reminded me of the previous two visits to the vets that didn't exactly go to plan.

Tales from the vets...

Last month it was time to booster up the pets for another year. Sitting in reception reminded me as to how serious some owners take these visits. 'Brandy' came in fully made-up tottering on her high heels with 'Precious' the Shih Tzu* in tow, sporting a pink bow in her hair. I felt like a new mum on the first day of school and knew that I had failed as a fur mummy.

* I originally spelt this as 'shit zoo' but thought it didn't look right...

Looking at Bonnie, I wished that I had brushed her and to make matters worse Bonnie started barking at Precious. I hoped the conversation went something like, 'Dude, you look really stupid in that bow.' I tried to ignore the sympathetic looks that Brandy kept giving me, whilst twirling her hair with her hand and re-applying her lipstick. Thankfully Casper hadn't weed and pooed in the cat carrier on this occasion (see below) and luckily the vet 'Henry' wasn't running too late so I quickly escaped from the waiting room.

Henry and I chatted about our normal topics of conversation which involved skiing and the forthcoming additions to our family of George and William the Alpacas.

As well as their boosters, Bonnie needed her anal glands releasing. She looked like she was about to bite Henry as he was trying not to gag from the smell but luckily I managed to use a headlock technique that I had been developing in case Mr H needed injections in his eye (more on this in a bit) so that Bonnie didn't bite him as he released them. In all honesty if someone tried to release mine, then I think I might try and bite them too... unless it was Henry the vet... but I digress. Henry warned me that Bonnie might try and rub her bottom on the car on the journey back and asked if I had anything to put down and that I would probably need to clean the car out when I got back home. I happily told him that we were in Mr H's car and that he didn't like me messing with it, so I would leave that for him to sort when he got back from work.

Lucy's leg tablets have gone up by 20p each, so she now costs £70 a month to keep her vertical, which is about the same amount that I spend on liquor each month to keep me horizontal. Life's ironies...

At least this time's visit wasn't quite as stressful as the last time that I went. On that occasion Casper and Lucy were both in the car with me. Lucy needed a check-up so that I could re-order her meds and Casper had had a fight with a squirrel and won but unfortunately had been bitten on the cheek in the process. It had turned septic, puffed into a great big ball and exploded all over the kitchen floor the night before.

To make sure that he didn't infect it further I had kept him in overnight in anticipation of the trip to the vets. Obviously the litter tray was not his usual toilet (he normally goes in the Farmer's back garden) so he had held it in. As the 20 minute journey to the vets was about five minutes in, Casper decided that he could no longer hold in his poo and I was sniffing the air with a, 'Where is that smell coming from?' I finally worked out that it was coming from the cat carrier. Another give away was

Casper clinging to the front of the carrier trying not to lie in it.

I pulled over into the layby on the A449 and used one of Lucy's doggy poo bags to try and scoop it up. So there's me trying not to heave from the smell and simultaneously trying to get the poo out of the carrier whilst trying to stop Casper from escaping, otherwise Lucy would surely eat him. Being a woman I can thankfully multi task, so with dog and cat both in one piece we continued on our journey.

As we got closer to the vets I started to smell something else and once again Casper was clinging to the front of the carrier trying to avoid the big puddle of wee now sloshing at the bottom of the cat carrier. In the vet's car park I managed to use one of Lucy's poo bags as a make shift rubber glove and tissues that I always keep in the car (thankfully) and mopped up the biggest amount of wee in the world. I'm surprised that Casper didn't shrink in size after the amount that he had done. Unfortunately, Casper's efforts to cling to the front of the carrier and avoid the puddle of wee weren't entirely successful and his tail and bottom were soaked with wee.

Luckily for Henry he wasn't working that day and 'Duncan' the vet was trying not to gag as he handled a piss-soaked Casper to inspect the pus on his face. Unfortunately for Duncan he didn't anticipate that Casper would do a dog-like shake and Casper proceeded to fling wee all over his computer in an attempt to rid himself of the smell. I mumbled some sort of apology for the state of him and left as quickly as I could afterwards. Thankfully Brandy and Precious weren't in that day to give me even more sympathetic looks. (Although, I wished they were after encountering the couple below.)

There was a couple sitting in the waiting room opposite me and I was trying to ear wig on their conversation to work out whether they were mother and son or husband and wife. She was a lot older than him but they didn't look like each other. She was skinny and all of eight stone, whereas he was tall and all of 25 stone. Their dog was a small terrier type breed and she had put it on the bench next to her when she sat down. There was nearly a nasty incident of 'dog killed by bum crack' as he went to sit down and didn't notice that the dog was there. I'm not sure that the dog would have survived his bottom landing on it. There was a sharp intake of breath from everyone in the room when it happened and an equally loud exhaling when we all realised that the crisis had been averted as she picked the dog up just in time.

The guy kept touching and stroking the woman (in an inappropriate fashion). I like to pride myself on being broad minded but the location of his touching, in my opinion, was just wrong.

1. We were in the vets and
2. He really shouldn't be touching her 'there' on her body.

I covered Lucy's eyes at one point. OK, I'm lying. I covered my own eyes and told Lucy that she was on her own. I came to the conclusion that they were husband and wife. It turned out that I was wrong though. As he went to look at the dog toys hanging on the display rack across the other side of the waiting room he called out, "Mum - do you think Gemma would like this?" I was absolutely horrified! As was everyone else in the room. I mean, who calls their dog Gemma?

Upon arriving home I did contemplate pretending that I didn't know that Casper was soaked in wee until Mr H got home from work and then exclaiming, "Well I don't know how that happened?!!" in the hope that Mr H would have to wash him. Casper is, after all, his cat. However, given that Casper likes to lie on my side of the bed I weighed up the pros and cons and decided that I would need to wash him straight away.

Ever tried to wash a cat in a wet room? No? Well don't. It's like that short story of 'how to give a cat a pill'. It's never going to end well. Unsurprisingly I think that I got more wet (I know that's bad grammar) than Casper and I'm not convinced I made one bit of difference to the smell of wee as I was trying to pull him back from clinging to the sink to wash his rear end under the shower head. After I finally made some progress, I vowed that next time I might as well wash him naked (me – not him. Obviously he was already naked) as I was soaked from head to toe. Mr H came home as I was shedding my soaked clothes to the floor whilst watching Casper furiously washing himself and said, "Successful trip to the vets then?" I swear that both Casper and I looked up at him with the same expression of, 'Just. Don't. Ask.'

Next time Mr H can make the trip to the vets...

Tuesday 15th March

Mission for today:

- *Research how many words my book needs to have and get cracking on writing*

Tales from Kent...

I had a lovely chat via text with our friend Letitia this morning. Letitia lives in Kent where it is extremely posh. If you have ever been there then I'm sure that you will agree. We went to stay there for one weekend last year and as we approached the border I did expect to undertake some sort of passport control process to see whether we were worthy enough to come into the county. I remember looking down at my £9.99 New Look jeans thinking my choice of clothing might let me down. Luckily Mr H was wearing his 'Joules' jacket that I had bought him for his birthday, so I knew that he would be ok.

We spent one of the nights at a local village's 'got talent' competition, like the programme *Britain's got Talent*. I knew that we were far removed from Wolverhampton when children taking part had names like 'Orlando Cobblestone'. Not one 'Beyoncé-Chantelle Smith' to be had here. We also drank wine out of proper glasses. I momentarily forget what to do and was pulling at an imaginary plastic lid on the top of my glass.

I also noticed a marked difference in the 'toilet chatter' in the ladies loos at the interval. In Wolverhampton, you are likely to hear, "Does this top make my tits look good?" or, "Do you think I could take her?" whereas in Kent it was, "Remind me to tune my ukulele". The only way that Wolverhampton beats Kent is that its name has four syllables. However, the people of Kent crucially know what that means...

We went out on the Sunday to a lovely vineyard and in one of the barns there were two shiny new bright red tractors. Mr H leant on the gate to the barn staring wistfully at them. (He's never looked so fondly at me like that.) I left him there as I went to wander up and down the vines. He was still there when I came back around 20 minutes later, in exactly the same position with exactly the same look on his face. One of the vineyard workers said, "Is he alright? He's been standing here a long time. I wasn't sure if he was supposed to be out on his own, or whether he was…ermmm… out with… you know…" "Carers?" I finished his sentence for him.

"No – it's just my husband. He really really wants a tractor. But if I had have known that these were here yesterday then I would have dropped him off in the morning and picked him back up again at night. You should think about starting a crèche for husbands. I really think it could take off."

Letitia has invited us back to go again so I think that we successfully conned everyone into thinking that we were posher than we are. I think Mr H's Audi had something to do with it, so I was mentally congratulating us on our choice of car. (Although I think the vineyard took a photo of Mr H and he is now on their 'watch list' so we might not be able to go back there again.)

Something else I probably should have told you in the introduction, is that Mr H cannot sleep without his favourite pillow. Luckily I managed to convince him not to bring it with him to Kent. (I'm not sure it would have got through the border quarantine screening process, as it is really manky and looks like Ebola is living in it.) However, the downside to not bringing his favourite pillow meant that he didn't sleep well for the two nights that we were here and I had to listen to him moan for four hours in the car on the way back. (Well, I would have done but he hadn't noticed that I put my headphones in and turned my music up – so he was actually moaning to himself.)

Anyway, back to home...

Mr H has tried to be helpful with the writing of this book. I like to think it's because he has unconditional love and support for the love of his life but really it's because of the tractor. So actually I was right, it is 'unconditional love and support for the love of his life!'

I said to him, "How long do you think this book needs to be? I've been on Google and it says the average book is about 60,000 words and if it's a thriller then it could be 100,000."

Trying to be helpful he said, "I don't think it should be any length of those, after all, if it was it would get incredibly repetitive. I know what will help."

He disappeared off and went into the bathroom to get some books out of the magazine rack. Looking very pleased with himself he said, "These are the sorts of books you should be aiming for." Unfortunately, two of them were 'Off The Leash' and consisted only of pictures of dog cartoons. I thanked him for his help though - it's important to praise men when they try to do nice things, otherwise they tend not to do them again.

Facebook reminded me that 'on this day' I had posted pictures of me with Dec (of Ant and Dec fame). This reminded me about my celebrity interactions...

Tales of stalking celebrities...

One of our favourite pastimes over the last five years has been to see how many selfies or interaction we can get with celebrities. The list is up to 32 at the moment and my most treasured moments are being kissed on each cheek by Simon Cowell. I didn't wash for about a week afterwards. He was incredibly charming and I blathered like a village idiot. I'm sure he thought that I had some special needs.

Dec is my phone screen saver and if I say so we really look good together. We managed to meet him when we had tickets to go and see *Britain's Got Talent*. I was so star struck though that I forgot to tell him that (at the time) he was number one on my laminated list (see later for an explanation of this) and that we could have a no-strings attached liaison, should he so wish. In all honesty, it is probably a blessing that I didn't as I'm not convinced that he would have taken me up on the offer and I probably would now not be allowed within 200 feet of him due to an injunction.

We got tickets to watch *Celebrity Juice* a few years ago and I was determined that we would get Keith, Holly and Fearne's signatures. I knew I was on to a winner when I produced three banners, 'Keith, please sign my wet pussy', 'Holly, please sign my big cock' and 'Fearne, please sign my boy tits'. Obviously the pictures were a cat soaked with water in the bath, a small man and a large cockerel and two baby blue tit birds. They worked! We got noticed in the audience and got our signatures. The reason that we got to meet Simon Cowell was also due to our banners... I said to Mr H, "Do you think I would make a good professional celebrity stalker?" He had a very useful point when he replied, "I'm not sure how you will make money out of it though."

We have also appeared twice on telly in the audience of *Stand Up for The Week*. We have a fail-safe strategy for getting the cameras to focus on us. As this was a comedy show we made sure that we laughed very loudly and cheered and clapped at every opportunity. The first time we were in the audience I shouted out to Jon Richardson (who was the host at the time), "Will you marry me Jon?" He asked if I was a tidy person and Mr H piped up, "Oh yes! She's really tidy, it's really annoying." Jon decided that two tidy people together just wouldn't work. I'm sure Mr H's tears were of laughter and not sadness that he hadn't been able to palm me off on someone else.

The second time that we went Paul Choudhry was the host. We had already had a bit of banter at the start with him. He then asked the audience where they had come from. I piped up, "Wolverhampton" (much to Mr H's disgust as he insists that we do not live there) and later on an audience member – we'll call him Dick - was trying to get noticed by Paul.

Dick piped up, "I have been on telly lots of times before you know".

Paul politely said, "Oh yes? When was that then?"

I spontaneously shouted out, "Crimewatch" and was surprised at the number of laughs that went around the room.

To be fair we had been there a while by now and there was a bar, so I think people were a little drunk as it really wasn't that funny. Dick took offence to this and was blathering away at Paul trying to get his attention back.

Paul helpfully said, "Mate – Wolverhampton has got the laughs, just leave it."

I felt like a minor celebrity when I went to the loo as a few of the girls said, "Oh? You're Wolverhampton – you go girl!"

When we watched the programme on the Friday, there was a massive close up of me, Mr H and our friend Jade laughing hysterically. Unfortunately, they had edited that bit in for a joke that was totally unfunny. All of our Facebook friends then took the piss out of us for laughing at such a poor joke.

As well as these cameo appearances on telly, we have actually starred in a programme of our own. Mr H's mum saw an advert in the local Express & Star that said that the BBC (for *Nick Knowles' Original Features*), were looking for families in Staffordshire that were restoring old properties for their new series.

Knowing how long Mr H had taken so far in the restoration of our farmhouse, she suggested to us that we might like to get in touch. Filming was such a laugh and it did kick-start my diet following my ruptured Achilles incident (more on this in a bit). Everyone knows that the camera adds ten pounds and I already was carrying an excess of two stone. As I lost weight during the five months that they filmed us, I did hope that it would be edited in order. Otherwise, I was going to look like I was fat, slim for a bit, then fat again when the programme was shown.

Meeting Nick was good fun – he is really tall! My sister gave me a copy of an article in Heat or it could have been Hello! magazine about him and how he had given up smoking for his girlfriend as he just didn't want to do it anymore. She said to me, "Awwww isn't that sweet." I told her that I thought that the article might have been written a fair while ago as the second time he came to film with us he smoked like a chimney. Thinking about it though, he didn't smoke the first time so there is of course the possibility that he had given up smoking and then after meeting me he felt the need to start up again. Sorry Nick…

We went through a phase of getting tickets to go and watch *The X Factor*. We were lucky enough to get tickets to watch one of the live Saturday night shows and later that month we got tickets to the live final at Wembley. Unfortunately on this occasion it meant that we had to queue for about five hours in the freezing cold and weren't actually guaranteed to get in. As luck would have it, we did get in but were in a block with loads of other people that had started drinking about three days prior, it seemed. We didn't actually hear much of the show itself because people like 'Paul' were talking on their phones constantly saying things like, "Yeh mate. Can you see me waving on TV to you? I know mate! It's been an awesome day. It's been free booze all day."

When I got home I emailed Dido Harding, Talk Talk's Chief Exec. (who were sponsors of *The X Factor*) and told her of our experience. She was brilliant as she had replied within 20 minutes and by the next morning we had been told that we had free tickets to see the tour and back stage passes to meet the acts. Mr H did go a bit gaga over Little Mix and Amelia Lily... It's a bit embarrassing to watch a 50-something star struck but he's my 50-something and I do love him... just not enough to buy him a tractor.

Wednesday 16th March

Mission for today:

- *Book Mr H in for his eye check*

Tales from the eye hospital...

Mr H had an eye scare a few weeks ago when his vision went blurry and is off back to the consultant this Saturday to check whether his blockage (the technical term is a 'retinal vein occlusion' (get me for remembering that)) has gone. When it happened he got a fast track appointment to the hospital to see what was going on.

The waiting room in there was like the programme *Waiting for God*. The average age of people in there was around 83. As I wandered in, I felt like the new girl in class as a great hush descended and arm nudging ensued. I tried to busy myself in the work I had brought with me to avoid the stares. 'Gladys' was happily telling everyone that her two husbands were dead.

"The first one died from lung cancer. But that came as no great surprise as he smoked woodbines like a chimney. The second one died of a heart attack and I wasn't prepared for that! I don't think that I'll marry again." I didn't like to point out that at her age the odds of someone else marrying her would be quite unlikely.

'Dora' was moaning to her husband 'Albert' about the length of time that they had been waiting.

"I mean we've been here 20 minutes already, it's shocking!" Albert looked very uncomfortable with her constant moaning and when the nurse called him for his eye test he seemed to leap like a teenager out of the chair to escape Dora. I'm pretty sure that 'Frank', sitting in the corner, had been breaking wind for the last half an hour.

Mr H didn't seem to notice anyone else in the waiting room, but this is probably because there was a magazine on the table called 'Farmer's Weekly'. He went to grab it at the same time as 'Arnold' spied it but Mr H had youth on his side. Mr H's eyes went wide eyed (well, one of them did) when he saw it. Arnold took three attempts to get himself out of the chair and by the time he got to the table with the magazines on the only one left was something called 'Menopausal Nightmares.' (OK – I don't think it was called that but judging by the picture on the front and the topics listed, it did not look like a happy read.) Arnold took it nonetheless and seemed to be quite engrossed in it.

Mr H seemed to enjoy reading Farmer's Weekly. He sighed numerous times. I think this was due to the pictures of shiny farm machinery and not the fact that we had been waiting a while.

Thankfully, after about an hour we got called in to see the consultant. I felt the eyes of 20 old people burning into my back as we left the room. The consultant showed us a picture of Mr H's eye and said that it didn't look too bad and that we would need eye drops for his dodgy eye for three weeks and then needed to go back to see him again as to whether he would need eye injections. We were shown a comparison of someone else's eye which was in a rather poor state of health. I think it was farting Frank's from the waiting room.

I did think it ironic that as we left the eye hospital a cleaner with a sick sense of humour had laid out a slalom course of 'caution cleaning in progress' signs. Given that we had passed at least three people with white sticks in there, I thought this very un-pc. Although thinking about it, it did slow people down somewhat, so maybe it was their cunning plan to reduce waiting time in the waiting room.

After the appointment we spent around ten hours* driving round approximately 6 billion* chemists to find one that stocked his eye drops.

* I might have slightly exaggerated these figures.

Whilst we were in Sainsbury's hunting down the elusive drops, I took the opportunity to do a bit of shopping whilst Mr H tackled the pharmacy. About ten minutes later I got a phone call from him asking where I was as he couldn't find me. We met up in the toilet roll aisle and he said, "No wonder I couldn't find you, I was looking for a woman wearing a light blue coat." I was wearing dark purple. Luckily there were no other women wearing light blue coats as he would likely have gone home with them.

I'm not convinced about his sight and to avoid a repeat performance I made a mental note to only wear my light blue coat in the near future. We have good friends, as Jade has offered to host us a pirate themed party if his eye turns out to be gammy.

We filled up with diesel before we ran out from having to travel around all the chemists and luckily I accidentally broke off the fuel filler cap to Mr H's car. I say that this was a lucky incident as this momentarily made him forget about the possible eye injections as he kept mumbling under his breath that I had 'broken his car'.

On the plus side, it turns out that Mr H's eye is fine. He doesn't need to have injections. This is a blessing, as I was Googling self-defence classes in order to learn how to pin him down. In the nurse's own words, "You're not very good with your eyes are you?" and I'm sure that I saw the doctor strike out the box on his medical records that said 'adult' and tick 'child' instead.

Thursday 17ᵗʰ March

Mission for today:

- *Reminisce about skiing holidays and don't get depressed as we won't be going again until next year*

Tales from skiing...

We went skiing last week with lots of our friends and after all the fun me and Mr H had we have felt a bit despondent today. So to cheer us up I decided to reminisce about our skiing holidays. Since hitting 40, I decided that 'work less, live more' was a mantra I would start to live by. Because of this, Mr H and I have decided to go on two skiing holidays a year from now on.

In January we went skiing to Austria with my work wife, Alexandra. We stayed at a lovely hotel which was run by Klaus and Mrs Klaus (we never knew her name). Klaus would have been perfect to play a villain in a James Bond film, as he has that 'Gestapo, skinny, evil doctor with torture implements' look going on. I'm thinking of tweeting them to let them know.

Whilst on one of the chair lifts, Alexandra decided to see what would happen if she took her skis off. As predicted, due to our excellent knowledge of Physics, they fell to the piste below. Luckily, no one was skiing underneath at the time. She then had the hard task of disembarking the chairlift without skis on her feet. I'm sure that I saw the chairlift technician mouth something in Austrian that resembled, "Bloody English."

We put on ski tracker and had burned 28 calories by 10:30am, sadly we ate around 900 calories at breakfast, so had a long way to go. We momentarily got excited when one hour later Alexandra announced that we had burned 1,000 calories. Our excitement was short lived though when she realised that she had mis-read it and it was actually only 100. I remind you about what I said in the introduction about her knowledge of maths.

Thursday was 'old people's cheap day' on the slopes. This turned out not to be a good thing as old people are just like little kids on the slopes. They have no spatial awareness, talk really loudly and pretend that it wasn't them that had farted in the gondola. One old man kept trying to spear my leg with his poles whilst getting on the chairlift and another tried to take me out when we were getting off. I made a mental note to avoid getting on a chairlift with anyone over the age of 60 for the rest of the day.

I am learning to snowboard (one of those mid-life crisis things). It is hard, very painful but hysterically funny when you catch someone face planting* on video and then post it on Facebook. Mr H chuckled as I did a huge face plant in the snow but karma kicked in as he had forgotten to press record.

* Face planting is where you catch the front edge of your board on the snow and catapult face forwards and your face basically acts like a snow plough as you fall head first down the slope. (I have clarified this phrase as Mummykins (remember from the introduction that's my name for my Mum) has been doing a first read through of the book for me and she didn't understand what I meant.)

Although we all arrived home technically in one piece, I'm pretty sure that I've got whiplash from my spectacular falls on the snowboard. If any of you get one of those calls, "Have you had an accident in the last three years?" then please pass their number onto me, as I need to sue the mountain.

There was a group skiing lesson of little kids going down the mountain on one of the days and one of them laughed and pointed at me when I was sitting on my bum on the snow on my snowboard. I had the last laugh though as further down the mountain karma had tripped the kid up (it wasn't me, honestly) and I gracefully boarded past while they were crying for their mum. The ski instructor was 70 metres down the slope before he realised that he had lost one of his kids and was mumbling something that definitely sounded like swear words in Austrian as he had to hike back up the slope to pick the kid up. Personally, I think there should simply be a 'survival of the fittest' rule on the slopes and he should have left him there.

The only breakage on the mountain that day was the zip on my salopettes, which I concluded was due to the number of falls I had on the snowboard but another possibility was the amount that I ate for breakfast...

We had a lovely waitress in our hotel and I asked Kimberley, "What part of England are you from?"

"Wales."

Luckily though, she wasn't offended and contacted her Austrian friend to find the kick ass version of Lemsip over here (which is probably illegal in England) as I was coming down with a cold.

On day three the lurgy struck badly. (I say 'the lurgy' but you might remember from the introduction that I think that Mr H is trying to kill me. There's a possibility that he was poisoning me and it wasn't the lurgy at all.) So like a good wife I sent Mr H out with Alexandra and her husband to ski with them for the day. I'm not convinced this was entirely a good idea. I texted him at lunchtime to ask if they were having a good day and he replied with, "Well, so far we have skied through a muddy farmer's field."

I forgot to mention in my introduction that Mr H's sense of direction is atrocious. He has to do a 'Joey in the map' in *Friends* to work out where he is. Alexandra's navigation skills are also pretty poor, so I did think that if they weren't back at dinner time then I might need to contact ski patrol to go and find them.

I managed to drag my broken body to the chemist to get the 'kick ass Lemsip' and some throat sweets. Unfortunately, I had forgotten that they have weird opening times in Austria and I was 30 minutes late and they were going to be shut for the next two hours. Not one to be put off I traipsed through town to find a convenience store and with my knowledge of the Austrian language at zero, I reverted to sign language to try and explain my snotty nose and sore throat to the girl on the counter. It worked and I paid the extortionate three euros for a pack of throat sweets but luckily the pocket tissues were only 49c for a huge bag. I also took a carrier bag to get my money's worth.

Back at the hotel I caught up with 'Scottish Bob'. It had been his 72nd birthday the night before and he generously bought everyone in the hotel a whisky to celebrate. He looked very hung over. Funnily enough he didn't want to kiss me with my snotty cold. (Last night it was Scottish kisses galore and he was trying to get me to leave Mr H for him.)

Coming back through border control at Salzburg airport was fun. Passport control did the usual look of, 'Flip me! You don't look like your picture!' I am blonde on my passport but was dark browny-purple on this holiday. I change my hair colour a lot - you'll find some tales from the hairdressers in this book. The passport control guy pointed to my hair and said, "Three hours, 200 euros?" and then pointed to Mr H's hair and said, "Four euros?" Mr H got told off by security on the x-ray machine as he had forgotten that he still had two juice boxes in his rucksack. Despite my pleas, they wouldn't arrest him.

So as I said at the start of today's tales, we went skiing with our group of 14 friends to France last week. There were many happy tales to tell from this week...

On day one it was Melanie's birthday - we actually had four birthdays in the chalet this year - and in true birthday fashion she skied with three pink 'birthday girl' balloons attached to her helmet. Unfortunately, one of them got stuck in the chairlift and went very flaccid for the rest of the day. I hadn't tightened my camel pack up properly in my rucksack and Melanie noticed water trickling down my bottom as we were skiing down a run. She delicately asked me if I had a water pack in my rucksack. I think this was in case I was just having normal middle aged lady issues. After depositing the rest of the water onto the slopes from my rucksack I had to ski with a wet bottom.

Luckily it soon turned to icicles so I didn't look foolish for all of the day.

Day three was interesting as one of the gondolas that we got in smelled of marijuana. This had the effect of enhancing all of our skiing abilities as we were chased down the slopes by dragons.

When we go skiing in the day we don't often ski as one big group but break up into smaller groups. I'm in the 'ski a bit, stop for coffee, ski for a bit, stop for another coffee, ski for a bit, stop for lunch, ski for a bit, stop for beer' group. At the end of the day Alexandra (who was in the 'ski for your life' group) regaled us of one of their exciting tales of the day. Apparently, they had come across a piste that said 'unpacked' and Alexandra, using logic of the English language, concluded that this meant that it was a quiet piste that no one went down. Sadly it turned out that it meant that it wasn't pisted, so they spent the next half an hour skiing through a mogul* field. At my age, I can't cope with mogul fields, unless I am wearing Tena Ladies.

* A mogul field is a slope that is full of big mounds of snow and usually lots of skiers lying on the floor as they can be hard to negotiate.

As the weather was fantastic on Wednesday, we stayed out on the slopes until after 5:30pm. We took the 'scary' up and over chair lift over the other side of the mountain. Usually chairlifts only go up in line with the contours of the mountain but this one drops you over the edge of the mountain and goes down the one side before eventually going up the other. This is why we call it the scary chairlift. It feels like you are going to drop off the edge of the mountain and as you can't see the land as it drops you over the edge you feel like you're freefalling. I think that we all did well with the lift. Some of us closed our eyes, others screamed, we all coped in our unique ways.

Before skiing back to the chalet we had stopped to have a beer higher up the slopes to take in the gorgeous views. I had a large beer and had forgotten that we still needed to ski home. On the way back you have to ski through a tunnel. My lack of knowledge of Physics once again let me down. I approached the tunnel at speed, forgot to remove my sunglasses and ended up blindly skiing through the tunnel which was full of mogully snow.

The inevitable happened and as I turned the corner of the tunnel, I lost my footing and my head bounced off the wall of the tunnel as I collapsed in a heap. Thankfully, my helmet took the brunt of the crash and the beer meant I didn't tense up so the rest of my body was fine as well. Mr H came flying past me in the tunnel and I could hear him call out from the other end, "You are okay aren't you?" I struggled to get up and had to use my helmet and hands to walk up the wall to right myself. As Alexandra said when I told her what had happened, "Well... skiing through a dark tunnel with sunglasses on is never going to end well is it?" She says such wise things.

It was 'International Women's Day' whilst we were out there and Letitia and I always tried to ditch Mr H and Sam on the lifts when there was a fit Frenchman on his own. We were giggling like two school girls as this hot French guy got into the bucket lift with us. When we were due to disembark he gestured to us and said, "It is International Ladies' Day, please go first" in his gorgeous French accent. We hopped off waiting for his chivalry to continue but alas that's where it ended. He strode off without helping us with our skis so we quickly went off him.

Restaurants on the slopes are always a rip-off. Six euros 60c for a diet coke meant that we all resolved to drink beer for the rest of the week. As if that wasn't bad enough they charge you a further 50c to use the toilet. I did the typically English thing and used as much loo paper as possible (even contemplating shoving some down my salopettes) to get my money's worth and decided to go shopping in town later for some Tena Ladies. (To slightly digress, me and my sister came up with a fab slogan for advertising these a few years ago, 'If you piss when you sneeze, you need these!' We thought this was really catchy.) Mr H couldn't get used to his new gloves that had 'kiddy wrist' attachments and accidentally weed in them. He was thinking of asking for his 50c back.

One of the restaurants gave you a 'wee token'. If you ate your lunch there you didn't have to pay the 50c charge. Alexandra and I noticed that they just kept them in a basket near the bar. Luckily the fact that we can't do maths in our head was our friend in this situation, as we mis-counted how many we would need for the 11 of us and had two left over. We vowed to use them on another day. We went to the resort of Alpe D'Huez three years ago and when we got back home I found one of the 'wee tokens' we had left over from that trip. I hit my fist on my head saying 'D'oh' that I should have taken it this year but then realised that they must change the colour of the tokens so that people don't do that very thing. Three years ago the tokens were red and this year they were brown. Honestly! How stingy are the French?

There were lots of dogs in the resort this year. Mr H tried to make friends with a golden retriever but it snubbed him and wandered off. It seems even the French dogs haven't forgiven us for the war...

We travelled back on my birthday and in order to help poor Melanie with her leg we opted to go on the 6am coach to the airport. Melanie had sadly injured her leg on her birthday and had been resigned to the chalet for the rest of the week. She had drawn up a slave roster though so that we could all pitch in to help her with what she needed. She said that the injury was from falling whilst skiing but we have our suspicions that it might have been down to the après ski drinking...

The first excitement of the day was coming down to breakfast at 5:20am to see a random drunk girl sprawled across the settee in the chalet. Mr H joked 'Happy birthday Honey! Look what I got you as a present' as he pointed at her.

Apparently, the chalet host had discovered her on the slopes at 4:45am. She had no idea where her hotel was and her friends appeared to have ditched her at some point in the night. She could just about remember that her name was Nicky. Initially we thought that this was comical as we could give her a totally new identity and tuck her up in one of the rooms we had just vacated and I posted her picture on Facebook asking if anyone wanted her if no one claimed her. As predicted, one of our single male friends asked us to put his phone number on a piece of paper and slot it in her jacket pocket. I didn't do this. She smelled of sick and I didn't want to get that close to her.

But then the seriousness kicked in. She could have died from hypothermia and could also have been attacked out there on her own. We all decided that her friends were very bad for leaving her out there. The London lot didn't leave the chalet until midday and apparently she still had no idea where her hotel was at that point. Nicky - if by any chance you are reading this then I hope that you finally got back to your hotel. Will you tweet me and let me know, please?

Ironically, as we were at the airport early for our flight we got to check in first and were allocated the extra legroom seats. Poor Melanie had no such luck on her flight. I did feel guilty about this.

After check-in we made our way to the French border control and apparently they adore me! One of them gave me a stamp on my passport, so it would show my birthday (which in itself offends a whole host of EU law, I'm sure) and security on the x-ray machine sang happy birthday to me in English. It did occur to me that if I was some terrorist or smuggler then now would have been the time to do it as they were so engrossed in their harmonies that they didn't watch my belongings going through the machine. You never know how dangerous an Estée Lauder eye pencil can be...

On the downside, Damian, the devil child, was playing merry hell in duty free and we (as in everyone in the tiny departure lounge) were all praying that he wasn't on our flight. Sadly our prayers were not answered but he did nearly get swallowed up by the conveyor belt back at Birmingham airport. His parents looked horrified, but I wasn't sure whether that was because he didn't get swallowed up.

Picking up the dogs after holibobs always makes me chuckle. Lucy goes off to Dad's when we are away and Bonnie goes to Mum's. Lucy puts on lots of weight and does the most disgusting farts for at least three days. It doesn't matter how many Schmackos go with her, Dad always has to buy more as 'you didn't put enough in again.' Apparently, a pack of 20 (when she has a maximum of two a day with her medicine for her eight day stay) isn't enough. Despite maths not lying, Dad still insists he is right. Bonnie always comes back trimmer and fitter (gold star to Mummykins) due to her proper allocation of treats and long walks. Given that Lucy is Mr H's dog then should she have bottie problems, I happily remind him of this fact and let him sort it.

Before dropping Bonnie off at Mum's she had diarrhoea. I did contemplate pretending that I hadn't noticed it but concluded that it would be mean that Mum would have to wash her on arrival. I'm pretty sure some of my friends have done the same with their babies though and dropped them off at the baby's grandparents with a dirty nappy, swearing that they had only just done it. I must confess that one time Lucy had been sick on the hall rug I pretended that I hadn't noticed it so Mr H had to clean it up when he got in. I felt slightly guilty at this as Lucy nearly trod in it a few times throughout the day. Bonnie has a habit of rubbing her bottom on the floor. (Bless her, she suffers with her anal glands). I did heave the other day though when she did it and Lucy promptly went to lick where she had done it. I suspect that this is another reason as to why Lucy's breath is so bad...

Our 78 year old neighbour (the Farmer's wife) was in charge of the chickens and ducks whilst we were away and said that 'the brown one' kept trying to escape when she went into the pen. I did chuckle at the thought of her chasing a chicken around the garden or having to pretend that it had died if she lost it. The Farmer's geese have been using our lawn whilst we were away and we were nearly eating goose pie for the next month when Lucy spied them on her return. Again I reminded Mr H that she is his dog and that he would have to break the bad news to the Farmer.

We've been having a wild male and female duck on our lawn for a while now. I told Mr H that I was going to name them Sheldon and Amy (out of The Big Bang Theory). Mr H said, "Why? Is it because they never have sex?" I thought it slightly strange that he had been watching them so much of the time that he could tell that they hadn't. "No," I said. "It's because normally the boy ducks let the girls eat first but she lets him eat first and he has his own spot under the tree." I do wonder whether we sometimes think a bit too deeply about some things.

Friday 18th March

Missions for today:

- *Try and avoid contact with Mr H as he has man-flu (and is being very annoying)*
- *Go and visit my friend in Solihull (and try and remember to talk with a posh accent, in case they try and throw me out)*

Tales from home...

Since arriving back Mr H has had man flu, so I have been trying to keep his spirits up by generally using one-up-man-ship when he moans. Yesterday he said, "Your throat would be sore too if you had just spent two solid hours talking." Given that I regularly talk for six hours a day, training adults, this really wasn't the best thing he could have said. My retort of, "Once you've talked for three days solid with a sore throat, then I might have some sympathy for you" seemed to go down well though. I think these little pep talks have helped him immensely in his return to health. At any rate his moaning seems to have subsided.

Tales from Solihull...

To escape the moaning about his cold I went to visit a friend and her baby in Solihull yesterday. The first stop was to the new Marks & Spencer food hall in Cannock to pick up some provisions for lunch. As I wandered in you could see the wide-eyed stares from the customers at what heaven had arrived here. It was the most exciting thing that had happened since they built the landfill site down the road. As I was browsing in the salad aisle, a 20-something boyfriend and girlfriend were picking out lunch and I heard her say to him, "You do love me, don't you?" Me and 'Doris' - the 80 year old stood next to me - quickly stole a glance at each other as we pretended to busy ourselves choosing olives, eagerly awaiting his response. Sadly he did the worst thing possible in the situation and paused before answering. Doris loudly sucked on her false teeth, tutted and vigorously shook her head at him. He looked back at her with a 'What did I do?' expression on his face. I sloped off quietly to go and choose some bread but could still hear Doris muttering under her breath. She was clicking her teeth and still grumbling to herself as I passed her in the queue to pay.

I have realised that we are all born with a certain amount of patience in life. Unfortunately, mine ran out at the age of 41. To this end, I chose to pay on the M6 toll rather than face the inevitable queues on the M6. This was a much calmer journey until I saw the sign that said the toll booth was approaching. I suddenly remembered how Mr H always has trouble reaching the credit card machine from the driver's seat and has to do some 'bouncing' type manoeuvre to reach to put the card in. As the car was getting closer, I was starting to panic a bit. I'm a lot shorter than Mr H so surely I would have even more trouble than him?

I needn't have worried though. I positioned the car perfectly and didn't even have to stretch to reach the machine. As I drove through the barrier I congratulated myself on the ease of it and made a mental note to take the piss out of Mr H when I got back home. On the plus side the scratch down the right hand side of the car is virtually unnoticeable.

I knew that I had arrived in Solihull when every other car was an SUV with a private number plate and all the dogs being walked were either Retrievers or Labradors. No Staffies or Pitbulls here. Rachel and I went to one of the retail parks for some shopping and coffee and I noticed that the women of Solihull generally have trouble parking their SUVs. Most of them park at a diagonal angle across two spaces. Initially, I thought that this was sheer ignorance and bad parking, but it transpires that by doing this they don't scratch their Mulberry handbags on the cars next to them. They really do think of everything here.

I arrived back home to find Mr H still complaining of his man flu. Unluckily for him I did the best one-up-man-ship possible in the situation and the next night I got food poisoning. He suddenly stopped whinging about his sore throat when I was chucking up the McDonalds milkshake, which I had concluded was the perpetrator in this dastardly deed*. I will spare you the details apart from the hallucinations it gave me. Luckily neither of them involved buying a tractor.

* I tweeted McDonalds and after looking into things they assured me that all their health and safety procedures were followed that night. They sent me a £10 voucher though. I'm back to thinking that maybe Mr H is poisoning me...?

Saturday 19th March

Missions for today:

- *Try and avoid Mr H's gloating smile, now that I am sick*
- *Try not to hurl from the smell when I'm sitting on the loo with Bottie McTrottie*

Tales from the sick-pit...

I have since been in the sick-pit with no energy and even watching Shemar Moore in *Criminal Minds* didn't seem to perk me up. Funnily enough Mr H's man flu seems to have gone now that I need him to nurse me.

Mr H seems to like it when I'm in the sick-pit. I think it's because I'm contained in one place and therefore can't hide his things, which he insists that I do (which I don't) and can't upset his routine, which he also insists that I do (which I also don't). I swear that when I came downstairs he said to Bonnie, "Oh great! Mummy's up - ready to annoy Daddy." I'm pretty sure that Bonnie's look in return was, 'I don't care - just feed me.'

I also came to this conclusion when I told him this morning that Bottie McTrottie had come to visit me and I would be lying on the settee all day. I swear that I saw the glimmer of a smile on his lips. At one point Casper came to watch over me by jumping on my lap but within a minute had hopped off and settled on the settee opposite. I did think about getting offended. After all, maybe I hadn't had a shower that morning but surely the smell couldn't have put him off that much? I've seen him eat the entrails of a mouse before and rub his face in fox poo.

Mum messaged me today to say that she had an embarrassing encounter with my dentist in the Co-op near them. This reminded me of my visit to the dentist last month...

Tales from the dentist...

My teeth are one of the parts of my body that generally work brilliantly and have never caused me any problems (apart from the usual fillings as a child). I say this because at aged 23 my thyroid packed up and at age 25 I had a blood clot in my right leg. I think work was trying to kill me. On both occasions the doctors said, "You are a bit young for this to happen". I should really think about donating my body for medical science, as it is unique. I am pleased therefore when one part of my body doesn't cause me any problems.

Imagine my horror then when a quick trip to the dentist resulted in him saying that I needed a wisdom tooth out. Apparently I had a hole in it and it would be hard to fill and probably wouldn't last long if it was filled. According to him, "Your mouth isn't big enough for your teeth." Mr H chuckled at this, "How can your mouth not be big enough?" I think that this was some rude reference to the fact that I am quite a noisy person.

The dentist actually wanted to take it out there and then but when he saw the startled rabbit in the headlights look in my eye, he said, "Think about it and come back to me." Mr H also laughed at the fact that I didn't just have it out there and then.

"But I was driving, and I didn't know whether I would be groggy from the anaesthetic."

"It was only a tooth for goodness sake. You would be fine to drive. I have them out all the time." (This of course is true. Due to his love of puddings and sweet things, Mr H's teeth are appalling.)

I never trust Mr H when he says things like this. Once we were building a greenhouse. Well, when I say that 'we' were building it, I was mostly sat on a recliner drinking Pimms and lemonade, overseeing things whilst Mr H did the hard stuff. These are the times that I totally disagree with sexual equality. Mr H would say something like, "Aren't you going to help?" And I would say, "I can't – this is man's work."

Anyway, the reason why I don't tend to trust him when he says things like this is because after he had built the frame it was getting late and he decided to stop work and continue fitting the glass in the morning. I said, "Don't you need to weigh the frame down at all? They've predicted high winds tonight." His response was, "No! Don't be silly, the wind will just blow through it." I bet you can guess what happened the next morning. We woke up to find a crumpled heap of metal that had nearly blown into the farmer's field next to us. I don't like to rub Mr H's nose in it when he's wrong, so I didn't put a picture up on Facebook, tagging him in it with a summary of the story - that would be mean... (Ok, I totally did... but the ribbing he got from our friends was so worth it).

Anyway, back to the dentist then...

Mum was much more sympathetic when I told her about having to have my wisdom tooth out. She didn't laugh at me like Mr H. She offered to come with me when I had it taken out. This turned out to be twice. The first time was a non-event. I had happily posted on Facebook that I was going to the dentist to have my tooth out and that it had been nice knowing people, when one of my friends commented that she was surprised that they were going to be taking it out with me flying only two days later. When I told the dentist about my flight he decided that as my teeth were very compacted then he might need to break the tooth to get it out and that cabin pressure in the plane could make the hole bleed. As I have a history of blood clots too then he decided not to take the risk. So back we had to trot when we came back from holiday.

I'm sure that the dentist thought that I was a complete loon. There I was, a 41 year old professional woman (my words – not his), with my mum sitting in the chair in the corner as I didn't want to be on my own in case anything went wrong. Thankfully it all went to plan and he asked me whether he wanted him to dispose of my tooth. "Are you crazy?" I said. "A tooth that size has got to be worth at least £50 from the tooth fairy!" I also asked him if I could have a sticker for being so good.

At least he knows where my lunacy comes from. Mum bumped into him in the local Supermarket this week and to begin with she couldn't work out where she knew him from. I dread to think what she said to him as she sent me a message on Messenger of, 'I think your dentist thinks I need psychiatric help.' I have made a note on my to-do list to Google a new dentist...

Monday 21st March

Missions for today:

- *Google 'poisons' and check the pantry and under the sink for suspicious bottles*
- *Get out of the sick-pit*

Tales from the sick-pit continued...

Again I started to wonder whether Mr H was trying to poison me as I didn't seem to be getting better. So when he wasn't looking I got out our life insurance policy but I was relieved to see that if your spouse kills you then it won't pay out. Dad has been over at our house helping us with the renovation of the spare rooms and I dismissed the idea that Mr H was trying to kill me as he would be silly to do it with a witness present.

Having said that, I'm not convinced that Dad's powers of observation are that great. Seeing me huddled under a blanket on the settee, in my dressing gown and looking like death, he did exclaim, "Are you not well then?" I think I might highlight the part of the life policy that says that your spouse won't profit if they kill you and leave it out for Mr H, just in case.

It's funny how even at the age of 42 I still feel like a small child in front of Dad. The last time that he came over I snuck a cheeky glass of white wine after lunch and spent the rest of the afternoon trying to hide it from him.

I have been too tired today to write anything else. I really need this bug to go, otherwise this is going to be the most boring book ever...

Wednesday 23rd March

Mission for today:

- *Go shopping to Sainsbury's and encounter some bonkers people*

Tales from Sainsbury's...

Today I actually managed to get properly out of the sick-pit and decided to try and go food shopping at Sainsbo's (this is the local term for Sainsbury's - I think it's because people in Wolves struggle with spelling long words), in an attempt to kick start my system.

Wolverhampton is always such an interesting place. Luckily today it was quiet and didn't seem to be 'old people's day out' so that I wasn't constantly trying to dodge the abandoned trolleys in the middle of aisles or pretending that I couldn't smell their farts when they silently broke wind (although there was one old lady in there – see below).

One strange thing did happen whereby an old man kept staring at me while I was choosing Mr H's bionic-yogurty drink things for his dodgy tummy. I couldn't decide whether he a) thought that I was famous b) thought that he knew me, or c) was just staring because I hadn't put any make up on and was scaring him. I didn't stop to ask him and at one point I thought that he was following me around the store but I seemed to lose him in the kitchen roll aisle.

Whilst I was wandering around Sainsbo's, I started to categorise the shoppers that were in there today. We had:

1. The Aggressive OAP

   She barged her way through other people browsing in the aisles and bashed her shopping trolley into any others that dared to be in her way. When she went to do it to me, I assumed the brace position and being the heavy person that I am she bounced off my trolley and ricocheted into a display stand with chocolate hobnobs on. She looked at me suspiciously but I just gave her the 'I have no idea how that happened' look and she actually apologised. I'm sure I saw one of the other customers give me a nod of approval.

2. The stressed out Mummy

   I don't think that it takes a genius to know what she was like. She had a screaming, crying, wailing toddler strapped into the seat of the trolley that was opening up her handbag and throwing things on the floor. Toddlers are excellent multi-taskers I have to say. It was managing to scream, "I want sweeties Mummy. I want them now! I don't like that man that's staring at me Mummy, make him go away…" and carefully pick out embarrassing things from his Mum's handbag, all at the same time.

She looked haggard, bless her. "Tommy darling – that's Mummy's special juice that you're drinking there. You know you're not allowed to have that." Tommy had given up on flinging things out of her bag and had pulled out a mysterious looking bottle and proceeded to drink from it. I think that Mummy's special juice had a bit of a kick to it though as Tommy was fast asleep by the time they made the 'sweetie' aisle. His mum at least started to look a little more relaxed, bless her.

3. The lost-in-the-loo-roll-aisle older man

I actually took a shine to him. He was in his 70s and I suspected that his wife had just come out of hospital and he was looking after her and had gone to do the shopping. I could tell that he was a supermarket virgin. He didn't have a basket and was wrestling with an arm full of items. He didn't have any 'bags for life' on him and he didn't understand the one way system in operation down the aisles but did some zig-zagging manoeuvre from side-to-side. He looked like someone's sweet old Grandpa (well until he dropped his bread and the naughty 'f' word escaped his lips).

Dad told us that he 'dinged' his car last night. Although he swears that he put the handbrake on properly, the car rolling down the drive and hitting the edge of the wall suggests otherwise. We chuckled as I suggested that maybe the car didn't want to be with him anymore and was trying to leave, or had seen a cute car on the road that it was trying to follow. I had to move his car today in order to get mine out to go to Sainsbo's and although he is only two inches shorter than me I don't know how he manages to drive. My legs were virtually around my ears as I was lifting up the clutch and trying to reverse. When I got back in the house Dad said, "So do you like my car?" I tactfully responded that I thought it was designed for smaller people and that I had left it in gear just in case it tried to make a bolt for it again.

Mr H has gone off to play badminton tonight. Funnily enough his man flu only seems to stop him doing jobs that he doesn't want to do. Just before he left he asked me what I was doing on the laptop. I told him that I was writing my book and that if he wanted that tractor then he shouldn't disturb me. He gave me a thumbs up and quietly disappeared. I have now realised that this is a superpower! However, it is probably one with a limited timescale. I'm now pondering as to how long I can get away with using that sentence, so that he leaves me alone. I'm thinking probably a year, by which time he will realise that there is no hope of getting his tractor.

Back to Sainsbo's though. I made the shopping faux pas of not putting the 'next customer' divider after my shopping on the conveyor belt at the till and my bread and lettuce were still sitting on the end. 'Glynis' (who was about 70) behind me had to ask, "Is this your bread and lettuce?" before moving it along the conveyor and exaggeratingly putting the 'next customer' sign down on the belt. She gave me a conceited look as if to say, 'Love, I'm much older than you, I know what I'm doing here'. I felt like an amateur shopper. She quickly forgave me though as the till operator asked me whether I was collecting the 'fitness for fat kids' vouchers (I can't remember their proper name) but having offended Glynis I offered them to her. She seemed quite thrilled to have them. As I handed over all of my money off vouchers and nectar card, one of the vouchers wouldn't go through as the till insisted it was out of date. This meant that I had to venture to customer services to get them to give me my 120 nectar points. I normally wouldn't bother but given that I wasn't in a hurry I decided to queue up.

Watching the woman serving behind the customer service till reminded me that companies must go through some extra training with the staff before they are let loose at this desk. Grumpy McGrumpy (I don't think this was her real name) did not crack a smile the whole time she was serving me. I always see this as a challenge and it makes me overly happy and smiley in return.

She quizzed me on which till hadn't accepted the voucher and I'm sure I saw her eyes narrow suspiciously when I offered to walk back up the store and call out to her and wave when I had reached the one that I had gone through. I can do the 'innocent - I'm a bit dim' look so well that she wasn't sure whether I was being sarcastic or not. I'm sure that one of the questions on the application form for this role says, 'Do you hate the general public?' and if you tick 'yes' then you instantly have the job.

As I was leaving the store and walking back through the car park I was reminded about the difference between the older male generation and the youngsters coming through. The new generation bring with it some welcome changes to the stereotypical world. It makes me smile that when I park in Sainsbo's carpark there are still a number of cars that have men sitting in the driver's seats reading newspapers, whilst their wives do the shopping.

Thankfully Mr H isn't like this. Although I think this is where we both have adopted the opposite gender. Mr H does most of the food shopping in our house as I hate food shopping and used to nearly have panic attacks when the trolley started getting too full. Mr H shops sensibly as well. He looks at the date of fresh fruit and veg and other products to make sure they have a long shelf life whereas I shop like a man. One time I went shopping Mr H asked, "Where are the milk and the tea bags?" My shopping bags consisted of crisps, beer, chocolate and toilet paper and nothing sensible in sight.

I always forget to use my nectar points when I go shopping. So when it was Christmas I made the decision to try and remember to redeem them. I managed to buy £83 worth of food for £18 after using every voucher and nectar point that I had. As the till operator said out loud what the savings were, the two people in the queue behind me promptly gave me a round of applause and one of them exclaimed, "Jammy devil". Only in Wolverhampton does this constitute an achievement worthy of applause.

Friday 25th March

Mission for today:

- *Catch up with friends for lunch*

Tales from meeting friends...

Today my good friends Aimee and Jill took me out for a belated birthday lunch. They enquired about my book and how it was going and I told them that Mr H wasn't happy that I was going to give away 11 free copies to the people on Facebook that had encouraged me to write it. They both promised to put a donation into the tractor fund and Aimee said, "He does know that he isn't really getting a tractor, doesn't he?" I told her not to tell him this as it would dash his dreams.

It took us around an hour to actually find somewhere for lunch. We should have realised that the 'Fox and Anchor' wasn't the best place to go when the front door was actually locked. We could see people inside though and not ones to be put off we snuck through the fire escape and enquired as to whether they were serving food. Hearing, "Yes we are but there's at least an hour's wait" made up our minds to get back on the road. We hypothesized that this was probably the reason as to why they had locked the door.

Our next stop was the golf club but that was all in darkness. Third time lucky and we ended up at Table Table. I must admit that we should have gone there first as they do at-seat table service. I've hit that age where I can't be doing with queuing at a bar to order food so this really was a good choice. Aimee said that table service didn't worry her as she was going to send me to order the food anyway. They also do free Pepsi refills here so we resolved in the four hours that we were there to drink as much as possible to get our money's worth. I'm sure the number of refills didn't all show up on the bill as it only showed that we had 12 between us and we had counted at least 16.

The biggest excitement of the afternoon was the waitress going crazy when she saw something run across the floor. Luckily it turned out to be a spider and not an errant toddler. I'm not sure that Aimee and Jill will want to go out with me again soon as I made both of them cry over the course of the meal. I also made Jill cry again two days later. I had been telling them about *Employable Me* that me and Mr H had been watching on TV and Brett who had Autism and Paul who had Tourette's. There wasn't a dry eye in our house when we had been watching it. Jill texted me to tell me that was twice in one week that I had made her cry now. I'm a good friend like that...

Lucy hasn't been sleeping well since she came back from Dad's. She keeps waking up at 1:30am and then again at 5am. Unfortunately, I lost to 'Rock, Paper, Scissors, Lizard, Spock' (you'll notice that we play this a lot) and I had to get up at 1:30am to let her out and Mr H got the 5am shift. I think this is karma for all of my friends that have babies and young children. They often post on Facebook statuses such as, 'Am I ever going to sleep past 6:30am again?' to which I normally helpfully comment, 'No.' Not having children of my own allows me to ridicule those that do and buy totally annoying presents for their children's birthdays such as drum kits. I often Google, 'What toy is the noisiest for a two year old?' Obviously I am joking... I let Mr H do both the 1:30am and 5:00am shift, as Lucy is his dog.

Saturday 26th March

Mission for today:

- *Book hotels and trains for forthcoming trip to smelly London*

Mum messaged me today to see when I was heading down to London for work. This reminded me of one of the times that she came with me on the train to help me out.

Tales from the riots... (You'll understand where I'm going with this in a minute).

On the 30th June 2011 I ruptured my Achilles tendon playing netball. I should really have known better as netball had tried to kill me once before. When I was 13 years old I broke my wrist and got concussion when my head bounced off the court. Now at the age of 37, it was going for its second opportunity to kill me. Luckily it failed again.

Sitting in A&E at midnight with my foot looking like it was dropping off from the rest of my leg, the doctor categorically announced, "Your tendon has snapped." He let me feel where it used to be and cheerily piped up, "It's probably half way up your leg". I had a temporary plaster put on my leg and had to come back to the fracture clinic the next morning for a permanent one to be applied.

Unfortunately, the next day was Mr H's first day at his new work club, so Little Wren picked me up and took me to the fracture clinic. You could tell that Thursday night had been 'sports night' due to the type of patients in the waiting room. Most were between 20-40 and still wearing their shorts and trainers from the previous night, with the gentle but unmistakable waft of 'eau de B.O.' circling around the room. I had to keep discreetly sniffing my own armpits as I was convinced it was coming from me at one point. If ever you have had a limb in plaster then you will know that it's a huge effort to get undressed and dressed again. Looking around the room, and realising my fate, I knew that wet wipes were going to become my best friend for the next month or so.

The doctor examined my droopy foot and said, "You need to be plastered from your hip right the way down to your foot and you won't be able to walk on it for six weeks. You will need your plaster changing every three weeks and you will be in plaster in total for 12 weeks. Oh, and you'll need to take your nail varnish off your toes so we can check that they aren't going purple and that you haven't got a blood clot."

At this point the shock of the situation hit me (I think it was the removal of the nail varnish comment that was the straw that broke the camel's back).

"Erm… No! I can't be in plaster for 12 weeks – I'm training in London next week and I work for myself, if I don't work then I don't get paid. I'm in London next week, I can't have a plaster all the way to my hip. I'm in London next week... London… London."

Fearing that I was about to have some sort of panic attack and maybe start throwing things around the room, I'm sure I saw him reach for the security red button on the wall - or maybe it was for a syringe of something to calm me down.

"Look. In that case we won't plaster you from the hip. I'll do it from below the knee. Recent research has shown that it doesn't make a difference in long term healing."

I think the 'recent research' that he was referring to was my irrational outburst and that he wanted to get me out of his clinic as fast as he could before I started to upset the other patients in the plaster room. He didn't help himself though when he pointed out, "Of course, you are exactly in the right category of people that have this sort of injury – middle age."

Middle age?! Middle age?! Apparently, according to government statistics we are middle aged between 30-50. This piece of information, along with the nail varnish comment, sent me into the depression pit quicker than the injury itself. Mr H's work club had ended so he came to pick me up. I was a bit of a jabbering wreck. The look on his face was, 'What on earth happened in here?' The doctor piped up, "I think it was something to do with nail varnish and middle age." Mr H gave an, 'Ah... I see' before shaking his head and sighing at the doctor.

I must admit that this is the one point in my life where I did have some really low moments. I'll admit that I lost my sparkle for a bit. I'm a heavy person and trying to drag my body from the lounge, along the hall, through the kitchen, to the toilet, all the time not being able to put weight on my left foot was like running the 100 metres. By the time I got back I needed another wee again and it was an ever continuing circle. Summer was just around the corner and I was going to be confined to shuffling around on crutches. I was really glum.

Hiring a wheelchair for a week was one of the best decisions we made as I was struggling to carry things in my cleavage. Hot drinks were particularly challenging. When we worked out that I would be in plaster for 12 weeks we took the decision to buy one. Little Wren brought me lots of stickers and other bits to brighten it up.

You might be wondering why this was entitled *Tales from the riots*. Were there riots at the hospital with patients attacking staff with crutches due to long waiting times? No, there weren't and I'm getting to the riots in a bit, I promise.

You realise who are good friends in situations like this. My (sort of) little sister Nicky was an absolute star. Virtually every week she came to take me out and we would go shopping or have lunch. I think she really enjoyed pushing me round in a wheelchair.

When I was in the wheelchair we realised that our house is pretty wheelchair friendly. We don't ever want to move but being in the wheelchair got me to thinking about what would happen if we couldn't get upstairs anymore. Because of this we plumbed in a wet room downstairs so that we could live downstairs if we needed to. We also congratulated ourselves as when we did the kitchen we didn't put units high up on the wall but all units are waist high, except for the Welsh dresser. The only items in the dresser are wine glasses. Mr H joked saying, "That would be no good for you! You wouldn't be able to drink wine!" Being the resourceful woman that I am, I decided that I would simply use beer glasses as they were in one of the low level units, or maybe a straw as they are in one of the drawers.

OK, so I'm getting to the riots. I am the main bread winner in this house and I couldn't afford to be off work for 12 weeks with no income. I started thinking that I would have to let Mr H go. Usually this wouldn't have bothered me, but at this moment in time he was my carer and I was relying on him. We also didn't have the container back then for him to live in. Doing the maths though it still worked out cheaper to keep him rather than let him go and employ a nurse. This meant that I needed to go to London. My mum and mother in law shared the duties of coming with me on these trips to help out. One trip will always stick in my mind.

The riots had started to happen across the country due to the shooting of Mark Duggan, in Tottenham. Wolverhampton loves any excuse to get involved in anarchy and it was a particular hotspot for looting. I was due to go to London for a few days as the rioting had just begun. As our car pulled into Wolverhampton train station, with me in the front seat with my leg in plaster, Mr H driving and mum sitting in the back, we noticed riot police on the perimeter and kids with masks pulled over their faces wandering round with laptops and other stolen goods in their hands. Inside the station, the Virgin Trains guy said, "Can you get to another station? It's a bit dangerous here and I'm worried about you being a vulnerable passenger," as he looked down at me in the wheelchair with my plastered leg sticking straight out on the leg adaptor attached to the wheelchair.

We decided that the rioters wouldn't be bothered with me and that they were coming to Wolverhampton, rather than going to London on the train, so we sat it out in the waiting room before our train rolled in. Mr H was not happy when he got back to the car in the car park as another car had dinged his door. Personally, given that there were youths running around with face masks and riot police everywhere, I would say that this was a minor inconvenience. He was lucky that the car was still there! It is obviously still very raw with him though, even to this day.

When he said, "Have you written about the riots yet, in your book?" I said, "Not yet, but it's on my list." He said, "Well don't forget about my car door getting dinged in the carpark." Men always get their priorities right (man-logic) and I can rely on him to focus on the most important aspect of this story. I'll tell you the rest of what happened and then we'll see whether you think that his 'dinged door' was the worst thing to happen that night!

Mum and me were safely on the train and breathed a sigh of relief as we left Coventry. This was for two reasons. 1) The train was quiet with no rioters in sight and 2) Everyone breathes a sigh of relief on leaving Coventry. It's an automatic reflex that you can't stop. We both relaxed, me sitting in the special wheelchair place on the train, which was basically a gap at the end of the carriage and mum on a seat in front. I'm sure Mum said something like, "Well at least that's all the excitement done for today." Someone with a sick sense of humour decided that we obviously hadn't had enough excitement and decided to throw some more our way. This was in the form of concrete ballasts strewn across the tracks, after thieves had stolen copper wiring from the side of the railway line.

Picture the scene: The train is going at 125 mph and suddenly it brakes. Underneath our carriage we hear a noise that I can only describe as gravel and rocks going round an empty cement mixer, which seemed to last forever and the train starts to shift violently. Mum is doing her best to make light of the situation so as not to alarm me but that was totally unnecessary as a big burly guy further down the carriage exclaimed "F***ing hell – what on earth is that? I think we're going to de-rail!" Now, we'll just pause there for a second and remember Mr H's most important memory of the night of the riots. Not the fact that the love of his life might have been killed in a high speed train crash. Oh no! The fact that someone 'dinged' his door in the train station car park. "Well, I'd only just had it," he just said again. I don't think he is ever going to get over this...

The train manager flew into our carriage and said, "Did you all hear that?" I was tempted to reply, "Sorry, what did you say? I couldn't hear you over the loud clanging and banging coming from underneath the carriage that sounds like the train is ripping apart."

Luckily we didn't de-rail and the train just gradually started slowing down until it rolled at a snail's pace into Rugby and finally came to a standstill. We waited whilst three engineers with torches looked underneath our carriage. Personally, I don't think it needed one and a half hours and three engineers to tell us that the train was broken, I could have told them that in the space of one minute. The train manager came over the tannoy to tell us that the concrete ballast had severed three brake lines and that the train would be terminating at Rugby. Luckily though another train to Euston had just pulled into the station and would be waiting for us to disembark this one and get on it.

I could tell that the train manager had successfully completed his diversity training as his announcement continued, "...and the lady that needs special assistance, please be assured that 'Deborah' and her team are on the way over with a ramp to help you off the train and board the other one." In a way it would have been more fun if he hadn't done his diversity training and had made a totally un-pc announcement, which is exactly what happened with one of the guys getting me off the train.

The Virgin Trains special assistance crew boarded the train and one of the guys, 'Steve', grabbed the handles on the wheelchair and said, "Shall I take you backwards?" My reply of "What - with my mum watching?" made him go a rather scarlet colour and I could see Deborah was trying to stifle a grin. He didn't say anything else for fear of putting his foot in it again until we boarded the next train. This train was rammed with people and for once I was pleased that I had my own chair to sit in. The allotted wheelchair space was taken up by loads of suitcases and at the direction of the Virgin Trains staff, "Get these suitcases moved, we need this wheelchair space!" they all quickly disappeared. Steve, having now got over his earlier embarrassment parked my wheelchair and said, "Is this good for you?" to which I piped up "Steve, I had the ride of my life." Poor Steve scuttled away his face once again burning.

Thankfully the rest of the journey was uneventful and we finally arrived into Euston approaching 11:30pm.

We thought that enough excitement had been bestowed on us for this trip, but it wasn't to end there. On the way back from work the next day, the heavens opened. Luckily being the organised person that I am, I had purchased a wheelchair cover (imagine a pram cover but only bigger) that would cover me and the wheelchair up if it decided to rain. People at the venue where I was working did chuckle when they saw me but to be fair I did look like 'Andy' from *Little Britain*. Mum and I got soaked on our way back to the hotel and to make matters worse the rioting was still continuing. Not ones to be deterred by such events, after all, we had survived a near miss of a high speed rail crash the night before, we still met up with some friends for dinner near Euston. We all played 'spot the rioter' and I think Mum won.

I needed the toilet on the train on the way back. I really should have just held it in. Going to the toilet when the train is doing 125mph and tilting is hard enough when you have the use of both legs. Trying to go when you are on crutches and can't put one of your feet down is nigh on impossible. Mum volunteered to come in with me but being the brave solider that I am, I decided to go on my own and Mum waited outside in case I had any problems. I only bounced off the wall a couple of times so concluded my trip a success.

I also managed to actually wee down the toilet itself. This made me think as to why men seem to have such a problem with their aim. After all I didn't have any hose pipe attachment to help with my aim and was struggling to sit (well, hover, you know why girls) with my one leg stretched out in a plaster cast - and then I had to try and wipe as well. I have come to the conclusion that men are just simply lazy and can't be bothered.

On one of the journeys down to London there was a blind disabled guy in our carriage travelling alone. He was calling out that he needed the toilet but there were no staff around. Mum decided to do a 'RAOK' (random act of kindness) and offered to take him to the loo. I joked when she got back that he probably wasn't blind or disabled at all and that he was probably some toilet pervert and this was an act that he did on a regular basis. She disagreed but said, "I did find it strange though that he needed me to hold it for him..." Mum says that I misunderstood this comment and she didn't mean that she held his 'thing' but that she meant his white stick. Yeh... yeh... the lady doth protest too much methinks...

But once again I think we need to pause and have a minute's silence for Mr H's worst moment of the riots... lest we forget he dinged his car door that night....

Sunday 27th March

Mission for today:

- *Meet up with friends and have witty banter and alcohol (lots of both)*

Tales from Shifnal...

On Easter Sunday we went out for a meal and drinks with eight of our friends. All of them are in their late 20s and two of them are twins. I am telling you this important information for two reasons.

1) We like to hang out with people younger than us. This is advantageous as no one in the group has kids to get back to and it enhances our knowledge of what the 'yoof of today' are up to and, quite frankly, we enjoy it and don't feel any older than them (apart from the toilet incident which I will re-count in a minute).

2) The second reason that I am telling you this is that Mr H cannot tell the twins apart - ever. He has only known them for around four years now. It is hysterical to watch and again allows me that one time that I can totally take the piss out of him.

We will of course have to ditch any of them and find new friends to hang around with as soon as they start popping out babies though.

Tonight's trip out to Shifnal has provided much fodder for my tales.

Carrie was telling us about her morning in charge of her 12 year old step daughter. Mark had given her a list of instructions (but being a man we all agreed that they were pretty scant) as to what to do with her in the morning. He gave strict instructions to make sure that she was up at 9am as she wouldn't sleep properly the next night and with the clocks having changed they had already 'lost' an hour.

I do find this 'losing' an hour thing complete nonsense. I certainly did not lose an hour as I just stayed in bed an hour longer and tonight will still have my eight hours sleep. The only annoying aspect of changing the clocks is the three hours it takes me to wander round the house to change every clock that we have. I groan when I get in my car to see that there is another one I have to change, but I often leave that one.

Every six months I forget how to change it and only ever succeed in changing the language of the car to Portuguese. The clocks changing is always a comical topic with Dad. He always insists that his medicine must be taken at 6 o'clock every night. Once I said to him, "What happens when the clocks change, Dad? It won't really be 6 o'clock." I'd never seen such a look of horror on his face until that moment.

Anyway, back to Carrie's morning. Carrie's story of how she managed to wake her up was worthy of a call to ChildLine. She started with a gentle coo-ing in the ear. This was followed by gentle tickling of the feet and when none of that worked she said that the only way to wake her was to vigorously shake her. We all had visions of Carrie on top of her step daughter straddled legs either side of her shaking her so much so that to an outsider looking in it would look like she was trying to strangle her. Thankfully her step daughter did not see it like this and therefore *Tales from Social Services* will not be a later chapter in this book.

The next step on the instruction sheet was to 'give her a proper breakfast'. Carrie admitted that she was played by the twelve year old as she announced that she didn't want a proper breakfast but would have a banana and some juice instead. When Mark got back his daughter announced to him that Carrie had not given her a 'proper' breakfast. We all decided that this was entirely his fault. Really he should have provided a flowchart for this and any responsible Dad should know this.

It would start with the question, 'Do you want breakfast?' If answered, 'Yes' it would then move to, 'Give the child a proper breakfast'. If answered, 'No' then it would also move to the box, 'Give the child a proper breakfast.' We all empathised with Carrie that Mark's deficiencies in his instructions were entirely to blame and that a banana and juice was actually pretty good going for Easter Sunday. She could have asked for chocolate (which is what I had for breakfast).

Apparently Carrie made a further wrong move later on in the day. The cake that the daughter had been eating was half eaten and the rest was sitting on the side. Not having children, Carrie took this to mean that she could eat the cake. If any of you have children then you will know what a rookie mistake this was. If cake is abandoned by a child, it still belongs to the child and the rule is that you simply do not touch it.

Carrie also told us that she had managed to sell her spare Adele tickets to a guy called 'Miles' from Bristol. We helpfully joked that she would be sitting next to some really fat, smelly guy that would take up three seats. She seemed grateful for our comments.

The bar we were initially in had a lone male singer in his 20s doing a gig. We were all enjoying his singing and I spotted a lone female in her 20s looking a bit bored sitting at the table in front of him. We pondered as to whether this was his girlfriend supporting him, or maybe it could be his sister. We got our answer when he was packing up his things and had his tongue down her throat.

Carrie said, "I think we can safely say it was his girlfriend after all."

"Or a very inappropriate relationship with his sibling," I countered.

One of our Facebook friends helpfully commented that maybe they were from Norfolk, and if so then she probably was both his sister and his girlfriend (and possibly his daughter too).

We chatted about George and William the Alpacas joining us sometime in the next few months and Carrie has decided that she wants a pig to be named after her, if we are going to branch out into other livestock. We are thinking of having some lambs and pigs as well as the Alpacas. Mr H told her not to be greedy as she already had a chicken named after her, but then we both realised that that chicken had actually died, so we have agreed that she can be a pig or a lamb.

The bar wasn't serving food and as Mr H kept telling everyone (we counted at least three times), "I've only eaten a yogurt today, as I knew we were out for food", we finished our drinks and headed off in search of food. Third time lucky and we found a bar still serving food and as luck would have it they also had live music on for the night.

I always find going to the toilet in a pub a venture that will provide me with a comical tale. These toilets were no exception. The sign on the door said, 'There are smoke detectors fitted in these toilets and if you smoke then you will set them off.' I'm not a smoker but I like a challenge as much as the next person. But obviously, being the law abiding citizen that I am, I didn't flout their rule. I did however, realise why the sign was there. As I was tinkling on the toilet I realised that there was no toilet roll holder in front of me and none to either side of me either.

I started to panic (us ladies do not like to do the shake manoeuvre) before I twisted around to see that the toilet roll holder was high up on the wall behind me. All I could think of was that the pub was either trying to cut down on the amount that was being used or was trying to discourage older ladies from venturing into the establishment, as only the nimble could twist to reach it. I'm thinking that this is where the 'no smoking' sign came in as the whole episode of reaching, stretching and twisting to get the loo roll made me feel like I wanted a fag to celebrate. I did feel a great sense of achievement that I was still young enough to be one of the bar's clientele and it was only afterwards that I remembered the tissues in my bag that I could have used instead.

Faz was with us tonight and Faz is my second husband (he doesn't know this yet). Should anything happen to Mr H then he will immediately move in to look after George and William the Alpacas. Being a lot younger than Mr H then prudence dictates that I should be sensible and have someone in reserve for the future.

However, there are two slight flaws in this plan. Mr H doesn't really drink so tonight he was the chauffeur for the night. Faz drinks like a fish and I'm not really his type (he is gay – in all honesty though, even if he was straight then I don't think I would be his type - I'm not really anyone's...) so maybe I need to have another spare husband in reserve. Hmmmmm... I will have to re-think this one.

Monday 28th March

Mission for today:

- *Catch up on Criminal Minds*

Tales from a bank holiday...

Being self-employed, it is unusual for me not to be working over Easter. I don't see the point in trying to go places when the world and his brother are on the roads and in the pubs, so I often carry on working from home. This year though I am up to date with work so have actually enjoyed the four day break.

Hurricane Katie was ferocious last night though and has washed away a lot of our drive. Mr H is going to borrow the Farmer's tractor later to try and put it back together. As you can see, it doesn't take much for him to need to borrow the tractor. I'm sure I've seen him hanging from a broken tree branch before to try and pull the branch onto the drive just so he can borrow the tractor to remove it (man logic). Unfortunately though the tractor has a small leak in the pipe so Matt needs to come down to tighten it up before Mr H can use it. Miranda (Matt's wife) texted Mr H to say, 'Matt will be down later to tighten it up but make sure you're not being idle in the meantime.'

(Miranda keeps her horses down the farm, so we see her regularly.)

We have good friends. Even Miranda keeps on top of Mr H's antics. She also keeps an eye on him when I'm in London to make sure he isn't slacking. To be honest though, she needn't bother. Our neighbours, the Farmer, 93 and his wife 78 are as good as any police surveillance operation.

I remember once I was away in London from Monday to Friday. On the Saturday morning, the Farmer's wife said to me, "Mr H had a female visitor on Tuesday at 6pm. She didn't leave until 8pm. Your mother and father in law came over, I think she took your ironing away and brought it back, and we knew that you were back last night as all the lights were on in the house as Graham went from room to room. I suspect he was cleaning and vacuuming before you came back." I thanked her for her contemporaneous notes and did assure her that I knew who the female was and that she did not need to set the dogs on her if she came again. Old people make me chuckle. I have wondered whether they have webcams set up in our house as they always know what we are up to.

Mr H is currently outside with the dogs as there a massive pool of water by the container that is higher than the door of the container. The container is the equivalent of a 'man shed'. It's 40 foot and if he ever annoys me then it's big enough for him to live in. He bought a pump recently so that he could pump the water away and to stop it flooding into the container. Unfortunately, he didn't think through where he should store the pump and it is in the container itself. He now has the problem that he needs the pump to remove the water to get into the container but he needs to get into the container to get the pump to remove the water. I helpfully suggested that once he has managed to get the pump out then it might be better to store it in the shed in the future. He grunted which I took to mean, 'Thank you, Honey. That's a really helpful solution to the pickle that I got myself into.'

When Mr H popped in for a cup of tea, between water pumping, I was watching *Criminal Minds* whilst working on my book (multi-tasking is another crucial difference between men and women. Men simply cannot concentrate on more than one task at the same time. I manage to iron, whilst watching telly, whilst also facetiming my sister).

I exclaimed, "Oh no!"

Mr H said, "What? What's happened?"

I said, "JJ and her boyfriend are splitting up."

Mr H said, "Oh good! I might now have a chance with her."
I made a mental note to book him in at the doctors to
check the state of his mind.

The tractor is now fixed and Mr H has skipped like a kid in
a toyshop to go and sort out the drive. I'm sure that there
is nothing wrong with the drive but it will keep him out of
my hair for a couple of hours, so who am I to argue?

Tuesday 29th March

Missions for today:

- *Get my nails done*
- *Have a fun night out with Mummykins and StepDaddykins*

Tales from working from home...

I do love working from home. It means that I can flex my time so that I can also do those important necessary day jobs, like go and get my nails done, and work at night instead. Usually my people-watching skills are at their finest in the nail salon. Unfortunately, today there was only me and one other lady in there, so interesting topics of conversation were a bit sparse. I made a mental note to ask them when they will be at their busiest in the future and make sure that I book in again at a busy time. One exciting thing did happen when the beautician asked me if I had any drugs on me. It turned out that she had a headache and simply meant Nurofen (I knew that).

Before heading off to get my nails done, I had a typical bizarre phone conversation. We used to run a Caravan Club CL site. We closed it down at the end of December in order that we could accommodate George and William the Alpacas. In all honesty, I do prefer animals to people and it's been a good decision. However, we are still getting phone calls asking if we are taking bookings.

Today a man called up to ask, "Is this the camping site?"

"I'm afraid that we closed it down at the end of December, so we aren't taking bookings anymore."

"So does that mean that I can't come?"

"Yes, that's right... we are now closed."

"So I won't be able to come at all?"

"Yes, that's right... we are permanently closed."

"Oh! Do you know of any others in the area?"

I told him of a couple that were nearby but that he would have to check the Caravan Club's website to make sure they were still open and taking bookings.

"Do you think they will take me?"

"I'm sorry – what do you mean?"

"Well – I have a van and it's the same model as the Gypsies have and I'm not sure whether they will take me."

"You will have to phone them up and check."

"Well, would you take me?"

"As I said, we are closed, so you will need to find out from the other sites themselves." I resisted the urge to say, "No, I'm happily married thank you."

"Well, can you give me their phone numbers then?"

"I'm afraid I don't have their phone numbers, you will have to find them from the Caravan Club website."

"So you can't give me their numbers?"

"No, I'm afraid not."

"Well, I am actually thinking of selling my caravan and getting a different one. Do you think I should do this?"

I resisted the urge to say that I thought that he should immediately sell his caravan, emigrate and never come back to the UK again but just made some crackling noises and said, "You're breaking up... I.... c-a-a-n-n-'-t he---ar you..." and put the phone down.

That was five minutes of my life that I will never get back ('and mine' I hear you say).

Casper has been a good boy today. He seems to be coming out of his 'SAD' (Seasonal affected disorder) and is back to serial killing ways. He seems to stop in the winter months but makes up for it once Spring is in full flow. Unfortunately, this was a bird and not a rodent. I had a long chat with him last year about picking the right type of victim, so I am disappointed that he has chosen to ignore my advice. If any of you have cats then you will know that they do exactly what they want, when they want and how they want. It's cat law. Once he killed a woodpecker and put it under our bed. We didn't notice for four days.

In a typical, 'I am cat. I shall kill whatever I like' type of way he decided to eat all of today's bird in front of me except the legs and five feathers. I think this is some sort of satanic symbolism in cat world.

I have had a massive headache today. This is ironic as I didn't drink any alcohol last night (or maybe it is alcohol withdrawal...) I always want lots of hugs when I have a headache. Mr H is very obliging in these circumstances, "I hope your headache goes soon, I'm fed up with having to give you all of these hugs." He is such a star.

As we were driving up the drive today, I exclaimed, "Oh look! It's the pelican-y, stork thingy," pointing at the big bird sitting in the middle of the paddock.

Mr H said, "You mean the heron."

"Yes that's right! Look! There's its mate on the fence post!"

"That's a buzzard."

I think that I need to stop watching *Criminal Minds* for a bit and turn over to the Nature Channel (if there is indeed any such thing) as I think that my knowledge of wildlife is a bit lacking and is making me look stupid.

Tonight we went out for a belated birthday meal with Mummykins and SDK (Stepdaddykins). Mummykins has kindly offered to read the 17,000 words that I have written so far and provide me with some critical feedback. It's a good job that she is reading it and not listening to it though, as when I told her about security at the airport 'swabbing' my handbag for explosives (you'll read about this in a bit), she exclaimed, "They swapped your handbag for some explosives?" Yes that's right mum! They took my handbag off me, gave me some explosives and said, "Have a nice flight, madam." She also mis-heard when I told her about security at Belfast airport and the 'being on a farm' issue (again you will read about this in a bit). Mum said, "They wanted to swap your shoes for foot and mouth?" Once again, yes Mum.

We joked that my book would become an international bestseller and SDK said, "So which morning show would you do, if it did? Would you go on 'BBC Breakfast' or 'This Morning'?" Mr H broke out into laughter and said, "She wouldn't be able to get up that early, she would have to do 'Loose Women'!" He is such a supportive husband.

There is some critical piece of information that I have neglected to tell you about Mr H. He has a sweeter tooth than a three year old and every pudding he orders in a pub or restaurant will never meet his expectations. We all groaned when he said, "I'll have the treacle tart - that sounds delicious." As predicted, the treacle tart was not up to expectations. It did not consist of treacle but was full of apple. What then followed was a ten minute discussion finding out the ingredients from the chef. As we were leaving the restaurant, we saw the waitress re-write the sign on the pudding board to say 'Apple treacle tart'. I think I'm going to have to ban him from ordering puddings in the future.

On a happy note, our purchase of extra land has gone through today so George and William the Alpacas are getting closer to moving in. I still think Mr H is trying to kill me though. At the bottom of the mug of this morning's latte was a paperclip. I have no idea how it got there. One of our Facebook friends helpfully said, 'Do you think that's why he wants the extra land?' I don't really think it's to dispose of my body but then again when the fence guy came this morning to give us a quote he did measure my height. He claimed it was to gauge the height of the new fence but I'm not so sure... One of my Facebook friends said, 'Was he also wearing a black suit and did he arrive in a long black limo?' I'm not sure about the car as I never saw that but he was suspiciously dressed in all black.

The new bit of land that we have bought has a big mound on it. I asked the Farmer whether I was likely to find any gold or hidden treasures in it. "No but there are two dead horses in there." I wasn't as thrilled by this news as I don't think there is a market for dead horses. Although I might advertise them on eBay - people will buy anything these days...

One of our friends, Bobby, asked whether we were going to call the mount 'Mount Graham', so that they could ask, "Has Jo gone out to Mount Graham?" I told him that I was going to steal that phrase for my book and he's been muttering nonsense about 'royalties' ever since. I did say that he could have 1p from every book sale. I think that it's safe to say that he won't become a millionaire anytime soon. Of course I'm joking, I told him he couldn't have a penny...

Wednesday 30th March

Mission for today:

- *Message my girlfriends to look at booking another girls' weekend away*

A memory has popped up on my Facebook timeline today about a girls' weekend away a few years ago. Girls' weekends away will always provide me with many tales to tell.

Tales from girls' weekends...

A few years ago Mr H bought me a girls' weekend away to stay in a swanky hotel in London with three of my besties. I like to think that this was a totally selfless gift and had nothing to do with the fact that I hadn't been working in London much at that time and that he needed a break so had to send me away for a bit. Jade, Aimee and Little Wren (remember she is my sort of little sister) accompanied me for a weekend of cocktails, a few more cocktails with a bit of celebrity stalking thrown into the mix and a few more cocktails.

One of the discussions on this weekend away was the 'laminated list'. If you don't know what the laminated list is then you need to YouTube the episode of *Friends* with

Ross, guest starring Isabella Rosselini. The 'laminated list' is basically a list of ten celebrities that you are allowed to have no-strings attached sex (or whatever you fancy really) without it affecting your current relationship. I suppose some people call it the 'free pass'.

It's always interesting to compare who features on someone's laminated list. Jade (in her own words) has a weird taste in men, so her top two at the time were Steve Backshall and Bryan Adams. When quizzed as to why Steve topped the list, she admitted that as he was generally away with work for around nine months of the year, then he was the perfect man. The rest of us went silent with awe, thinking that we might have to re-think our choices. I have to point out that Steve is no longer top of Jade's list as he is now engaged to an Olympic rower and in Jade's own words, "I'm not going to try and compete with that, she could easily take me."

Since this time she has gone for someone else equally dedicated to their work but more achievable, Noel Fitzpatrick. We have managed to successfully stalk him twice now at the Pet Show and both got selfies with him two years in a row. I must admit in this year's picture he is starting to look more tired with dark circles under the eyes – I have made a mental note to ask him at next year's Pet Show whether he is looking after himself properly and that if he is worried about the dark circles then I've heard that rubbing pile cream on them can reduce them. I'm sure he will appreciate this thoughtful advice.

I must admit that the first time that we went to the Pet Show we actually spent longer drinking lager in Wetherspoons in the NEC foyer than actually in the show itself (not that we confessed this to our husbands). I think we were both so excited at having got a selfie with Noel that we needed celebratory alcohol to bask in the glory. When Noel was posing with us for our selfies, he said, "What would your husbands think about this?" Both Jade and I looked at each other and silently mouthed, "What husbands?" – we are so in tune with each other.

It was also at the Pet Show that gave me the idea of having two Alpacas. Mr H was not very thrilled at this news, but didn't seem to mind about the selfie. I think he has been secretly trying to offload me onto someone else for years. Jade and I have also been thinking of ways to get to see Noel at Supervet's surgery in Surrey. We have concluded that the only way to get to see him for longer than a selfie is to take one of our pets there. All of our pets are relatively healthy though so we are on the lookout for a broken pet so that we can go there.

I have digressed a bit – so back to girls' weekends away...

One other topic of conversation we often have is who would be on our laminated list if we were lesbians. I have absolutely no hesitation whatsoever in saying that Sandra Bullock would top my list. Not the *Miss Congeniality* SB but more the *A Time to Kill* SB. Men simply won't do this. A few of us were sitting around once and we asked the men to say who would be top of their list if they were gay. None of them would admit as to who would be up there.

Last year we went to Liverpool for Aimee's hen weekend. In true hen weekend fashion I bought a helium inflatable willy balloon which Aimee had to carry on the train and around Liverpool. We are good friends like that. It was actually really handy. When we lost her in Debenhams we only had to look up and play 'spot the willy balloon.'

Apparently, the professionally offended were out in Liverpool that day as when we were munching our way through lunch in TGI Fridays, 'Mr Willy' had to be taken to the manager's office as there were some children in the restaurant that could get offended. Personally, I was offended by some of the children in the restaurant that day but I didn't see anyone putting them in a room out the back. (Obviously this is a joke.)

I do find it comical though that if you are of a certain age and don't have biological children yourself then you are tarnished with some 'child hater' badge. I do confess to being a bit naughty and playing up to this. If we go to family catch ups, I will always get the inevitable, "So don't you want children then, don't you like them?" My answer of, "Well, I couldn't eat a whole one" is usually enough for them to leave me alone and not broach the topic again.

Back to Aimee's hen weekend though...

In true celebrity stalking fashion, Jade noticed on Twitter that Calum Best was staying in the same hotel as us. Having successfully stalked him we managed to get some selfies with him. Unfortunately for Little Wren, this was the point that she had wandered three metres away to the hotel bar to get some more champagne. During her two minutes away from us we had approached Calum, had pictures taken with him and were basking in our glory. She had missed all of this. It was a bit like the Kit Kat panda advert with the photographer. We did feel sorry for her but obviously not sorry enough at the time to make sure that she had seen what we were doing.

On the Saturday night we went to see some strippers. They were called something like 'Delicious Lads' (to be honest, I can't remember because we had had a lot to drink in the limousine by this point). I did think of contacting trading standards afterwards as they were not delicious and definitely not lads. But the night was more entertaining due to the drunken exploits of the 50-something mother of one of the 'hens' there who was heckling and trying to cop a feel of all the men on stage. When the fire-fighting act came on we did have visions of her launching herself onto the stage and setting herself on fire. If I'm honest, I think we were all a bit disappointed that she didn't.

It was that weekend that we introduced Primark (or Primarni as we call it) to Aimee and Jill. Jill was a Primark virgin and needed to cut her teeth. Little Wren and I are what I would call 'expert level' Primark shoppers. Primark shoppers start at 'entry' level, proceed to 'amateur', then to 'advanced' and finally to 'expert'. We are proud to be at the top level. Within 20 minutes we were in, had collected two massive brown bags worth of stuff, had paid and were out the door again. I think it might have been one of our personal bests.

Little Wren's boyfriend Alan does not like visiting Primark with her, "She was in there for at least two hours - I had four fags whilst I was waiting for her." At this news I did wonder if their relationship was okay, as she never takes that long with me... Alan also made the mistake of saying to her, "Do you really need any more handbags?" Men say the silliest of things sometimes! If Mr H says that to me then I say, "It's like you men never having enough cars... or tractors." Oh? Wait.... that doesn't really work.

I won't buy anything over 15 quid though - who are they trying to rip off?! When my vest tops went up from £1.50 each to £2, I remember thinking of boycotting them. I remember saying to Mr H, "I mean - that's daylight robbery. It's nearly a 50% increase!"

A few years ago Little Wren and I went away to London for the weekend and thought we would try some celebrity spotting. Off we trotted to the Champagne bar at the Savoy Hotel. Our waitress Gemma told us that we had just that second missed Patsy Kensit.

The clientele of the Champagne bar made us chuckle and others made us roll our eyes. Some of the women in there were what I affectionately call 'hoity toity'. Hoity toity people are so up themselves that they seem to think that they don't need to use manners. Our waitress really liked us (although seeing us nurse a £15 cocktail for two hours, I think she realised that we probably wouldn't be the biggest tippers in the world) as we chatted to her and had fun with her. The older ladies in the corner clicked their fingers in the air to summon her and dismissed her with a wave of their hands. Is it wrong that I really wished some awful tragedy would befall these odious women? I made a mental note to give myself a big slap on the chops if ever I won the lottery and started to act like them.

One of the ladies complained to Gemma, "Does the piano really have to be that loud? I can't hear myself talking." I was grateful that the piano was that loud as I really did not want to hear her talking. I also thought about requesting that the piano player play some power ballads to drown her out further.

A group of men at one table had ordered a £2,000 bottle of pink Champagne but hadn't drunk it all. Gemma sneaked a couple of glasses leftover from it and gave them to us for free. Each glass was worth around £50. Poor Little Wren doesn't really like Champagne and was trying not to scrunch her face up as she drank it.

The toilets there were so posh that we took lots of selfies of ourselves in there. I think the staff thought that we might try and steal some of the ornaments or face towels though as a cleaner mysteriously arrived while we were in there and pretended to busy herself folding the face towels and brushing away non-existent dust.

Friday 1st April

Mission for today:

- *Wind up Mr H that I'm going to buy him a tractor*

Tales from April Fool's Day...

Each year I am tempted to put a picture of an ultrasound scan of a baby up on Facebook and announce to the world that I'm pregnant. However, even I won't joke about that. Mr H's mum would definitely think it was real and I couldn't have her in floods of tears on the phone (tears of joy I assure you) to have to then confess and tell her that it was some awful joke. So this year I decided to joke about something that wouldn't hurt anyone. I set my Facebook status as, 'OK, I have finally given into peer pressure... #tractor4graham'.

Amazingly quite a few of my friends thought that it was true and that I was buying him a tractor. Once they realised it was an April fool, 'cruel' and 'mean', were words that stood out in the comments. I think he's forgiven me. I say 'think' as he hasn't actually spoken to me since getting in from work. But I have made a note to do this again. The peace and quiet has been lovely.

Lots of our friends have been helpfully putting pictures of tractors up on Facebook all day and tagging Mr H in them. I didn't realise how much they hated him! How cruel to rub his nose in it. One of our friends found a pair of high-heeled ladies shoes with 'Jack Deere' written on them and a picture of a tractor. She asked whether I would wear them if Mr H got his tractor. Since rupturing my Achilles I can't wear high heels for any length of time but Mr H replied to say that he was more likely to wear them.

Sadly this is true. Mr H seems to like dressing up as a woman. So far he has been a pink lady from *Grease*, a belly dancer and a transsexual vampire. Any fancy dress party is an excuse for him to put on his wig and high heels.

I remember when I was looking for some red high heeled shoes for him for his transsexual vampire costume. I went into Lichfield and started with the charity shops. This was my first mistake as Lichfield is a lot posher than Wolverhampton and the shoes in the charity shops weren't cheap. Also women in Lichfield are much daintier than the women of Wolverhampton, so there were no wide fitting size eight shoes to be found.

I chastised myself for not going to Wolves. However, as luck would have it my perseverance paid off as I wandered into Dorothy Perkins. Sitting on a shoe rack looking up at me were some size eight high heeled red shoes. They were perfect for this outfit. As I walked towards them my excitement grew as I realised that they were a wide fitting. At £7.95 they were also cheaper than most of the shoes in the charity shops. I grabbed them quickly before anyone else could get their mitts on them and took them to the till.

I asked the shop assistant if she thought that they would fit a man and was about to recount my tale about how it was for a fancy dress murder mystery night and that he wasn't really a cross dresser. I didn't even get to say any of that as she immediately looked at me and without the hint of sarcasm or a knowing smile she just said, "We sell a lot of those to men, they're really popular because of the wide fitting."

At that point, I then remembered why I had gone to Lichfield to find his high heels. Lichfield is posh and has a lot of judges and barristers residing there. I had remembered seeing a story about how it was often men in these highly paid professions that were secret cross dressers. That was why I had chosen Lichfield and not Wolverhampton - gangsters just don't have the same predilections. As I was driving home I was trying to remember where I had seen the story but then it came to me, it was on an episode of *Inspector Morse* and was nothing to do with Lichfield. Never mind though my mission was accomplished.

Saturday 2nd to Sunday 3rd April

Mission for the weekend:

- *Have a fabulous weekend with friends*

Tales from Aimee and Lad's one year anniversary...

This weekend was the first year wedding anniversary of two of our fabulous friends. I had been chief bridesmaid last year and Mr H was head groomsman. As a surprise for Aimee we had organised a weekend away back at the hotel where they had had their wedding breakfast, with lots of their close friends. This weekend has provided me with many stories for the book, some of which I really can't put in print!

Mr H wanted to take his favourite pillow but I assured him that as we had booked a newly refurbished, executive room then the pillows would be just fine. When we arrived, the first thing he did was plump them one-by-one and move them around whilst sighing and making sucking noises. It looked like he was a football manager trying to position his players. It took him five minutes to do this. (In that time I had already had my first glass of wine. When he went to the bathroom I deliberately moved them all around. My evil inner twin likes to rear her head every so often.)

By upgrading to the 'executive' rooms they gave us extra cushions on the bed, bottles of water in the fridge, the smell of fresh paint and an ambient blue light in the bathroom. Aimee naively said, "Awwww wasn't that romantic - the lovely blue light?" Jack said, "You do realise why they put blue lights in bathrooms, don't you?" We all did but Aimee didn't. "It's so that drug addicts can't find their veins to inject themselves." I think that Aimee was horrified by this revelation and the fact that the blue lights were only in the executive rooms and not the standard rooms. We all concluded that it was more likely to be the wealthy that could afford to take the drugs and that's why the lights were only in the executive rooms.

One weird consequence of the blue light was the colour of your poo. Over breakfast Aimee and I had a chat about how we had both thought that we must be ill as the blue light meant that your poo looked a purple-ey/blackcurrant type of colour. At the time (and after a fair amount of alcohol) it is a freaky thing to see. I was merrily wiping away and as I turned around to flush the toilet I exclaimed, "What the frigg is that?!" Apparently, Aimee had done exactly the same thing. Jack disappeared for a while after that conversation and I'm sure he was back in his room trying to do one just to see what the fuss was all about. When I checked out and the receptionist said, "Did you enjoy your stay?" I did bite my tongue and decided not to talk about the purple poo incident.

There was a lot of 'poo' talk at breakfast, as mum had sent me a video of Lucy wandering around the garden first thing in the morning. As I watched it and saw Lucy squat to go to the toilet, I did think it a bit strange at her video of choice.

She said on Messenger, 'Did you like the video of Lucy?' and I thought, 'Oh here we go, she's getting like Dad, as he always counts how many poos Lucy does when she stays with him.'

So I said, 'What? The video of her going to the toilet?'

Mum said, 'No it wasn't, I was showing you how sprightly she was and how well her legs were doing. She wasn't going to the toilet you daft ape-eth*!'

Now all my friends think my mum sent a video to me of our dog doing a poo... I might tell them at some point it wasn't.

* During her first read through, Mum said, "You don't spell it like that. It's ha'p'orth." I really do learn something new every day. I thought the saying meant that you were acting like a monkey and being stupid.

I asked Mr H how he had slept and he said, "I'm glad I sorted through the pillows. I slept like a log. And you laugh at me for doing it." That really wasn't why I was laughing at him...

Jill had the delight of unintentionally seeing a naked man over the weekend. She swore blind that we had told her that we were in room 101 and on her way to the bar she rapped loudly on the door of room 101 shouting, "Oi! Lazy Graham! Get out of the shower now, you're late for dinner." Unfortunately for her we were in room 110 and the man that answered the door of room 101, having just been disturbed in the shower, was not best pleased to see her. Her, "Oh?! You're not Graham, sorry!" and running away down the corridor seemed to be the only thing that she could do under the circumstances. Personally, I would have said, "Nice todger!" winked at him and then run away. Men are rarely angry with you after receiving compliments about their tackle.

Aimee and Lad were lucky to have the presence of a celebrity for their anniversary. We like to pretend that we had specifically organised it, but it was a lucky coincidence that he lived down the road from the hotel. Glynn Purnell of Purnell's in Birmingham was having a quiet dinner with his family - well he was - until Mr H accosted him and asked him if he would have a pic with Aimee and Lad for their anniversary. He was lovely though and very amenable and none of us have been slapped with an injunction so we considered it a successful stalking event.

We had had to pre-order our meals for the night and I was the one with the list of what everyone had ordered.

Unfortunately, it all went to pot when I took a wee break and people were fighting over the chocolate brownies that arrived for dessert. Normally I would pass the mantle to Mr H but the last time that happened he misread the list and all hell had broken loose, so I thought it safest to take the list with me. I was wrong. Mr H ended up eating a child's Rocky Road dessert.

After dinner we retreated to the bar to chat about what Aimee and Lad had discovered from their first year of marriage. We expected things like, "He's really romantic and does...." or, "She is such a good wife as she...." What none of us expected was, "Well, I've been working on his timekeeping. It's really not good and I've been having to nag him to keep him to time." Lad was equally as complimentary, "Well she's a lot less patient than she used to be..." We tried to rapidly change the subject before this can of worms multiplied. Alan didn't help the situation though as he piped up, "Well you do realise that Little Wren is the kiss of death don't you?" Apparently, she has been a bridesmaid for five couples so far and four of them are now divorced. Aimee and Lad are the only ones that are still together. Jill and Jack have just got engaged and I'm sure I overheard them say that Little Wren was most definitely not going to be a bridesmaid for them.

Lucy and Bonnie had been to Mum's for the night as Dad was away and couldn't have Lucy. We haven't yet broken the news to him as to where Lucy went and I hope he won't remember to ask when he gets back (and is unlikely to read my book, so I think the secret is safe). He would be distraught to think that he might not have her again. Mum said that Lucy did follow her everywhere when she had food. I think that Grandad spoils Lucy when she goes to stay with him and probably shares all of his food with her. Unluckily for Lucy, Grandma was not going to share her food. I like to think it's because it isn't good for Lucy but I once made the mistake of trying to share Mum's food and she nearly bit me...

The day after our surprise wedding anniversary shenanigans we all sat around outside in the beer garden of the hotel. Obviously we were all shivering under our coats but determined that as it was now April then we would enjoy the sunshine. The conversation turned to blood pressure. None of us can remember how the topic came up. Interestingly, all the men there had high blood pressure and all the women's was perfect. I think I heard Jack mutter something about, "You women stressing us men out." Personally, I think that if they didn't have us then their blood pressure would be far worse. Mr H can never find anything and I always know where everything is. If he didn't have me then his blood pressure would be through the roof with the stress of hunting for his things.

Hughie and Elly told us that they nearly had trouble checking into the hotel the day before. I had done everyone's bookings and although each room was in the name of one of the couple, the hotel had gone with a very sexist view and all the rooms had the men's name on them. Well, this was apart from ours which said 'Jo and Graham' - but I think they weren't sure whether we were an all-male couple, so were hedging their bets. As Hughie was checking in he thought they were all booked under my name but couldn't remember my surname. Funnily enough the hotel didn't have a booking under the name 'Joanne New-Shoes', despite him asking.

We got back from the weekend completely exhausted from chatting, laughing and staying up late. We were hoping to have a nice relax on the settee but didn't get any peace and quiet as we heard shots ringing out across the lawn. I swear that I heard some of it ricocheting off our log shack on the front garden. Apparently some Canada geese had decided to move in on the farm so the 93 year old Farmer had decided to 'shoo' them off with his shotgun. Our friend Miranda texted to say, 'If I was you I wouldn't come outside as his aim isn't that good'. I looked through the window to see the Farmer leaning on his cane and trying to aim his gun and ducked as I heard more shot ricocheting off somewhere. I checked that all the pets were safely inside and promptly sent Mr H out on the garden to investigate.

Monday 4th April

Missions for today:

- *Hope that there isn't a dead goose in the moat when I wake up (this isn't a mission as such but a 'wish')*
- *Pack for smelly London*

Sadly, the next day I woke up to find a dead goose floating around our side of the moat. It appeared that the Farmer's aim was better than I thought. Luckily I am heading off to smelly London later so I won't have to keep seeing it. I'm hoping that Mr H will have managed to get it out with a rake before I come back. Mind you, my money is on him slipping in the moat whilst trying to scoop it up. On the plus side, as long as it's an accident then I get to claim on the life insurance. I like to look on the bright side of life...

Mr H asked what train I was going to be on today and I said, "I'm going early so that I'll be in time to have dinner with Alexandra." He said, "Oh! So you don't want to have dinner with me then before you go?" I didn't bother to answer him. After 25 years he should know by now not to ask such stupid questions. I always put make up on before heading out to catch the train. If I am ever involved in some high speed crash, I really want to look my best. A year ago I decided to invest in some decent make up and swapped my cheap stuff for Estée Lauder. I did this after a waiter asked me, "What can I get you to eat Sir? Oh?! I'm sorry Madam..."

Mr H loves it when I go to London. He always pretends to look sad when he drops me off at Wolverhampton train station but I'm sure I see him doing a fist bump* in the air as I turn to wave goodbye.

* I always remember the wrong word. Apparently, it is a fist pump, according to the latest Tesco advert.

Just before leaving home, I asked Mr H if he would help me set up the Facebook page 'Tractor4Graham'. I'm hoping that if I can canvass interest in the book before it comes out then it will increase sales. He will then get his tractor and therefore stop his eternal moaning. It's a win-win for both of us if that happens. In typical fashion this resulted in an argument.

I was happily inviting my friends to 'like' the page when Mr H said, "What are you doing?!! You don't want them to like it yet - there's nothing to like! You need to fill the page first, otherwise no one else will like it with nothing on there to see." Just as he had finished his rant, a notification pops up, 'Sheila has liked your page'.

"See!" He exclaimed, "...and now when Sheila's friends see it pop up on her timeline and they visit the page then they won't like it because there's nothing there." Before he had finished his second rant at least three more friends had liked the page. I was trying not to smirk, well okay, I didn't really try at all as his getting more agitated made me chuckle to myself all the more. (I think I might need therapy, I seem to delight in annoying him...)

This resulted in him grunting something and he left me to it and went off to hang the washing out. In the space of ten minutes, 28 friends had already liked the page (and I will say that I am feeling the love, thank you!) Not to upset Mr H any further - although to be fair I was heading off to London for a few days, so wasn't actually that concerned about whether he was going to have a long sulky strop - I rapidly began copying some bits from the book to fill up the page on the off chance that some random person visited it and wanted to see what it was all about. (They didn't.)

What fascinated me the most about how rapidly my friends were liking the page, was the 'profession' order in which it happened. I concluded that it must be a slow day for the NHS as those of my friends that worked in that sector seemed to be hot off the mark. I had visions of some poor woman with her bits on show having a catheter fitted, whilst one of my nursing friends was saying, "Just a minute, hang on a sec" as they got their mobile phone out of their pocket to 'like' the page.

Teachers were in the second category of 'liking' the page. But I belatedly remembered that it was the Easter holidays so decided not to chastise them for having their mobiles on in class. Surprisingly, the retired were not as quick off the mark. Thinking about it though, it made sense really. 1) They were probably having an afternoon nap, or 2) The technology of the situation was just too much for them to cope with.

Trying to pick out some short, funny bits from the book to upload to the page was quite hard. Something I have noticed though, through scanning what I have written so far, is that a lot of the stories involve toilets and poo and me being a suspected terrorist. As I was happily copying some of my 'tales from the airport' to the Facebook page I did wonder whether the Facebook Police would shut me down for inappropriate use of words or maybe Mr H will facetime me tonight and say, "I'm sure I saw a drone flying above our house earlier."

Tales from Virgin Trains...

I am now sitting on the train to London, having nearly missed it. I blame the Virgin Trains guy in charge of the first class* lounge at Wolves. As he was seeing a train off from the platform, he quite clearly couldn't multi task and it took him four minutes to let me, and another woman that was waiting, into the lounge. I was starting to get anxious as he was severely eating into my 'fleecing the lounge of all its food and drink' time. I only had chance to grab a latte, a banana and a bag of crisps. I have made a mental note to leave earlier next time.

* I explain at the end of this day why I travel first class, so don't get all judgemental and think that I'm posh. I'm as tight as the next Midland-er. But I manage to bag a bargain with First Class tickets, which you will see later.

Whilst in the lounge I was hoping to have time to browse through the visitor book to see if there were any funny comments from passengers to add to my tales. Being a bit strapped for time I only had chance to glance down one page. One comment immediately caught my attention though as it was written in shouty-capital letters.

It was a comment from a passenger (whose name was unfortunately indecipherable) that said, 'NO GOOD FOR FOREIGNERS AT ALL!!!! AND THE WIFI WASN'T WORKING.' I was trying to work out what was meant by this? The lounge is basically settees, a telly in the corner, a coffee machine and assorted snacks such as crisps, fruit and popcorn and a fridge with soft drinks and water in it.

I couldn't work out whether the 'foreigners' that they were referring to were anyone that lived outside of

Wolverhampton. If that was the case, then that didn't make sense at all as the food of choice in Wolverhampton is curry, so the snacks on offer here would be perfect for non-Wolves peeps and wouldn't suit locals at all. Unfortunately, due to this passenger's capitalisation of his rantings there was no room for me to write a reply to them underneath to ask them for clarification. But if by some chance that person is reading this book, can you please let me know what you meant, as I am intrigued? Just to clarify, I understood the Wi-Fi point and yes, I can never get the Wi-Fi to work.

I just got irrationally momentarily excited when I just looked at the word count and realise that I have now written 30,000 words in this book and Facebook has just told me that 39 of my friends like the page. It reminded me of the time that we were on the M5 and drove past an Eddie Stobart lorry with the name 'Joanne Louise'. I screamed, "Look it's called Joanne Louise, that's my name!" (The last part of my exclamation was superfluous, as Mr H does know my name after being together for 25 years...) Mr H was driving and nearly had a heart attack. I do wonder how many Eddie Stobart lorries cause motorway accidents. Mr H was a meany though as he wouldn't reverse back up the motorway so that I could get a selfie with my name in the background. Sorry to go off topic... back to the journey to London.

Today has seen a lot of my friends posting on my Facebook timeline with which actors they want to be played by if by some miracle my book is ever made into a film. Jack has decided that he wants George Clooney to play him. A good choice as I will definitely play myself! Hughie wants Nick Frost (comedian with a big bushy beard) to play him. My friend Miranda wants to play herself - this is probably because she often chastises Mr H and as he wants to play himself I think she wants to do it on the big screen. Also, if there are a number of 'takes' to get a particular scene right then I think she relishes the chance to do it over and over again. Alexandra wants to play herself too. I think she decided this when Jack said that George Clooney could play him... and as he (George, not Jack) is on her laminated list she would get the chance to sleep with him.

I knew that I had arrived in London when the heavens opened. London always conspires against me. Being the seasoned traveller that I am though, I was cleverly wearing my waterproof coat with hood. Looking around me most of the people rushing along the pavements did not have coats with hoods and were getting drenched from the rain. I suspect that they all hate their jobs so much that they were hoping to come down with the flu so they could phone in sick. One woman who didn't want to get ill had a Sainsbury's carrier bag tied around her head. She probably thought that it was the cheapest way to buy an umbrella as it would only have cost her 5p. She was wrong. I got mine free from Primark when I bought Mr H a pack of his man pants.

The best thing about smelly London today was catching up with my work wife Alexandra. Our conversations are always totally hilarious and we often find random strangers trying to join in our fun. We only let them if they buy us a drink. Obviously, I'm kidding! Being two vulnerable women on our own you have to be careful. We make them buy us at least two...

We went to dinner at Poppadom Express as we both had a BOGO voucher from the hotel. This actually stands for 'Be Our Guest Offer'. Poppadom Express has moved premises and is back in the breakfast room at the Tavistock hotel where we used to stay. "The guests at breakfast won't be thrilled with the smell of curry", Alexandra astutely noted.

We moved to the President hotel after working out that the extra £3 a night was worth it to get Wi-Fi in the room and an extra five minute lie-in in the morning as it is slightly closer to the bus stop. You also get proper shower gel and not just a bar of soap. We are, after all, girls with standards.

We think that there were some virgin Poppadom Express-ers in there. A young couple were sat at the table next to us and seemed to copy our every move for the night. When we went up to the buffet table to choose our starters they followed. Four of us crowding around a small space resulted in a lot of, "Oh, excuse me", "Can I just grab a poppadom?", "Oh sorry, were you wanting that pakora?" etc. Given that we were the only ones in there they really could have waited but we think that they were scared to go up on their own.

The same thing happened with the main meals. We knew they waited for us again as we took our time before heading for the main meals. So, lo and behold, as we went to get our curry and rice there they were again. Normally it is me doing the stalking of others and I was bit unnerved having it done to me. I tried to outfox them with making a trip back to the starters and Alexandra went to the pudding area to throw them off the scent.

Our normal highly intellectual conversations then ensued. One topic was, 'What would we do if our husbands died?' We decided that we would use the life insurance to buy a skiing chalet but in honour of our husbands we would name it after them. We couldn't decide between 'Andgrah' (which would obviously have a silent 'h' on the end) or 'Grandrew' (with a silent second 'r'. We like to get details sorted). I preferred the latter and Alexandra the former. We said that they would have to have died as they wouldn't leave us for other women as they obviously couldn't do any better than us. We laughed and laughed at the thought of this. (When I got home I told Mr H this story and he said, "Why didn't you just call it 'Grand' – that has the 'Gra' from 'Graham' and the 'And' from 'Andrew'?" I gave him a look of, 'No one likes a show off'.)

Alexandra helpfully said, "Of course you know the saying, if your husband dies then you marry the carpenter or your neighbour." We concluded that that really wouldn't work in my situation as our carpenter was my Dad (and I wasn't from Norfolk) and our neighbour was a 93 year old Farmer. "And he is already married", Alexandra helpfully said. I contemplated this for a second but concluded that this wasn't that relevant as I reckon I could easily take a 78 year old if I needed to.

We concluded the 'husbands dying' conversation with the fact that we both would be unlikely to bother to find new men if it did happen and that we might try lesbianism instead. Men are such hard work and it would be nice to have someone living with us that we actually understand and think like us. Later on I decided that I couldn't even be bothered with that and would just add batteries to my regular Amazon 'subscribe and save' order.

Alexandra asked if her expertise at Maths was in the book and I assured her that it was in the introduction. Luckily for me, Alexandra is just as good at Physics as I am. She said that if there was a bomb outside then the safest place to be would be right by the window. This is because the glass would be in its biggest pieces at that point and not hurt so much when it hit you. If you were standing at the far end of the room then by the time the glass had reached its optimum speed (after all it wasn't a Lamborghini and wouldn't go from nought to sixty in a few seconds) it would be in lots of little pieces and would cause you more damage. I was wide eyed with amazement and thought that this made total sense but apparently it's not true. Maybe the glass wouldn't kill you but apparently the force from the bomb would.

We have both decided to avoid topics such as Maths and Physics in the future. (Once again I told this story to Mr H when I got back and he said, "Well. Surely if you stand beside the window but behind the wall then you would be protected from both?" For the second time that night I gave him the 'No one likes a show off' look and have decided to stop telling him my stories. He is just trying to make me look dim.)

Tales from first class...

I'll now tell you why I travel first class.

People think that I'm posh because I travel from Wolverhampton to Euston on the train, first class. But this is where the maths totally makes sense. I travel off-peak and book my tickets in advance which means that I can go

131

first class for only £10 more than the price of a standard class ticket. Another reason as to why I travel first class is because, as already mentioned, I no longer have any patience, and being rammed into a vestibule area sandwiched between some sweaty guy and a very smelly toilet is something that I can no longer tolerate.

Being a girl from Chasetown, I make sure that I get my money's worth by fleecing the first class lounge at Wolves before I get on the train and then eat and drink as much as I can on the train. By the time I get off the train I am always satisfied that I have had my extra ten pounds worth. Travelling first class is an eye opener. There are usually lots of men in pinstripe suits on the train and they are generally the rudest. They never let you board the train before them. I will catch them looking up and down my hoody and jean clad figure mentally convinced that I am boarding the wrong carriage and will be evicted at some point by the train manager. Once the MP Michael Fabricant was in the carriage on the Lichfield to Euston route. I noted that he asked for a second bag of cheese crisps. I suspect these were for his second home...

Once when I was travelling back from London there was a mother with her two daughters in my carriage. The younger girl piped up to her mother, "I wish we could afford to travel first class all the time. If I marry a rich man when I'm older then I will be able to do that." The mother gave the type of responsible speech she should, which was, "No darling - you don't want to be reliant on a man to buy nice things. If you work hard in school and get a good job then you can buy yourself nice things." The younger girl not convinced by this turned to glance at me. At this point I mouthed, "Marry rich - work is overrated" at her. Her mother asked her what she was chuckling at and she answered, "Nothing mum" but gave me a wink. I like to think that I performed an important public service.

As I said at the start I bag a bargain with my first class tickets. Sometimes, the cheapest tickets are for the trains that have a 'change'. I prefer to get on a straight through train from Wolverhampton but if I can save a few quid by changing at Birmingham New Street then I will do it. The problem with the trains that change are the time they give you to get off one train and board the other. I had 13 minutes to get my connection. I had thought about hopping on an earlier train to make sure that I didn't miss my connection but having done that once before and being told off by the train police, I didn't dare do it again. Luckily, this journey was before the newly revamped Birmingham New Street, Grand Central Station had taken place. I would have been screwed if that had opened.

The first time I went to the new 'Grand Central' station I ended up going through about three ticket barriers and was wandering for about 20 minutes trying to work out how to get out.

Anyway, back to the story. Unfortunately for me my train from Wolves to Bham was running late and I was starting to panic that I wouldn't get my connection to London. I went on the train APP to find that my train was coming in on platform 2 and the London train was going from platform 7. I had one minute to hop off the train and peg it to platform 7 for the London train.

I did my best Usain Bolt impression and looked like a mad woman running for my life with my suitcase. At least my out of shape panting cleared the way of people in front of me and I didn't have to resort to shouting, "Bomb!"* to get them out of my way.

* Note for the professionally offended: Obviously I was not going to shout this, it's a joke...

I managed to throw myself on the train and find my seat. There were four other passengers on the train watching me trying to bring my breathing under control and when I could finally speak I told them that I had got on at Wolverhampton and had nearly missed the connection because my train was running late.

They cheerily piped up, "Oh yes! We were supposed to be on that train too but thought that it would be cutting it a bit fine so we got an earlier one." If I hadn't have still been out of breath then I would have sworn. On a positive note the first class staff called me a 'hero' for making my mad dash and later brought me a free bottle of white wine with writing on it which went something like, 'To our best passenger of the day, for running for her life to catch the train.' I tweeted Virgin Trains as a thank you. Their staff really are great. One and a half hours later when my breathing finally came back, I managed to thank them properly.

Tuesday 5th April

Missions for today:

- *Have a successful day training adults in 'Presenting for Non-Presenters'*
- *Have a fabulous catch up with my work-wife*

Tales from training...

Today I was training adults in 'soft skills.' My Midlands accent is always a source of amusement in London and for those of them that haven't ventured North (and to clarify, this means past Watford) they think I must be representative of people in my area.

These days I generally regard a day's training as a success if no one cries (including me) and I still have the same number of people at the end of the day as the number that I started with. Once, when I was doing a training course at a hotel, a random guy wandered into the room at lunchtime and plonked himself down in a seat. He stayed for half an hour and none of us asked why he was there. Let's face it, you can't be right in the mind if you are voluntarily attending a training course, so we thought it best to ignore his presence. We never did find out where he came from. It was raining outside but in all honesty I think I would have stayed out in the rain. Maybe that's why he left after half an hour..?

Alexandra asked me where I wanted to go for dinner and I guess she knew what sort of day I had had when I said, "Anywhere that has 2-4-1 on alcohol." We headed off to Giraffe where they have their bar buddies offer on until 7pm. This means 50% off a lot of drinks. I ordered two beers and instructed the waiter to make sure that he came back at 6:55pm so that I could get my next order in before they went up to full price. Now I know what you're thinking. How unprofessional?! Well, I wasn't working the next day so I felt quite justified in having a couple of drinks.

I told Alexandra that my back was killing me from training today (part of the course had been to pretend that you were an animal. I really shouldn't have chosen a snake. Slithering across the floor at 42 is not going to end well). She happily piped up, "Oh, I couldn't be bothered to take the tube this morning so I took a cab." I, on the other hand, had walked to the bus stop and suffered the smell of wee and general hostility from the other passengers on the bus whilst she had been basking in comfort on the back seat of her fancy cab. I made a mental note to think about putting an advert on 'plentyofFish.com' for a new work wife. Of course I'm joking. I think you have to pay these days and I'm too tight for that.

Alexandra said, "Do you think Graham misses you while you're in London?" After I had finished five minutes of chuckling I managed to get out the words, "I doubt it!"

Just that second a Facebook notification popped up. Mr H had just updated his status, 'Forgot to get something out of the freezer for dinner. Ice cream and wine it is then!' We both concluded that he must miss me lots. The poor lamb obviously needed me there to get something out for dinner and now he was going to suffer terribly...

Over dinner our conversations were of the usual highly intelligent variety. Alexandra said, "How old do you think you would have been when you died if you had been born 200 years ago?" I paused for a bit. This important topic of conversation would require some thought...

Initially, I decided that I would have died at around five years of age when I had a stone thrown at me on the school playing fields that whacked me on the head (I still have the bump to this day). But as Alexandra pointed out I would have been in the work house and not in school, so that wouldn't have actually happened.

I then decided it would have been when I was around eight when I did a handspring on my bed and bashed my foot on my bedside locker and an infection crept up my leg. But again, as Alexandra quite rightly pointed out, I wouldn't have had a bedside locker back then (I wouldn't even have had a bed) so that wouldn't have happened either.

I then decided that it would have been when I was 23 and my thyroid packed in. That was probably caused by over-working and stress. Alexandra said that I would be weaving all day and that was probably quite relaxing, so that wouldn't have killed me either.

I then said that it probably would have been at 25 when I had a blood clot. But as I got that from driving a car then as Alexandra quite rightly, once again, hit the nail on the head, "You wouldn't have had a car so that wouldn't have happened either."

"That's great then!" I said, "I wouldn't actually be dead yet!"

"Oh yes you would - you'd have died in child birth at age 17." She's such a ray of sunshine... but she speaks the truth, so I love her.

During this intellectual conversation, Mr H texted me goodnight as he was going to bed early as Lucy had got him up three times during the night and he put around 30 kisses at the end of the text. I said to Alexandra, "Do you think that he's bought a tractor?" It turns out that he hadn't but he had bought a new sit-on lawnmower. I'm now thinking that I might need to chain him up when I work away and get Miranda and Carrie (Carrie also keeps horses down the farm) to pop in and feed him. On the plus side he said he saved 300 quid so Alexandra and I decided to buy a bottle of Champagne with the savings. I'm kidding! We stay in a cheap hotel, the Champagne is only £19.99.

Wednesday 6th April

Missions for today:

- *Catch up with my friend who's over from Japan*
- *Brave Primark (Primarni) in Oxford Street*

Tales from a day off in smelly London...

I stayed an extra night in the hotel as I was meeting a friend that was over from Japan and we arranged to meet up for the day. I chuckled at Helga's text when she said, 'The builder is sorting out my damp patch at 1pm, so should be on for a later afternoon meet up.' That reminded me - must put tampons on my shopping list.

I thought that smelly London might not provide me with many tales today but when the fire alarm went off in the hotel during the morning, I knew that I was wrong and was going to find lots of tales to tell.

Although I didn't have to get up early, being the good work wife that I am, I set the alarm for 6:30am so that I could have breakfast with Alexandra before she headed off to her job. I told her that I didn't mind getting up early as I had brought some work with me to do and I would do it before meeting Helga. Things didn't quite go to plan as I headed back up to my room at 7:45am and promptly fell back to sleep. You might have remembered from the introduction that I get my ability to sleep from my mum and it is a genetic quality that I am most grateful for (I'm less grateful for Dad's double chin). The fire alarm went off at 9:45am but this was a blessing as it woke me up and I would probably have slept through meeting Helga.

I decided that today would be 'smile at a Londoner' day. They all walk around as if the world is about to end so I decided to spread the joy with everyone that I met. I started with the concierge in the hotel and this resulted in me getting to store my bags for free. 'Excellent!' I thought, 'there's £1 extra in the shopping kitty'. You might laugh - but I was off to Primark (Primarni) and that would get me half a pair of sunglasses.

I also smiled at the bus driver and this resulted in him waiting for me to sit down before he moved off. They normally take great delight in pulling off sharply so that you go flying across the floor and as I was trying to balance two bags and a coffee I was definitely a candidate to end up spread-eagled on the floor. I have realised that my smile is a commodity that I really should patent. (When you read that word can you please pronounce it correctly as 'pat-unt'. It is not 'pay-tunt' and I get irrationally upset when adverts don't pronounce the word correctly. I blame my intellectual property lecturer at University for this freaky quirk of my personality that I now possess.) I reckon that I could make money from licensing out my smile. My smile has got me lots of free stuff in the past and today looked like being no exception.

First stop of the day was Costa. The woman in front of me in the queue had a handbag with a huge 'MK' logo on it. I was standing there thinking, 'Why on earth would someone want people to know that they came from Milton Keynes?' But then I don't want people in London to think that I come from here, so I could actually understand it. I contemplated that maybe I should wear a badge next time saying 'Made in Wolves'. There was something written under the logo on the woman's bag and I had to pretend to be perusing the blueberry muffins so that I could lean in closer. I bet Michael Kors is now wishing that he was called something else by his parents.

This also reminded me of one time that I was in the Costa in Wolverhampton. The barista had told me that it had already been an exciting morning (it was only 9:30am when I went in). Apparently she had had to throw a man out for coming in and licking* the newspapers and that a woman customer had been whinging to her about how she loved her dog more than her grandkids because the dog didn't mess up her dining table and wasn't as noisy. Whilst I was in there another customer had grabbed my hands and started stroking them saying, "Your nails are lovely. They're really beautiful." It took me at least 20 seconds to pull my hand free from her grasp. Needless to say that was the only time that I went in that Costa.

* Mum said, "Did you mean 'nicking' the newspapers? Is this an autocorrect fail." Sadly no. He was coming in to lick the newspapers. Apparently he did it every day.

Anyway, back to London. The next excitement of the day was the argument between the bus driver and a car driver. Obviously my smiley-ness had not chilled the bus driver out sufficiently. As we pulled into a bus stop on Oxford Street there was a broken down car with its hazards on. The bus driver could have left enough room to pull out from behind him but I knew we were in for some excitement when the bus driver pulled right up behind him. I thought to myself, 'This isn't going to end well.' And I was right.

When the bus was ready to pull off the bus driver bipped his horn at the car in front. To be fair though it was at an 'abandoned' angle on double yellow lines, so shouldn't have been there. The car driver did not move. One minute went by which was long enough for three passengers on the bus to huff and puff and ask the driver to let them off to catch another one that was pulling in behind us. It always amazes me as to how time driven Londoners are. If they have to wait longer than three minutes for a bus or tube they start to explode. They definitely would not cope in the Midlands. Buses only run every half an hour near us. They would be a physical wreck.

I was enjoying the entertainment and was waiting to see what happened between the drivers. I wasn't in a hurry. The car driver insisted that his car had broken down and he couldn't move it at all. The bus driver, after a lot of swearing, tried to reverse the bus so he could get round the car. Given his agitated state then it would have been wise for me to get off the bus but curiosity (or my genetic nosiness from Mum's side of the family) told me to stay put. The bus mounted the pavement as it reversed and I could hear something scraping down the side of it. I suspect that when the driver pulled into the bus depot later he would probably try and claim that he had hit a squirrel. 'Just one that was metal and shaped like a cycle rack,' I thought.

I actually thought that a fight was going to break out between the two drivers and realised that apart from an old guy asleep on the bus, I was the only one left and it would be down to me to diffuse the situation. Luckily though my calming negotiation skills were not required and apart from a massive amount of bad language between the two men the bus carried on its way.

I actually wondered whether the bus driver had done it deliberately to give me the bus to myself as he called out to me, "Have a nice day" as I departed at my stop. Maybe my smile really is gold...

As I was walking down Oxford Street a building was undergoing construction work and there was a sign on the scaffolding that read 'Considerate contractors care about appearance.' This obviously was the case as one of the contractors called out to me in his cockney accent, "Alright darlin'. You're looking good today!" I felt quite chuffed as I was wearing my new coat and called out, "Thank you! It was £49.99 from TK Maxx". I don't know why he looked so puzzled. I thought he just cared about my appearance as the sign had said.

The phone boxes in London are always full of signs too. A lot of them are of the rudey-nudey variety but one caught my eye because I thought, 'That's a bit strange!' It was a sign that said 'Tax is sexy'. I thought - it really isn't. If tax was a man it would be Donald Trump. Thankfully offshore and preferably living in a tax haven on his own. But as I got closer, I realised that I had mis-read it and it said 'Taxis Ex' – apparently it was advertising an executive taxi service. I did ponder that it was unfortunate that the sign was right next to 'Busty Beverley' advertising her wares... I'm not sure this was the image that the executive taxis were going for...

This wasn't the end of today's bizarre sightings. Outside Primarni in Oxford Street, a dog caused quite a stir. It was sitting in the passenger seat of a white van and leaning on the open window with its left arm (I know dogs don't have arms but that's what it looked like). Hordes of people suddenly stopped what they were doing to take its picture.

To begin with the dog took it all in its stride and did not move an inch. Helga and I thought that maybe it wasn't actually real, but it did finally turn its head. The only thing that would have made the picture perfect would have been if the dog had had a fag hanging out of its mouth. When I got home, Helga had found an article in the Daily Mail online about 'Roxy' the dog being a minor celebrity in London. I immediately regretted not getting a selfie and adding Roxy to the list of celebrities that I have had selfies with. I imagine that her breath was better than some of the celebrities I've had selfies with too... You really need to Google 'Roxy the Mastiff Daily Mail' to see the picture. Although as one of my friends said, "Your picture of the dog on Facebook was much better." She speaks the truth...

Just going back a bit to my visit to Primarni itself though. I wouldn't normally even consider venturing into the biggest Primarni in the UK in the Easter holidays. But my undies were looking a bit bedraggled and when I'm travelling I try to make sure that I'm not wearing ones that look like the colour of chewing gum with the elastic baggy-ing, just in case I end up in an accident in hospital and some random stranger therefore has to see them. If ever you watch *Holby City* you will see that the women always have on nice matching undies after being involved in an accident. My motto with Primarni is 'Get in. Get the job done and get out.' I suspect that this is also most men's philosophy when it comes to sex...

I was pleased with my 20 minute trip. I think this might have been a personal best. In this time I had covered all three floors and made all of my purchases. When I was at the till the sales assistant helpfully said, "You know that these are non-returnable, don't you?" as she held up my new knickers. "But what if they make me itch? You know, down there?" I gestured to her. Obviously I didn't say this... having said it to two other sales assistants in the past I didn't want to start becoming predictable.

As I wandered out of Primarni, Helga rocked up. We needed to go back into Primarni as she needed to buy a fluffy white ball. As she said this I was reminded of her visit from the builder this morning and said, "Did he sort your damp patch out?" Apparently it wasn't readily apparent what was causing it so she needs to monitor it for the next couple of weeks and then give him a call again so that he can re-inspect it.

I got home at 10:30pm and it always makes me smile that I can chart Mr H's movements around the house in the two days that I have been gone. He is like a human snail leaving a little trail behind him as he goes. The bed is never made but at least I know he hasn't secretly had a woman there while I've been gone. I put a picture of the unmade bed on Facebook and Miranda commented, 'Well who would sleep with him?' She speaks the truth. Mr H and I once decided that I have to live with him and he has to live with me for the sake of the rest of the world. No one else would put up with either one of us!

Men are comical human beings though. I am a tidy person so it frustrates me to see his trail of destruction when I get home. So I tend to tidy up whilst telling him about my time away in London. I put his breakfast things in the dishwasher and wipe down the work surfaces. I pick up his dirty undies from the floor and put them in the washing hamper and I run the shower around the shower tray and pick up the shower towel from the floor and hang it over the bath.

This is where random man-logic kicks in. After running the hand held bit of the shower around the tray, I often leave it sitting on the tray and don't put it back on the holder. Mr H comes into the bathroom and says, "Can't you ever put that back on its holder? It really annoys me when you leave it on the tray." Having just picked up lots of his crap from the floor and tidied up, I think he is taking the piss a bit. I just looked at him with that, 'Really?!' look. He looked bemused. Men! Just like cats they are totally hilarious, will do what they want and are also secretly plotting to kill you...

My knowledge of Physics once again let me down tonight. I went to put my phone in my front jeans pocket having forgotten that I had got changed into my jarmies.* So the phone promptly dropped down the inside front of my jarmie bottoms and fell to the floor. I was a little surprised that it didn't get caught in the bush as I hadn't waxed in a while.

* Just in case this is a local phrase that you don't understand – this means pyjamas.

This has just reminded me of the Tetley Redbush adverts a while ago. Me and my sister used to howl with laughter at them because all we could think of was that they were advertising ginger haired women's fru-fru's.*

* Just in case this is a local phrase, it means v....... No! I can't bring myself to write that word in my book. We will have to stick with bush and fru-fru (so to speak).

My sister sent me a message on Messenger today which was an article from The Sun which said, 'Jo Hughes shed eight stone in weight and now her family don't recognise her'. I love stories about people with the same name. Unfortunately, some people on Facebook didn't get the humour when I posted the picture with the caption, 'Well done me' and three 'crying with laughter' emoji's next to it. Someone 'shared' the post and another person said, 'Well done!' Woops! Note to self – not everyone realises when you're joking. I'm hoping all the readers of this book realise when I'm joking... (and when I'm not...)

Thursday 7th April

Mission for today:

- *Have a day off writing my book*

Tales from home...

I was pleased when I woke up this morning that the dead goose seems to have gone from the moat. Either Mr H has managed to remove it or maybe a fox has been and taken it. I must remember to ask him later.

I had a day off today so have spent a lot of time working on the book and eating all the chocolate that I had collected from first class on the train. I told Mr H that I didn't have any free alcohol from the trolley, as it came through the carriage, as I actually felt a bit nauseous on the train. He is tighter than me at times and said, "You really need to take some empty water bottles with you next time that happens so that you can still have two beers and pour them into the bottles to keep for the next day." I have decided that even I'm not that tight and it would be just my luck that if I did then I would end up having some accident, go to hospital and have the police or hospital staff rifle through my handbag thinking that I was some weirdo that carried her own urine around.

Something a bit strange on the train yesterday was when the alcohol trolley came round and I asked if they had some Diet Coke or Diet Pepsi - whichever one they had would be fine. The Virgin Trains guy said, "It's Pepsi Max, is that ok?" I answered with, "Yes – it's basically the same thing anyway." He then went into an animated state and answered, "Yes!!! I would say so too but I had a woman earlier who told me off that I should have told her that it was Pepsi Max and not Diet Pepsi." Part of me was thinking that I should just say, "That's nice" and hope that he just went on his way but again my genetic nosiness kicked in and I said, "Really? Why is that then?"

He said that the woman that had told him off was on Weight Watchers and that Diet Pepsi was zero points but Pepsi Max wasn't. The look I gave him confirmed what he also thought and he said, "Life really is too short to worry about things like that." Having bonded over the Pepsi story he then gave me a second Pepsi Max and two bags of peanuts. I think it was payment for my spontaneous therapy session with him. I really should Google how many points a Pepsi Max is on Weight Watchers but life really is too short...

Mr H has been in work today (I like to send him out to work occasionally so that I can have peace and quiet). My friend Helga sent me a message asking whether there was not one blade of grass left to be cut after Mr H had got his new mower yesterday. Unfortunately for Mr H the world was conspiring against him with the new mower (I think it was trying to tell him that he shouldn't have bought one.) He got stuck in traffic on the M6 yesterday going to fetch it, due to a tanker fire. This meant two hours of him and his son sitting going nowhere. I did chuckle to myself about this as Helga and I had been chatting yesterday about this. I had said to her that I would have paid the £100 extra to have it delivered. You can't put a price on time these days. I did think that Mr H would be sitting in the traffic not going anywhere hearing my voice in his head say, 'Why don't you just get it delivered?' Of course he wouldn't admit that I was right. But as I wasn't stuck in the traffic in the van with him then I didn't need to really gloat too much.

Mr H was back momentarily at lunchtime and again I'm sure the world is telling him that he shouldn't have bought a new mower. It was beautiful sunshine all morning and as soon as he wandered through the door the clouds broke and massive hail stones came down. This continued for the hour that he was here and as soon as he left to go back to work the sun came out again. I shouldn't laugh... whilst he was here Mr H said, "Are we going to go out to practise sign language tonight?"

I said, "I'm really tired and don't have the energy tonight."

He laughed and said, "You've only worked one day this week!"

"Yes – but I didn't get in until 10:30pm last night. We'll practise on our own tonight, I promise."

I then reminded him that I was out tomorrow with my sister, Dad and Uncle so we wouldn't be able to practise in the daytime.

He looked at me with that, 'Where are you going tomorrow?' look. I swear that he was there when my sister and I were talking about it but like a man he typically claims no knowledge of the discussion.

It was Dad's 75th birthday this week so we were taking him to his favourite football club, which is Birmingham City.

Friday 8ᵗʰ April

Missions for today:

- *Have a fun day out with my Sister, Dad and Uncle*
- *Try not to kill my Dad when he says that we should have taken the Chester Road*

As mentioned yesterday, today, my sister and I were taking Dad and the legend that is our Uncle Mick out for a surprise treat to have a tour around Birmingham City Football Club and lunch in a country pub afterwards.

Mr H was dropping me off at my sister's (after all I might need alcohol today) and I had specifically told him that we needed to leave at 8:10am. You will notice that I put the word 'specifically' in there. Mr H's timekeeping is atrocious and I always have to tell him that we need to leave ten minutes before we really have to as he is always running late.

So at 8:13, I am standing outside the front door with keys in hand waiting for him to come back from walking the dogs. When we get in the car he says, "Look! It's only 8:14, we're early!"

"No we're not! I said that we needed to leave at 8:10!"

"No you didn't, you definitely said 8:15!"

I am pretty sure that this is a common discussion in millions of households across the UK. Men have a habit of hearing what they want to hear. Mr H does not listen – which ironically I have to tell him all the time.

When I got to my sister's, her morning had been just as comical. She didn't need to get up early but her husband had wanted to catch the 7am train. The night before they had had a discussion about setting the alarm because she had reminded him that she didn't need to get up early. After setting the alarm for an early time, he proceeded to hit 'snooze' and said, "I think that I'll catch the later train after all." Luckily she hadn't smothered him with a pillow and he was alive and well and on the train to work when I rocked up. Karma kicked in though as the trains were running late, so he will now learn the value of not hitting the 'snooze' button.

She then said, "Did I actually hug you?" She hadn't – but she had got a poo bag filled with kitten poo in her hand at the time she had opened the door. Now she was poo-less I gave her a hug.

We went to pick Dad up and something that you need to know about Dad is that he loves the Chester Road. On a previous car journey with Dad we were in the car heading down the M6 when we hit a queue for five minutes. Dad piped up, "You should have taken the Chester Road. This is disastrous!" We now deliberately never take the

Chester Road just to watch his reaction. We also take bets as to how long it will take him from getting in the car to say, "Which way are you going to go?" and then proceed to tell us that our choice of route is the worst one that we could have chosen.

As he didn't know where we were going today, we thought that we would be spared this. But when the satnav piped up that we were going to Chelmsley Wood, He said, "Well, I wouldn't have chosen this route to Birmingham." Who had 33 minutes on the sweep stake? Even though it was his surprise birthday treat we did think about dropping him off on the hard shoulder of the A38. Of course we didn't! That would make us mean daughters. If we were going to drop him off we'd at least wait until we got to the Belfry so he didn't have to stand in the rain waiting for a ride home.

The roads were thankfully clear so we got to Uncle Mick's in good time and had chance for a cuppa. Dad pipes up, "How's Pat these days Mick?"

"Pat passed away over a year ago."

"Oh?! How's Tony then?"

"He's dead too."

We asked Dad if he could pick someone that he knew was still alive so that we could have a less depressing conversation.

Tales from Birmingham City's Football ground...

We were early at the football ground so we went to look around the Club Shop. I got Dad a polo shirt. They were all reduced in the sale and as Dad is tiny and Birmingham supporters are generally XXXXXXL, we were in luck as there were only small sizes in the sale. I have made a mental note of this as this could sort his birthday and Christmas presents going forwards.

The tour was good fun and even us girls enjoyed it. This was apart from when we got to see the changing rooms. We went into the 'Away Team's' changing room first. Wandering in there I had flashbacks from High School PE with the lesbian gym instructor staring at you as you got showered and changed. Our tour guide, Rick, said that a woman on the tour earlier in the week had wanted a selfie next to the urinal because apparently she wanted to stand where Cristiano Ronaldo had been. He thought that this was strange. I did slope off discreetly to take a look though.

You never know when the cleaner might have missed an errant pubic hair. I'm sure that one of those would sell quite well on eBay and raise enough money for a tractor.

I thought that maybe this would be an easier way to raise money for Mr H's tractor, then banking on sales from my book. I also thought about stealing one of Mr H's when we got back and trying to pass it off as some famous footballers - but that's just wrong. I didn't fancy getting out the tweezers. Also, Mr H's pain threshold is non-existent. I couldn't cope with his crying tonight.

Apparently I was sitting in the seat in the changing room that Wayne Rooney had sat in when they had come to play. I had to move quickly upon hearing that news. Rick commented that the changing rooms might have been a bit basic but they were equipped with everything a team might need. I disagreed but chose to keep my views to myself. There was only one power socket in the room. How on earth would the footballers be able to update their Twitter if their iPhones ran out of power?

The Home Team's changing room was slightly posher but there was still the smell of 13 year old boy lingering in there as we wandered in. In this changing room there were slightly more power sockets I noticed and a biro stuck to the wall of the showers. I pondered as to why that was there and thought that maybe it was so that the footballers could write what number they played on their hands as they came out of the shower to get changed. It would be awkward if they couldn't remember what number shirt to put on and put the wrong one on.

We also got shown the police detention area where unruly fans were put if they kicked off during a match. This was the scuzziest* place in the ground and there was a plastic seat in the waiting area which had some sticky questionable yellow liquid on it. We didn't like to think any further about what this was and made a mental note not to sit down.

* Mum says that I've made up the word 'scuzziest', or in her words it is 'a Jo-ism'. Just to clarify, it means scutty/gross/disgusting/a place you never want to go. It's a bit like Wolverhampton being voted the scuzziest place to live in the UK. How a place with 12 take-aways within a one mile radius can come within this category is a mystery to me. Although for the sake of my weight, I really could do with legislation making online ordering and home delivery of fish 'n' chips being made illegal except on a Friday night. No wonder more children leave school in Wolverhampton obese than have any GCSEs. Although there's probably a GCSE in obesity here...

After the tour we went and had lunch, well it was around 4pm, so wasn't exactly lunch and unfortunately I was not going to make sign language practice tonight. But Mr H would be going as normal.

Tales from sign language...

Mr H and I started learning sign language this year. Hitting 40 two years ago made me re-evaluate life and what's important. Mr H had a deaf client in work club that he wanted to be able to communicate with and I have always wanted to learn it.

I seem to be in the naughty corner in class more often than most. But in my defence, if you are going to teach someone the sign for 'lady' and then follow it with the sign for 'boy' then you are simply asking for trouble. Apparently pointing at Mr H and signing 'ladyboy' was not ok. I blame the teacher for inciting such behaviour. Obviously this is just humour as our teacher is fab and makes learning such fun. She seems to love having me and Mr H in her class as each week towards the end of the session she has tears of laughter.

Mixing up the word 'black' with 'shit' also put me in the naughty corner but I was triumphant when it was Mr H that made the worst faux pas. Signing 'prostitutes' instead of 'hallelujah' apparently gives a totally different meaning to a sentence...

We have our final exam in June and one of the topics is to talk about our pets and we might need to give a five minute presentation on our hobbies. Being the clever student that I am, I have decided to use words that have very similar signs to ensure that I don't have to remember lots of different hard ones. I'm sure that my hobby of 'shopping for dead dogs' will go down a storm.

As George and William the Alpacas will hopefully be joining us in the next few months, the sign for 'Alpaca' has become one of our much used signs. I also use the signs for 'turtle' and 'helicopter' quite a lot too because they are cool signs. I try to avoid the sign for 'tractor' though as I don't want to encourage Mr H. Deaf people have a sign name so that they don't have to finger spell their name to people they meet. Unfortunately, everyone at sign language encouraged Mr H to have 'tractor' for his. I think they must hate me.

Anyway... I digress, so back to lunch...

Mr H messaged me whilst we were at lunch today to tell me that our second purchase of land had gone through today. George and William the Alpacas will hopefully be moving in once we have it fenced and have a shelter sorted for them.

Dad didn't question us on our choice of route for the journey home but I think he had run out of energy by then. Taking your parents out is a bit like taking a toddler out. They are excitable at the start of the day, need to stop to wee every five minutes and then fall asleep in the car on the way back drooling. What was sweet was we asked him if he had had a good time and he said, "It couldn't have been any better." Awwwww... bless him. He really does have low standards.

I bought a Euromillions ticket on the way home just on the off chance that today's fantastic day ended in style. It didn't. And Mr H is still tractor-less. So I'm sorry but you still need to encourage all of your friends to buy this book.

Saturday 9th April

Mission for today:

- *Book the doctors*

I was actually awake at 7:33am this morning. This is totally out of character as I am not a morning person and do not naturally wake up early. I think I might be coming down with something...

This reminded me that I need to book into the doctors to have blood tests for my repeat prescription of thyroxine. I groan at the thought of trying to book the doctors. They never have appointments when you phone up and I suspect I'm going to have to do what I've done on the last two occasions. I'm going to have to turn up early and wait.

Tales from the doctors...

Our doctors operate a system whereby you are guaranteed an appointment if you turn up from 8am. The first time I did this I was totally unprepared. By 8am there were already 15 people in the queue and I had to wait two hours for an appointment. I also was inappropriately dressed as I wasn't wearing sweat pants, Nike trainers and did not have my hair in a top knot. (This rule apparently applies to both genders.)

Having learned from this experience, I was determined that the next time I went I would be better prepared. I had to congratulate myself when I arrived at 7:45am and was second in the queue. It was a really cold day and my winter coat, ear muffs and latte in a flask were eagerly eyed up by other people as they joined the queue behind me. I was a little worried at one point that I would be mugged of these treasures but luckily the door opened before the crowd pounced on me. I was continuing to congratulate myself as I was first in to see my doctor and strategically positioned myself on the front row to avoid the two people behind me that seemed to be having a phlegm coughing competition. I mentally reminded myself to bring one of those face masks that they wear in the Far East next time.

I busied myself in my Kindle so that I didn't have to make eye contact with anyone. I wasn't certain that someone might try and trade my top slot with the doctor for a stolen mobile phone or the like. My Kindle seemed to cause some eyebrow raising, I don't think they read much in Wolverhampton. Twenty minutes later, Adrian was having an argument with the receptionists as to why he was going to have to wait two hours to see a doctor but he made the rookie mistake of grabbing a McDonald's breakfast on the way. As I was sitting there waiting for surgery to start I did think about how I could improve my performance in the future and started Googling 'Go Outdoors' for a pop up tent.

My visit in with the doctor was slightly unusual as we spent the first few minutes chatting about how the health and safety lady had just been in and had told him that 'his chair was killing people'. I think that this was probably a slight exaggeration as I hadn't noticed any patients going missing. We also chatted about snowboarding and he didn't know about wrist guards, so he was grateful for my visit. I seemed to spend a long time in with the doctor and as I was leaving Adrian was still arguing with the receptionists about having to wait for two hours. She helpfully said to him, "Well he is already running behind, so it will probably be longer than that." I quickly snuck out before he realised that I was the cause of that.

I remember when we first joined the doctors. We had to take samples of urine to them as part of their screening process as to whether they would accept us or not. This did make me wonder. If it turned out that you had some awful disease then were they more likely to accept you because they would probably receive more government funding to treat your illness, or did they want healthy patients that would rarely darken their door. I must remember to ask our friend Bobby as he works for the NHS.

Anyway – back to the urine samples. I had the job of taking both of them up to the doctors. Obviously being the clever person that I am, I had written my name and date of birth on the side of my bottle before I tried to wee in it. Mr H had not and after handing me his bottle (which felt decidedly sticky), I had to write his name and date of birth on the side. It took me three different pens before I found one that would write over his wee.

Anyway, I carefully put both bottles in a carrier bag and took them up to the doctors. I hadn't realised that it was half day closing (which coincidentally coincided with McDonald's half day-half price food offers) and thought, 'Rats! I'm going to have to come back up again'. There was a post box in the door but being the genius that I am I did not post them. As I looked through the glass doors, that the post box was in, there was a broken urine bottle on the floor with a really disgusting coloured liquid oozing out from it. I suspect that 'C Smith DOB 12.5.40' was not going to get good news from the doctors for a couple of reasons:

1. The doctors would probably bill them for the cleaning up of it (although it had brought a nice shine to the tiles so maybe they would bottle it and water it down and use it again to clean the floor...)

2. They would need to provide a new specimen to be tested (although it didn't take a genius to know that something was wrong there. I was a bit mesmerised for a while staring at it)

As I turned to leave, I saw a 20-something girl (eating out of a McDonald's bag) rock up. I told her that they were closed and she said, "Oh flip – if I hadn't have gone to McDonald's I would have caught them – never mind – I'll just post it through their letterbox." I decided to disappear off at this point but heard the unmistakable, "Oh f**k" escape her lips as I heard what I can only assume was a bottle breaking the other side of the door. The next time that I went to the doctors there was a big sign up saying, 'Do not post sample bottles through this letterbox.' Obviously this didn't work as the next time I went there was another sign that said 'Our letterbox is out of order' and there was a piece of wood nailed across it.

You have simply got to love Wolverhampton...

Sunday 10th April

Missions for today:

- *Successfully throw Mr H's pillow out without him knowing*
- *Order lots of Roxy stuff in their sale (and don't tell Mr H)*

Tales about Mr H...

I forgot to mention yesterday that I decided to change the bedding on the bed (I know – it doesn't sound very exciting but bear with me). Something else that I forgot to mention about Mr H is that he is a hoarder (I blame his mum). He hates having anything thrown away, except that he will happily have a new car, a new lawn mower or obviously a new tractor at the drop of a hat. But woe betide me if I want to throw out some of his manky underpants. He will pull a face like a toddler that has just been told that they can't have their dinner in their blue bowl because it's in the dishwasher and they will have to have the green one instead. He will say in a pathetic whiney voice, "They'll last at least another two months, they don't need throwing out yet". Man-logic again at its best.

Because of this I have to throw his old stuff out when he's not looking. As I was changing the bed I noticed that his favourite pillow had mould growing on it. He must have had both of his pillows for at least 11 years as I'm sure he had them in our old house and they are a disgusting yellowy colour and probably have Ebola or something living in them. I'm sure this is partly why he suffers with his tummy, but being a man he won't be told.

Knowing how much of a drama it would be to ask him if I could throw it out, I decided to take matters into my own hands. I couldn't be doing with the, 'Give it a wash, it will be fine' conversation or, 'Give it another wash – honestly, it will be as good as new soon'. New pillows are after all £2 from B&M (cheaper than a Starbucks latte). Once I had put one of my old pillows in the outside kennel for the dogs (obviously it did not have mould on it). He promptly took it out of the kennel and brought it back in the house. I had to tell him that Casper had thrown up on it in order to convince him to put it back in there. (He hadn't.)

Mr H freaks out enough if I accidentally put his bottom pillow on the top and his top favourite pillow on the bottom after changing the bedding. He will exaggeratingly put them back the right way round with a look of, 'See! That's how they are meant to go.' It's really a shame that his OCD is selective and doesn't follow through to other aspects of our lives. I would love for him to have an obsession for keeping the house clean.

So while he was out cutting wood I took the offending pillow and hid it in the bottom of the grey wheelie bin. I then took the rubbish out of the kitchen bin so that I could cover up the pillow in the bottom of the bin. I had to do this because once in the past I had made the rookie mistake of throwing something of his out and he went into the bin and got it back out. I didn't want to chance this happening again. To make doubly sure I poo-picked the front lawn and luckily as the Farmer's geese are residing there at the moment there was a lot of goose poo as well as dog poo. I spread the poo bags out so that they were on top of the rubbish and the rubbish was on top of the pillow. I was very pleased with my layering technique and after putting my torch on my iPhone on to sweep it round the bin, I was confident that if he looked in the bin he wouldn't be able to see the pillow to try and remove it. Just call me Sherlock Hughes.

Luckily we have lots of pillows in the house for when we have our paddock parties so I took one of them and put it on the as yet un-made bed. By 9pm I had forgotten that I hadn't re-made the bed and momentarily panicked that if Mr H helped me make the bed then he would see that I had killed his favourite pillow. He doesn't notice if the house is a tip, hasn't been vacuumed for a week and if one of the dogs has poo stuck to their bum but he can spot a new pillow a mile off.

So, I said to him, "I would really like a cup of tea Honey, so can you make me one while I make the bed?" I swear that I saw a flicker of the look of 'phew' cross his face as he said, "Of course, Honey. Whatever you want…" He doesn't like putting fresh bedding on the bed. Although he is much better at Physics than me this doesn't extend to being able to put a duvet in a duvet cover. It takes me about two minutes to make the bed and he will be wrapped up and still wrestling with the bedding after ten minutes (with lots of sighing and sometimes swear words).

As I wandered up the stairs he started whistling. I knew that he thought that he had won from not having to make the bed but I knew that secretly I had played him. I quite like this feeling. I momentarily felt bad for playing him like this but given it is so successful I have made a note to try it again soon with something else. Also, I have realised that this is a 'win win' situation. He thinks he's won but really I have. It really does help enhance our marriage.

So the new pillow was carefully concealed under a fresh pillow case and he hasn't noticed yet. I was going to ask him how he slept last night but I didn't want him to start thinking about why I was asking him. To be fair, it was unnecessary. When Lucy barked at 1am to go out to the toilet he was snoring like a baby and she didn't wake him up. Even my 'accidental' kicking him in the back of his legs didn't work. I think the new pillow is to blame. I'm now thinking that I might need to stuff some straw in it to make it less comfortable so that he wakes up when Lucy wants her wee trips in the middle of the night.

It's bin day tomorrow so I think it's safe that by the time Mr H reads this he won't be able to go and rescue the pillow. I'm just hoping that his weird hoardy-ness isn't so bad that he decides to take a trip to the landfill site to find it.

Yesterday we had a visit from our Alpaca sellers to chat about the land and how to design the shelter in the best way for them. We might now be having three boys instead of two. William is turning into a really good Alpaca for his fleece so he might be kept as a stud and it would be a shame to just have him come to us as a pet. Instead we might have George, Chester and Cyril. 'Chester Hughes' has a fab ring to it and I am looking forward to taking him to the vets. Brandy and Precious the Shih Tzu will be so jealous when they see me and Chester sitting in the waiting room. I might put a blue bandana round his neck. That will trump Precious's pink bow.

Mr H has been playing with his man-toys today, whilst I have been adding to my book. He loves his new bright yellow sit on lawn mower and Matt came over to have an ogle over it as well. I just don't understand this fascination with machines. They aren't fluffy, they aren't warm and do not give you unconditional love. I will totally understand Miranda and Carrie coming over to fawn over the Alpacas when they arrive. Mr H was happily telling Matt that his new mower will take a fraction of the time of the old one to cut the paddock. 'Nooooooo!' I thought. 'What have I done?' I might have to give in and buy him the tractor just to keep him busy and out of my hair.

After playing with his new mower Mr H decided to strim some of the new land that we had bought in anticipation of it being easier to get the fencing done. He was having real trouble starting the strimmer so he put it on the Rayburn to dry it out. I think this was what he was doing. To be honest I didn't like to ask as he was starting to bang about the kitchen and I could see he was going to have a moody strop soon because the strimmer wouldn't work.

To make matters worse Casper pulled it off the Rayburn by playing with the strap that you hang on your shoulder. I heard a clattering in the kitchen and saw Casper shoot out from the kitchen at the same time as a few choice swear words shot out of Mr H's mouth. I'm sure I then heard him ask the Siri equivalent on his Windows phone, "Why won't my f***ing strimmer start?" I don't think that Google had an answer to the problem. (Sorry for the profanity Mum – but it wasn't me that said it. You can tell Mr H off when you see him.)

I had an email a few days ago that Roxy were offering a 50% off in their sale to their loyal customers. Obviously, I am one of these due to the amount of skiing and snowboarding stuff that I buy from them. I had a good look through the items on sale and have now bought a new skiing coat, some base layers, a new snowboard bag and some presents for my work wife, Alexandra and some other goodies to put in my 'present' box. My present box (well boxes) is where I put things that I buy throughout the year. I often see something that will be perfect for family or friends and store it there until their birthdays or until Christmas comes around. I have a motto for shopping and it is, 'It was so cheap it would have been a crime not to buy it.'

The 50% off was after the other discounts that they were already offering. So my new snowboard bag at £35 compared with its full price of £100 was an absolute steal. I haven't actually told Mr H about all the purchases. He's not very good at taking in big volumes of information at a time so I filter things through to him in stages. I am such a good wife like that.

Monday 11th April

Missions for today:

- *Stop stressing about the pillow*
- *Get to Birmingham on time for work*

The pillow is gone… (I actually wrote this yesterday. Mum messaged me to say, 'You're being a bit previous and optimistic aren't you? But I was right ☺)

However, I think that karma is kicking me in the teeth as I was wide awake last night at 4:30am whilst Mr H was happily snoring away whilst hugging his new favourite pillow. I was doing some training in Birmingham today on presentation skills so needed to set the alarm for 5:50am so that I could get to the first class lounge at Wolves early enough to fleece it of its contents before boarding the train. Given that the days that I can lie in, Lucy decides to wake up early, I thought, 'It won't matter if she is up early today as I need to be too'. So the alarm goes off and I trot downstairs to get my toast and latte and Lucy is fast asleep, curled up in a ball, in her favourite spot at the bottom of the stairs, gently snoring.

I looked at her and looked back upstairs and realised how similar her and Mr H looked when they were deep in dreamland. When she broke wind, I thought, 'Yep – she's definitely his dog.'

She didn't wake up while I was making breakfast and only woke up just before I had to leave. 'Typical!' I thought. Of all the days that it wouldn't have mattered. To make matters worse I said to Mr H, "I wish she had woken early today and not yesterday." Mr H responded with, "Oh? Did she wake up in the night yesterday? I never woke up. In fact I've slept like a log the last two nights."

My eyes narrowed with suspicion that he knew that I had killed his pillow and was deliberately winding me up. I thought about double checking the wheelie bin to make sure that he hadn't found it and got it out, but I thought that would be classed as slightly weird behaviour. I'm sure that the pillow has gone to pillow heaven (well, Cannock landfill site). Also, Mr H has a 'liar' face. If he tells a lie he cannot stop his face making a particular expression. It's hard to describe but it is definitely the same expression every time that he tries to lie. It is a very useful thing and he didn't do it when talking about his sleep. I am confident that Pillowgate is now over.

Incidentally, last night I said to Mum on Messenger, 'Do you think that once the bin men have been that I should tell him about his pillow?' Her reaction was, 'No! Don't! He'll only start sleeping badly and then you'll never hear the end of it.' It's good to see that she's on my side and isn't one of those people that advocate honesty in a marriage. I nearly puke when I see people on Facebook say, 'I'm married to my best friend. We tell each other everything.' What a load of trot! Although if we were talking about work spouses then that would be the case, as me and Alexandra do tell each other everything. You can't tell husbands everything, there's just too many things in life that men can't handle. The pillow, for example, is one of those things. I thanked Mum for her reassuring and sensible advice.

At 6:20am there was a random lorry in the farmyard. I texted Miranda (she was in work so I knew I wouldn't be waking her up), to see if she was having anything delivered or whether I should go and get the shotgun. I thought it an odd time of the morning for a lorry to be in the yard and thought they might be vagabonds. Turns out it's been doing this every Monday for about the last year. I did mention in the introduction that I'm not a morning person and to be fair am not usually up at this time. Good job they weren't up to no good!

On the way to the station Heart FM cheerily announced that there were signalling problems at Birmingham New Street and that anyone travelling by train was being advised to find a different route. I groaned and once again reminded myself why I work from home for around 90% of the time and thought, 'Why does this happen to me when I'm travelling?' However, the train gods were shining on me as my train left Wolves on time and only arrived five minutes late.

Thinking about it, this is better than the normal service. Wolves has the benefit of being on a route with long distance trains. Local London Midland trains were being cancelled left, right and centre but my Wolves to Euston Virgin Train seemed to have priority on the line. I felt slightly* guilty as my train passed loads of others stationary in the tunnel at Birmingham New Street and happily pulled into its platform. And seeing a lot of my friends post on Facebook that they couldn't get in or were stuck in traffic should have made me feel even guiltier.

* I didn't feel guilty at all. Once again I had lost my opportunity to fleece the first class lounge of goodies.

Tales from Birmingham

Walking up New Street in Birmingham was interesting this morning. A lorry was delivering to one of the cycle shops and was half on the pavement. This meant that there was only room for one person to get past and as I started walking past the lorry, I could see a woman walking towards the lorry and me. She looked and realised that there was a one-way system in operation but that didn't make her decide to wait at the other end for me to get past. Because of this we were going to meet three quarters of the way along and one of us was going to have to give way. I could hear heavy footsteps behind me and turned to see two people following me. She had no one following her. Now common sense and the moral code of the situation should have dictated that she move to the side in one of the doorways to let us pass.

But from the look on her face that clearly wasn't going to happen. To avoid a crash between us, I quickly stepped to the side and stopped so that she could come past. The guy behind me nearly fell into me as he hadn't anticipated her not stopping and the guy behind him nearly crashed into him. I pictured us all on the floor like a game of human dominoes.

She didn't say thank you at all or sorry for what she had nearly caused but hurried on her way. Although I'm not a morning person, I don't presume that everyone else is either and I could forgive her ill manners. What I couldn't forgive though was the reaction of the guy behind me. He looked at me as were on the move again and said, "Bloody coloureds! They're all the same – no manners!" I wasn't going to let this one go and said, "I don't think this is a race issue (and refrained from pointing out his offensive description), I think it's more a person issue. Either you have manners or you don't." He looked me up and down, grunted something and flounced off. I didn't get chance to tell him that I categorise people into one of two categories. Either you're in the 'Tw*t' category or you're in the 'non-tw*t' category. He was most definitely in the former category... Sorry about using the 'T' word Mum, when you're doing your read-through. (And for the avoidance of doubt, it is not an 'I' that is missing from those words...)

As I was walking past the cathedral and heading down to the Jewellery Quarter, a guy wearing headphones was singing along to the song playing in his ears. He was singing, "It's alright... It's going to be alright... It's alright..." I then wondered whether actually it wasn't a song and was one of those self-help tapes to calm him down on a Monday morning and he was chanting it to make himself feel better. I smiled at him just in case it helped him on his route to cheery-ville.

I must admit that in general the people of Birmingham are much nicer than those in London. Apart from tw*t face (the guy behind me on the one way walk) all the other people that I interacted with today were really friendly and polite. I noticed how all the customers in Costa were really polite and cheery to the barrister. Whoops! Autocorrect fail. Although to be fair I think the baristas in Costa should be held in as high regard as a barrister. They supply me with my fix of caffeine, which keeps me sane and generally law abiding for the rest of the day.

I couldn't believe that it was only 7:48am and already so much had happened. If I had been working from home then the only thing that would have happened by this time would have been Lucy barking to go out for a wee. No wonder when I got home I was in my pjs and dressing gown by 6:30pm. I was exhausted. There were other reasons as to why I was in my pjs at such an early time though. The rest of today was quite a traumatic day.

On four occasions I had to dodge a tram that was trying to kill me (well I think it was four different trams). Who puts grass down and then has a tramline running through it? Honestly! It's just asking for trouble.

Another of today's tiring events was to do with the toilets in the building where I was training. There are a lot of new buildings in the Jewellery Quarter and they seem to have gone all 'hi-tech'. In order to get into the toilets you needed an electronic pass and there was only one pass for the boardroom that I was in. I mentioned that I was training adults on 'presentation skills'.

The poor attendees were having to do tag teaming when they needed a wee. This didn't seem to upset the girls as us girls are quite used to going to the loo in pairs. The men were not as used to doing this though and would say, "Does anyone else need the loo while I've got the pass?" which would generally be followed by a shrug of the shoulders in that sort of, 'You know – whatever – it's no big deal if you do or don't' kind of way.

The toilet issue was just plain strange. For the women's toilets you could get into them without a pass by pressing a green button on the wall but then you needed a pass to get back out. I've had enough weird experiences in toilets before to make me have a slight phobia about them. I had visions of being stuck in the toilets having forgotten to take the pass and then having to wait for someone else to come in and rescue me. I thought it odd as to why it wasn't the other way round. Why not have to use a pass to get in because at least you would know you had it on you if you then needed a pass to get out. But then I thought... actually it made loads of sense.

If someone had Bottie McTrottie visiting that day then they wouldn't want to risk that they hadn't got their pass and couldn't get into the toilet in time. I wondered whether it had happened in the past that some poor woman had ended up squatting in the corridor with uncontrollable trots because she had forgotten her pass. I now have visions of the film *Bridesmaids.*

You should YouTube this now if you haven't seen it – the food poisoning incident. I think it adequately explains the situation that I was picturing. This also reminded me of the time that my sister was walking down the street in London and she saw a tramp squat to the floor and do a big poo. She said it was hysterical how much of a wide berth people were giving it after he had sloped off. Yet if it had been dog poo most of them probably would have trodden in it.

I also had to go in the disabled toilet at one point as a cleaner was cleaning the other toilets. Whoever had designed it had a sick sense of humour. The red emergency pull cord was hanging right in front of the loo roll dispenser. I spent a few minutes like the game 'Operation' where I was trying to extricate some loo roll without setting off the emergency buzzer. Good job I was only having a wee, I thought.

Another weird thing about the venue today was that it was like Fort Knox. You couldn't even get in the lift without a security pass and you had to press which floor you wanted before you got in the lift. After you had pressed your floor the electronic console told you which lift you had to take, either A or B. Once you were in the lift there were no buttons in there so you had to rely on the lift to take you where you needed to go. It did feel a bit like *Terminator 3 – Rise of the Machines*, as I wasn't convinced that the lift was going to let me out again. I had visions of me riding up and down in it all day.

At one point there was a chap using one of the consoles and me using the other and my console told me to get lift A and his must have said lift B. They both arrived at the same time and I'm sure I saw the same thing flash across his face as mine. What if we switched lifts? Would the lifts know and some secret security alarm would go off that we were heading to a floor that we weren't authorised for? I think we both concluded that we didn't think the risk was worth it and duly headed to our respective lifts. But in all honesty it was lunchtime and I was really hungry. I didn't want to end up in lift jail without my lunchtime latte and chocolate.

This is why I am now in my pjs. Today has been a very strange day...

Tuesday 12th April

Today's missions have four objectives:

- *Don't get killed by a tram...*
- *Don't get stuck in the toilets...*
- *Don't get stuck in the lift...*
- *Stop stressing about the pillow...*

The day started well apart from the fact that I was once again wide awake at 4:30am. I'm sure that this pillow thing is conspiring against me. At this rate I'm going to have to have therapy, or make a trip to the landfill site myself. I have decided that this pillow fixation is not good for my health and have vowed to never mention it again. 'Thank goodness!' I hear you say.

Once again Lucy was fast asleep when I got up at 6am. You can guarantee that Saturday morning she will be up at 1am and 5am. As I was making breakfast I turned my back for two seconds and could hear a licking noise. It was Casper licking the Philadelphia off my toast. He didn't look best pleased when I banished him to the utility and gave him some of his food. The look he gave me was, 'You expect me to eat this while you gorge on cream cheese?' He sloped off through his cat flap and as he turned to look back at me his face said, 'I will kill you at some point my human slave.'

After scraping off his cat drool I ate my toast.

Once again the first class lounge was conspiring against me. I had just made it onto platform 4 and was congratulating myself on the eight minutes I had to fleece the lounge of food and drink and have a look through the visitor book. Just as I was walking along the platform the announcement came over the tannoy that my train was now going to go from platform 2. I missed the lounge again. I knew that I wouldn't have time to get into the lounge and back across to platform 2 in the time available as the lifts at Wolves are so slow. Damn you Cross Country Trains!

Tales from Cross Country trains...

On the train, 'Tracey' (the Cross Country catering manager) was chatting to 'Steve' (the Cross Country train manager) and asked him if he had a spare pen. "'Dave' will kill you if he knows you've forgotten your pen. In his eyes that's a sacking offence." In my eyes Dave sounded like a right nob. Personally, I would have thought that there much worse things that Tracey could have done, like spilling hot tea on a passenger or running over your foot with the alcohol trolley. Tracey asked me if I wanted a drink and I meant to ask for a cup of tea but my alcohol

Tourette's kicked in and 'scotch on the rocks' escaped my lips. Of course it didn't – I asked her to hold the rocks and make it a double. (Note for thickies: quite clearly this is a joke. I do not drink alcohol in the morning and especially not when I'm working. Although I did once have a lot of Bucks Fizz for breakfast when Mr H and I stayed at a swanky hotel near Buckingham Palace once, when we were on an anniversary trip away... but I think that's the law...)

I stopped at Costa on the way into work. I had worked up quite a sweat as I had power walked to the Jewellery Quarter. I don't weigh myself anymore. It's just too depressing when I eat like a sparrow for a week and only lose half a pound. I now go with the 'if my jeans are getting tight, then I cut down on the calories' philosophy. I think Mr H thinks I'm getting a bit porky. He went shopping and totally ignored the fact that I had written 'chocolate' on the food shopping list. And I had written it in capital letters. But having said that when I was power walking I did notice that the top of my thighs seemed to rub together so maybe he was right. I pondered this whilst drinking my large latte and eating my chocolate twist.

Mr H renewed our public liability insurance last night. I was starting to panic a bit that I would have to spend the day trying not to kill one of my attendees. It would be just my luck that today would be the day that I accidentally pushed one of them under a tram. It hadn't happened in the 13 years that I had been self-employed but you can guarantee that it would happen when the insurance had run out. Mr H would definitely not get his tractor then and we would have to live in our shipping container. As luck would have it though I did not accidentally kill one of them. It wasn't an accident...

It did make me think though. Included in the insurance is employer liability for employees. Mr H and I are employees of the company so maybe he is trying to kill me after all. If I happen to fall foul to some accident then he would be able to claim on the insurance and get his tractor. I think I'll read the terms and conditions carefully when I get home...

I successfully avoided being hit by a tram this morning even though the sneaky things tried to gang up on me. As I was busily looking to the right, another one came round the corner from the left at the same time. I wonder if Mr H knows the drivers and has paid them money to do away with me.

Mum did a read through of yesterday's tales and said they were funny. But she is my mum and is biased (love you Mummykins). I told her that not getting in until 6:30pm last night meant that I hadn't had chance to mess around* with them as much as I would have liked and that they were a bit raw. Apparently this made them better! I've made a mental note not to try and be comical as apparently it doesn't work.

* I mean edit of course

As I was writing my tales last night, Mr H put *University Challenge* on. I'm sure he does this just to make me look dim. As I was pretending to be engrossed in my book writing, a question about sheep cropped up and out of nowhere I piped up 'Suffolk', which happened to be the right answer. Even geeky Gerald from Cambridge got the wrong answer. Every so often I have a moment of genius. It's a shame that it's generally only about once every three months.

My tights have been annoying me today. They've been very itchy and keep falling down and going baggy around the crotch area. It's not very professional to have to keep hoisting them up – and definitely not when you're trying to give some training on presentation skills. Maybe I should add that to one of my slides...

I always try to do it when I think that no one's looking but there's always someone lurking around the corner to give me a quizzical look (or pretend they haven't seen me and quickly walk away). Also due to the itching I feel like I've been wriggling around on the chair whilst the attendees have been doing group work. I'm sure they think I have piles.

There is a possibility that my mother in law washed these tights. She is a star when we go on holiday as she will come over, collect our washing and return it nicely ironed. However, I think that I have become allergic to the washing powder that she uses or maybe the starch that she uses to iron everything. I suspected that these were ones that she had washed as they were as flat as a pancake when I took them out of the drawer this morning and nicely folded. As I only iron the bare minimum of things then mine would have been screwed up in a ball. I do find it strange that she irons socks and underpants. Thankfully I was wearing my new Primarni knickers. If my knickers had been washed and ironed by her I would have looked like a dog with fleas and worms.

I contemplated taking my tights off but my pasty white legs are likely to have been more offensive to the attendees than my writhing around. And before you think it, I didn't have time at lunch to go and buy some more tights. Tomorrow I will wear trousers and the adults on the course will think that I purchased some pile cream on the way home and all is well again 'down there'.

I told Mr H about my tights story but in true style he had to go one better. He had been back to the doctors for his prostate check. Now readers, I'm going to be really serious here for a minute. If you are a man (you will know if you are, I hope) then make sure that you go and have your prostate checked. Unfortunately for Mr H prostate cancer runs in his family.

His Uncle, Dad and eldest brother have all had it. Mr H just this second reminded me that his Grandad also had it. This is where I am truly grateful for my genetic double chin and not some genetic cancer. Mr H has his checked regularly and as his level is above what doctors have as their maximum limit then he needs to go back to the consultant at the hospital again. I squeezed his hand and said, "Is there anything that would make you feel better?" I immediately regretted my choice of words as he said, "Well a tractor would be nice," I have concluded from this that he's not that worried.

There is a new doctor at our surgery. So when Mr H was having his exam by our female doctor, she asked him if she could get the new doctor in as she was his mentor and was training him. So poor Mr H was poked up the bum by two people. In all honesty I am thinking that if he can sit on a tractor and suffer its bouncing without any pain at all, at this current moment in time, then I might actually get him one.

Before the new male doctor came in, Mr H said to our female doctor, "I'm glad the new guy is staying on here to become a permanent doctor. I haven't seen him yet but my wife said he was really good." She seemed pleased with this. Once again though I have realised that he doesn't listen to me. After I had seen the new doctor in the surgery I remember saying to Mr H, "He's a real fittie and really young. I'd like to go and see him again. I hope that he joins the practice." The old doctor was in his 60s. Oh? Wait... I've just realised that Mr H is right. It was Alexandra, Carrie and Miranda that I was telling about the new fit doctor in graphic detail. I hadn't imparted this information to Mr H. Just like the pillow, he wouldn't be able to handle it, so I had spared his feelings.

Wednesday 13th April

Missions for today

- *Leave early enough to fleece the first class lounge of food and drink*
- *Look through the first class lounge visitor book for funny comments*
- *Don't get run over by a tram*

I was going to put 'don't accidentally kill any of my attendees' as one of my missions but now the insurance is sorted I feel that it's unnecessary.

At least I didn't wake up at 4:30am today... it was 4:19am instead. Once again Mr H and Lucy slept like logs.

Today got off to an interesting start. When the alarm went off at 6am I went downstairs and stepped over a snoring Lucy. You might wonder why Bonnie hasn't featured in my morning stories. Bonnie is my dog and just like me she likes her sleep. She will wake up when I come downstairs but she will usually only open one eye and the look on her face is, 'It's far too early, if you think I'm getting up, you've got another thing* coming.' It's the same look that I give to Mr H if I don't need to be up early and he is banging noisily around the bedroom. Sometimes I also provide him with some complimentary swear words.

I call them complimentary as I give them for free. But that's not why this morning was interesting.

* Apparently this is supposed to be 'think'. Oh well, another of those things that I've been saying wrong for years. No wonder people look at me funny (although it's probably nothing to do with my grammar as to why they do...)

I could hear Casper in the utility so went to feed him as I didn't fancy scraping cat drool off my toast today. I didn't put the light on and could see that there was something big and grey in his cat food bowl. I thought that maybe he had been hunting in the night and had left me a present to happily wake up to*. I put my hand down to touch what it was and recoiled as I felt something slimy. I turned on the light to see what it was and it was the head of a fish.

* Note to the grammar police. I am from Wolverhampton and we like to end sentences with prepositions and split our infinitives, here.

Now remember that I'm not a morning person and being quite dim anyway I am even more stupid first thing in the morning. To begin with I couldn't work out how Casper had managed to get a fish out of the moat, chop its head off and bring it through the cat flap and have the presence of mind to drop it in his food bowl.

What I had forgotten was that Mr H had cooked me rainbow trout for dinner last night (I told you I think he thinks I'm getting porky. I wanted to get a chicken kebab on the way back from work but he wouldn't let me...) and he had taken the head off it and given it to Casper to eat. This has reassured me slightly as I am back to the opinion that Mr H isn't trying to poison me... but then again Casper didn't eat the fish head and he eats everything. OK... that's not exactly conclusive... I'm starting to get concerned again that Mr H might be poisoning me. I might have to get the fish head out of the bin when I get home and send it to one of my friends that works in forensics for the police. I'm sure they'll be able to test it for poison.

I also remembered to wear trousers today so that there would not be a repeat of the itchy tights drama from yesterday. I think the adults on my course will be grateful for this.

I was driving myself to the station today as I was meeting up with my friend Shane for dinner, after work. Mr H was off to badminton so wouldn't be able to pick me up from the station. I do think that Mr H needs to comply with 'car etiquette' a bit more though. He has started listening to 'Old FM' (OK... I don't think it is called that but it should be) and when I turned the key in the ignition it started spilling out music from the 1950s (anything before the 70s should really be made illegal). I am very good with car etiquette, as I re-tune the station back to Old FM in Mr H's car after I've driven it. I'm kidding of course! I can't actually change the radio to Heart FM in the first place as his car has so many dials and buttons and I can just about work out where the indicators are (which is more than BMW drivers can... *ducks for cover as BMW drivers bristle at my comment*)

Tales about other road users...

Other car drivers do make me laugh. Some of them are so impatient. (Mr H is in this category.) There were two buses in front of me on the road and one of them stopped at a bus stop to pick up a passenger. The other bus had to wait behind it and I was behind the bus. I looked to my right and there were road works on the right hand side of the road.

I deduced that I would be unlikely to get past both buses and then pull in without getting stuck on the wrong side of the road. Unfortunately, the div* of a male driver behind me did not come to the same conclusion and I was right and he was wrong. All he succeeded in doing was pulling around me and at this point the buses started to move off. He was then stuck on the wrong side of the road next to the road works and the buses were not going to let him in. He had to put his left hand indicator on and pull in front of me.

* 'div' is a local term for idiot or f***wit as we also often call them (sorry for swearing again Mum). Maybe I don't need to become a bestseller and should just have a swear box tractor fund...?

I shook my head in despair and just said to myself 'typical male driver'. Luckily I was driving myself. Mr H wouldn't have let him in and we would probably have ended up like racing cars side by side waiting for one of us to back off with me swearing at Mr H. I had the last laugh though as this driver obviously did not know the short cut to the ring road. As I pulled out in front of him further down the ring road I gave him a knowing-conceited smile. I like to enrich the lives of others wherever possible.

As I hadn't had to wait for Mr H to drive me, I was early for my train and getting excited at the prospect of completing one of my missions to fleece the first class lounge of food and drink. Luck was on my side for all of 20 seconds as I got into the lounge and started making a latte.

Just when I was congratulating myself on my achievement, the tannoy came over to announce that my train was being re-platformed to platform 2. Noooooooooo!! Not again. I decided that this was revenge for the conceited smile I had given earlier to the bad driver and left the lounge to get to platform 2. At least all this exercise will help me lose weight, I thought, as I was tucking into the blueberry muffin I had fleeced from the lounge. I didn't however complete one of my missions to have a look through the visitor book.

At Wolves station there are emergency electronic 'help' buttons on each platform. The instructions above them say that you should only press them in an emergency. Being that this is Wolverhampton, I suspect they mean that if you are being mugged or stabbed or you've dropped your kebab on the train tracks. There were A4 white paper signs taped to each of the buttons saying 'Out of Order'. I was really tempted to write underneath, 'So no one will hear you scream...' Obviously I didn't, I didn't have time with the re-platforming of my train.

On the plus side the Cross Country train staff today were very generous with the food and drink trolley and I got some cake, crisps and water to take away for the day. The difference in price between a standard class ticket and a first class ticket from Wolves to Bham is around £3 a day. I definitely get my money's worth in the food and drink that I get.

Another advantage is that generally the first class carriages are less crowded, so you get a seat and the smell in the carriage is expensive aftershave rather than the eau de B.O. that normally permeates the air in standard class. The CC lady also complimented me on my fluffy black and white pom-pom*. This was a present from Letitia for my birthday and it is now firmly attached to my work wheelie-case and accompanies me when I'm working. Last week in London a lady had said 'nice ball' to me. I told the CC lady this and she chuckled and said, "I think we should stick with calling it a pom-pom."

* Apparently it is spelt pompon. I don't really understand this as it isn't pronounced with an 'n' at the end. I shall continue to spell it with an 'm' at the end – I like to annoy autocorrect.

Dad sent me and my sister an email today thanking us for his lovely day out last week. I now feel bad for saying that we thought about dropping him off en route. Love you Dad xx

I tried to be healthy at lunch today because I knew that I was eating out. There is a 'little' Waitrose about a 15 minute walk away from the Jewellery Quarter where I was training (I don't know why they feel the need to tell you that it's little. You really could tell from the size of the building). I bought some prawns, some edamame beans and mango. A guy in the lift back at the training venue said, "What a healthy lunch." I nodded in that, 'I know, how good am I?' kind of way. I didn't like to tell him that I'd already eaten a bag of crisps and a chocolate bar (as well as the muffin and toast for breakfast).

Tales from the pub...

I went out for dinner with my friend Shane tonight. Dinner always produces some tales. We reminisced about one of our experiences a few years ago when I, Shane and a group of friends had gone to dinner at a curry house in Birmingham.

Something else you should know about me is that if I order a glass of white wine then I always order a diet coke at the same time. I really can't take my alcohol (despite alcoholism running in the family) so I make sure I am hydrated. I had done my usual order with the waitress of, "I'll have a Chardonnay* and Diet Coke please."

* I have since seen the light and become a Sauvignon Blanc girl.

Maybe the waitress was new or maybe she was just as dim as me, but either way what turned up was a wine glass with liquid in it the colour of coke. She happily announced, "White wine and Diet Coke". Needless to say I didn't try it and she had to call over her manager as she didn't understand what she had done wrong. Thankfully, tonight, we were in a bar that understood perfectly my request for a small* Sauvignon Blanc and a Diet Coke and they arrived as they should, in separate glasses.

* I was driving

I had a homemade pie for dinner and said to Shane, "What did the waiter say was in it? Was it wildebeest and something else?" Shane said, "Do you mean buffalo?" What then followed was a discussion of 'are all buffalo's wildebeests or are all wildebeest's buffalos?' Or were they actually totally different things? We asked Siri but after spending five minutes reading a post entitled 'Giles from Cambridge asked this question in January 2012' we concluded that Giles had not received a helpful answer, and neither had we, so we gave up. So if anyone knows the answer, I'd be very grateful.

The only strange thing to happen tonight was when the waiter whisked my serviette off my lap after he had collected in our empty plates. I hadn't seen him coming as he crept up on me from behind. As he whipped it off my lap I exclaimed, "Oo! It's been a long time since I've had a guy in his 20's down there." I don't think that he got the humour of the situation though as he said (in his broad Brummie accent), "I'm only 19"...

I told Shane about the sign up at Wolverhampton train station and he mentioned that the first class lounge at Coventry had been shut for ages and was being refurbished. Twice now signs had gone up to say, 'This lounge will be re-opening on...' and so far neither date had been stuck to. Apparently, the latest sign has gone up to say, 'The lounge will be re-opening on April 15th'.

Someone* had written underneath, 'Really? Will it? Like the trains... it's delayed.'

* I think 'someone' is Shane.

Tales from train stations...

As I was waiting for my Cross Country train at New Street, a Virgin Train pulled in first. The VT guy said to me, "Why don't you get on this one instead if you're heading to Wolverhampton?" I told him that I go Virgin to Euston first class as they give food and alcohol but that the trolley service never comes round between Birmingham and Wolves. Cross Country, however, do generally offer some cake and a drink between Birmingham and Wolves. I did actually hop on the Virgin Train though. I thought that karma might delay my Cross Country train and that would teach me the life lesson of 'gluttony' one of the seven deadly sins. As luck would have it though, the VT guy brought me six chocolates to my seat and said, "We can't have Cross Country being better than us. I did look for cake but there wasn't any but have these instead." I have made a mental note to try and play one off against the other when travelling in the future. We'll see if Cross Country try to outdo VT the next time that I travel with them.

When I got back to Wolves station and joined the queue to pay for the carpark, I nearly had heart failure when I saw the price. It's now £9 to park at the station for the day. Flip me! That's over three Starbucks coffees. And in all honesty it's really not worth £9. The stairwell smells of wee and the design of the multi storey means that a lot of cars bounce off the walls as they drive up the ramp to the next level as evidenced by the amount of scrapes and colours of paint. Obviously, being the superb driver that I am, I have no trouble at all. I generally park on level 1. I noticed that the sign in the car park says that that it's £8 to park. My keen knowledge of contract law kicked in at this point and I'm thinking of writing to them to get my £1 back. After all that will pay for the other half of my Primarni sunglasses that I bought last week.

Whilst I was waiting in the queue to pay, I heard a low growl behind me. Apparently a dog had taken offence to my pom-pom and was growling loudly at it and then started bouncing on the spot. The owner apologised and said, "He's got a fear of balls" (I didn't like to correct him that it was a pom-pom as the dog was clearly agitated and I didn't fancy writing, *'Tales from A&E'* in my book.) In all honesty I was more grateful that the dog didn't decide to cock his leg up my case. I don't think that Letitia anticipated that the pom-pom would cause so much excitement.

Thursday 14th April

Mission for today

- *Get to the first class lounge to look at the visitor book*

I'm a bit tired today so I have decided to aim low with my missions to complete. Unfortunately, I failed again. Mr H was dropping me off at the station, so due to his normal rubbish timekeeping standards we were running slightly late anyway. As I was heading straight to London from Birmingham New Street after work today I spent longer hugging him and kissing him goodbye. I'm sure he appreciated it. He just hides it well.

In the car journey to the station we had had one of our usual highly intelligent conversations. I told him that if ever I died quickly (and young) from some awful cancer then I would like him to meet someone else and be happy. I did caveat this with, "…after a suitable period of mourning obviously". I don't think that there is just one person for everyone. He didn't seem phased by this and that got me back to thinking that maybe I had just accelerated his program to poison me. Never mind, I wouldn't be back home until tomorrow night so that would give me two days longer to live. And being a man he would probably have forgotten about our discussion by then.

I missed the first class lounge again as the Cross Country train was once again re-platformed. But I did get cake and a cup of tea on the train so all wasn't lost. I think I need to stop smiling and look less approachable though. As the train was arriving into New Street the train manager decided to try out some jokes on me. I will only put two in here as I really do want you to read on.

"A cowboy arrives on Sunday, stays for three days and leaves on Sunday... How?" I asked him if this was a joke and he said no. He was right. Jokes are supposed to be funny. Another overly enthusiastic passenger piped up, "The horse was called Sunday". I smiled in that, 'Shoot me. Shoot me now!' kind of a way.

His second joke was, "What do you call a woman who destroys bills for a living?" I thought about this seriously for a minute and thought the answer should be 'clever'. I after all am a master at hiding what I've bought from Mr H. Apparently the correct answer was Bernadette. I was so relieved when the train came to a halt at the platform.

Tales about Christians....

It was raining when I came out of New Street. Every day this week there have been at least three Christians standing by Starbucks handing out pamphlets on Jesus and spreading the gospel. They weren't here today though, standing in the rain, I noticed. But then again didn't Jesus live in a desert so he probably didn't like the rain either. This obviously was universal throughout their religion as the Christians in the Jewellery Quarter were out at lunchtime but as soon as the heavens opened they packed up their board and scuttled to find shelter (ironically in a pub across the road). I thought to myself, 'Yep Jesus didn't like the rain and quite liked a glass or two of wine as well.'

I did my usual stop at Costa this morning and got tempted by the 565 calorie Cumberland sausage toastie. Given the amount of exercise I've had this week with trains changing platforms and going up and down in the building that I've been working in, I felt justified. I also thought that this would see me through until lunchtime. (If you count lunchtime starting at 10:40am then it did.)

You will notice that I didn't put, 'Don't get killed by a tram' as one of my missions for today. I decided that after three days I had this in hand. I was pondering this as I crossed the tracks and had to hurry as I saw one coming round the corner and heard the driver blare his horn. I would have been really annoyed if one had squished me today. I'd spent a lot of last night printing out power point slides on 'Life Coaching' and packing for London. If today was the day that I was meeting my maker then I would have spent the night doing something a lot more fun. I'd have spent it drinking instead.

My attendees were having an intellectual discussion about Brexit before we started our group work (initially I thought they said breakfast and wondered why they looked at me funny when I said that I had a toastie in Costa). One of them joked that they would have no one left in their office back in Cheltenham if we did leave the EU as all of them would be banished from the country. I thought this was a bit mean but after my toastie faux-pas I decided to keep my opinions to myself.

One of our friends, Bobby, had posted on Facebook today a train journey with a picture of a girl doing her make-up on his timeline and couldn't understand this as a phenomenon. Just to wind him up I took lots of pictures of me putting on make-up on the train today and put them on his Facebook wall. I really am starting to think that I have an evil twin in me that rears her head from time to time… I seem to enjoy winding Mr H up and now this is extending to other people's husbands. I reckon that some therapist would put it down to something that happened in my childhood. Personally, I put it down to men acting like morons a lot of the time…

One of Bobby's friends piped up, 'Oh! I was going to do the same but you've beaten me to it.' I replied to her to say, 'We are kindred spirits.' Unfortunately, autocorrect (or autocrapet as I call it) kicked in and said that we were kindred Doritos. She replied to say that she really liked Mexican food. Luckily I hadn't offended her. Autocorrect is very dangerous and I'm convinced that it will cause World War III.

Although Bobby says that he is on Mr H's side to get a tractor, I think that he must secretly hate him. He asked me how the book was going to conclude and said to me, 'Well I think that the obvious conclusion is that you get Mr H his tractor.' I told him that he was missing the point as the book needed to sell for Mr H to get it. He replied, 'Oh well. He's screwed then. He's never getting a tractor.' Sadly I think he speaks the truth...

Friday 15th April

Missions for today:

- *Smile at as many Londoners as possible**
- *Try not to fall over in the rain*
- *Drink as much free alcohol as possible in first class on the way home on the train*

Luckily I didn't wake up at 4:30am this morning. Instead it was 1:58am. I was convinced that I had heard Lucy barking but when I remembered that I was in a hotel, I knew that I was dreaming. (Although the other possibility is that there was a dog in the room next to me as I swear I also heard some whimpering this morning.)

I was partly successful in my smiling mission today. The 20-something bus driver winked at me as I said, "Morning" and smiled at him. I decided not to smile at the weird smelly guy on the bus who kept re-arranging his testicles in his jogging bottoms. After accidentally seeing him do it the first time I made sure that my eyes were firmly focussed looking outside the window.

* I decided at this point that the recipients of this mission would need to be selective.

I was also successful in my second mission. I don't know why but I have a tendency to do cartoon comedy slips in the rain in London. It doesn't tend to happen anywhere else so I put it down to the pollution and general scum that must coat the pavements and road. (The other possibility is the fact that I am accident prone.)

Once when I was training in London I did a massive comedy slip on the pavement and ended up nearly in the splits position on the floor with my bags strewn all around me. Initially I remembered being chuffed that I had nearly done the splits. After all I couldn't do the splits when I was a gymnast (…when I say 'gymnast' I mean when I was about five years old and went to after school gym classes and played on a gym mat in the garden – I obviously was never a professional gymnast).

But then I had the hard task of trying to get up out of that position. Never having been in the position before I really didn't know what to do. Luckily though I was in London, so I needn't have worried. There were so many people around so I was sure to have help. Being London though, most people decided to step over me and tut as I was spread eagled on the pavement. I was obviously delaying their journeys by at least five seconds.

Finally someone came to my aid and helped me up. Turned out they were from Yorkshire. I thanked him for his help and he said (remember to say this in a Yorkshire accent), "No problem lass. I grew up on a farm. Lots of cows getting stuck in ditches up there." As he winked at me and went on his way I wasn't sure whether he was joking or maybe whether he was hinting that it was time for me to go back on the diet...

Tales from eating breakfast...

As I made my way to EAT for breakfast near Marble Arch, there was a police car, ambulance and cyclist at the side of the road. Looking at his wrecked bike I think that he had come a cropper with a car. EAT gave free cups of tea to the Policeman (gold star for them) and I got some eye candy for the next 15 minutes whilst tucking into my bacon bap. Pride comes before a fall though. As I was busily watching the policemen through the window I had forgotten that my bacon bap had a poached egg in it. Just as I bit into it egg oozed out and dribbled down my trousers. And it dribbled down the worst bit that it could. Yes you guessed it, I now had egg on my fru-fru.

I'm sure the guy that was sitting across from me let out an accidental chuckle and then quickly looked away. For the next five minutes I sat there scraping poached egg off my trousers and I tried to wipe it away with a wet wipe and a tissue. I should have left it and let it dry as it was. All I had succeeded in doing was adding to the yellow colour with fluffy white bits of paper tissue that now looked like I had attached some granny's merkin* to my trousers . I put this down to the quality of tissue that I used. I had bought cheap ones from B&M. If I had not been so tight and bought some expensive ones from Boots, I don't think this would have happened.

* If you don't know what one of these is then I suggest that you don't 'Google Images' it... (I bet you're going to anyway).

The only other exciting thing to happen today was when I was giving a lecture on 'professionalism in the workplace' and one of the attendees knocked a glass off the boardroom table and it shattered all over the floor. Being the responsible person that I am I didn't let them pick up the pieces (which had gone everywhere). Instead I got down on the floor on my hands and knees and carefully picked up the large pieces of glass. I was grateful that I was wearing a long top as I don't think the attendees would have liked to have seen my builder's bum as I was scrabbling on all fours on the floor (and it would have been a great irony to my talk).

I was also grateful that we had renewed our employer's insurance. Today could easily have been the day that I did kill an attendee. I didn't attempt to pick up the small pieces but responsibly called a cleaner to sort out the rest. Sometimes I do actually have brains. I only had to pick two pieces of glass out of my trousers where I had knelt on them.

Even the adults on my course today were impressed with my first class train travel strategy. A few of them asked when I was travelling back and I told them that if I got the late train then I could travel back first class, for cheaper than a standard class ticket an hour earlier. They seemed impressed when I told them that I had bought the ticket in the Virgin Train 'flash sale' and that I was going back for £17. One of them had been on one of my 'team building' courses before and said, "Oh yes! I remember you telling us about getting white wine and wasn't it pretzels and 'Uglies' chocolates you got last time too?" It's amazing the things they remember. It's a shame that when I asked them about the team building course and whether they had enjoyed it, that they couldn't remember anything else about it... Mental note: Must make myself more memorable.

Given that today is Friday I decided to have for lunch exactly what I fancied. My lunch therefore consisted of a bag of Kettle Chips, a Cadbury creme egg and a donut. When I was a child I always remember adults saying to me, "These are the best years of your life. When you're older it's all downhill. When you're an adult you'll look back and realise how lucky you were."

Tales about being a child...

Now that I'm an adult I realise what utter bollocks that was. Being a child was rubbish! I have numerous reasons

215

as to why I hated being a child (and these are only a few of them):

1. Being the youngest, I had to wear my sister's clothes when they were no longer fashionable. Believe me, wearing a ra-ra skirt and sailor blouse was not considered 'retro' when it had gone out of fashion four years earlier. And when your sister is about seven inches taller than you it's no fun having to wear her swimming costume with the crotch hanging down to your knees.

   (I put this snippet up on the new Tractor4Graham Facebook page and one of my friends commented that it had been the same in her house. My sister commented to say that this was untrue as we had both had a new ra-ra skirt. She has missed the point though – this just meant that I was wearing one for eight years instead of four. Mum would buy clothes that were slightly too big for us and too long so that we got wear out of them. My ra-ra skirt started at ankle height and after four years only just about covered my fru-fru. At that point I would switch to wearing my sister's and the whole process would start all over again.)

2. Being a child meant you had to eat what you were given. School dinners consisted of green custard

and cabbage. Not on the same plate – but they may as well have.

3. There was nothing to do in our town except get drunk with your friends on Diamond White and wander the streets (obviously this was when I was much older).

4. I got the small box room in the house as bedroom size was always allocated on a FIFO (first in-first out) basis. (This is a little quip for my friends that are accountants.) I can now picture Mum reading this and probably feeling a bit guilty*. I did swear that if ever I had kids then I would give the last one the best of everything and the oldest would have to sleep in the kennel. (Obviously I'm joking – the kennel is Casper's.)

5. GHDs** weren't invented when I was a child so I had to go to school looking like Red out of Fraggle Rock with mad curly hair that was put into high bunches with elastic bands. (I think this hair practice by Mums has since been made illegal probably under the Geneva Convention or something.)

* I don't think it will last long. After reading this Mum said, "I thought you were going to say that as soon as you moved out I re-decorated your bedroom and turned it

into a sewing room." I had forgotten about that but thanks to her memory I have now been able to add it in.

** Something I forgot to mention in my introduction is the fact that I have naturally curly hair and used to be called 'Bubbles' by my Uncle. Well, he wasn't really my Uncle but that's what we called him. Now I know what you're thinking - and I'm sure that visions of Jimmy Savile have just popped into your head - but he was just a nice guy. If someone asks me what the greatest invention ever was then I categorically state 'GHDs'. I can see you curly haired ladies nodding vigorously in agreement at this. And if you have curly hair and are thinking, 'What the heck is she on about?' then immediately put down this book and Google 'GHDs' - I promise that they will change your life forever. I am often mentally straightening random stranger's curly hair when stood waiting for a train.

One of the other consequences of having naturally curly hair is that I often look like 'Monica in Barbados' if there is the tiniest amount of moisture in the air. If this cultural reference escapes you, then go to YouTube and look up this episode of *Friends*. Sometimes I nearly have heart failure in the morning when I look in the mirror. Although I wake up in the 21st century my hair occasionally decides to wake up in the 1980's. Carol Decker of T'Pau would be so proud.

Being an adult on the other hand is ace! I can drive. I can buy what I want to wear. I can eat what I want and I can go places for entertainment. And if I want to wander the streets with my drunken friends then I can... Oh? Wait...

Seriously though - I would love to bump into these people that warned me of the awful future to come and give them a slap. I love being an adult (apart from Mr H's constant whining about the tractor of course. That I could live without...)

I have just remembered one fun story of when I was a child, so I'll share it with you now.

Tales from being 15 years old...

Dad worked as a carpenter and joiner and for many years he worked on refurbishing pubs. The pubs would always have an open night for the workers that had worked on them and even better it was always open bar. Picture the scene. I was 15 years of age and my sister was 19. We really, really, really wanted to go to the opening night. Sadly Dad told us that we couldn't go and that it would just be him and Mum.

Not ones to be deterred we decided to go above Dad's head. His boss popped down to our house one night and we ran out to greet him saying, "It's a shame that we can't come to the open night." Dad's boss piped up, "Of course you can come girls!" Dad's eyes narrowed but he didn't want to look bad in front of his boss, so we were planning our outfits and slapping on make up very soon after.

Dad doesn't really drink so unlike the rest of the workers that were going by mini-bus, Dad drove us. The night was as expected. I was on the Malibu and lemonade and my sister was on Taboo (or 'Saboo' as Dad thought it was called.) I was merrily being chatted up by a 27 year old electrician but my sister got the short straw with the 40-something. Mum was on the Guinness and Dad was on 'daughter patrol'. Needless to say, we three girls drank too much and Dad was not best pleased to be chauffeur to us. The best part of the night was us three girls trying to harmonise to California Dreamin' by the Mamas and Papas, on the way home in the car, when it came on the radio.

Needless to say, that was the one and only time that we went to opening night of one of the pubs...

Saturday 16th April

Missions for today:

- *Unpack and re-pack for going back down to smelly London tomorrow*
- *Have a shower and wash away smelly London (don't get freaked by the dirt that comes out of my hair and nose)*
- *Write some of my book*

I've tried to keep my missions down to things that are achievable. Although, in all honesty I'm not too bothered about mission number two. I'm back to smelly London tomorrow so there isn't really much point in getting clean.

I was actually awake quite early this morning and it had snowed overnight. At 8am I took a picture and put it on Facebook. My friends were less bothered about snow in April but more concerned that I was up at that time of the morning. I'm now thinking that maybe it always snows in April. By 10am the snow had gone. I'm not usually up before 10am so for all I know it could snow every day in April and I would have no clue. When I first saw the snow I did wonder if I had slept for a really long time and had missed the rest of Spring, Summer and Autumn; and had woken up in Winter.

Mr H had not slept well (I thought he might have sussed the changed pillow) but luckily it was only because I had stolen the covers and was snoring (according to him) and that was the reason that he had woken up at 6am.

I have realised that yesterday's tales appear to finish at lunchtime. But there were a few other weird things that happened later that day...

After I had finished work yesterday I had headed back to catch the train home. It was absolutely pissing it down and I really should have shelled out for a cab instead of trying to squeeze onto the bus with the rest of London on Oxford Street (trying to avoid their glares because I dared to bring a suitcase on the bus was a challenge in itself). But given that most London taxi drivers are miserable b***ards I decided to take the bus.

Tales about my pom-pom...

I was soaked before I even got to the bus stop. My furry pom-pom was also soaked and I think it must have started to smell funny. I was followed by a stray dog at one point and was starting to get anxious that it thought that the pom-pom was its Mummy. I needn't have worried though as quite clearly this is not what the dog thought as it proceeded to try and hump my bag. I tried to pretend that the dog was nothing to do with me as I hurried along the pavement but a five year old child pointing, "Mummy!

Look at that lady giving her dog a lift on her case" did not help my cause. I was in luck though. Being London, most people didn't even raise an eyebrow at the dog hanging off my case. I am starting to think that this pom-pom is becoming a bit of a liability. Letitia will be delighted that her present is causing so much fun. When I got home both Lucy and Bonnie started sniffing the pom-pom. They gave me a look as if to say, 'We smell other dog. You've been unfaithful haven't you?' as they turned their backs on me.

As I was heading to Euston an older man and his wife were huddling under an umbrella as they scuttled across the concourse outside. Very loudly she said, "Dennis! Can you stop bouncing the umbrella off my head and hold it higher? How many times do I need to tell you this? You really can't do anything can you?" Poor Dennis replied, "I'm sorry Judith, I'm trying to hold it higher but then you moan that it's too high and then you get wet." Judith huffed and puffed and strode off so that he had to jog alongside her to keep up and keep her covered by the umbrella.

She had been so vocal that a lot of people had stopped what they were doing and had turned to look at them. I gave Dennis a sympathetic look and thought that it wouldn't have just been an umbrella that I would have been bouncing off Judith's head, it would have been a sledgehammer. I have made a mental note to check the Evening Standard when I'm back down just in case the headline is, 'Woman found dead with umbrella shoved up her bum.' I would know that it was Dennis. But don't worry Dennis, I won't tell anyone. You looked like a nice guy and deserve happiness.

As usual I stopped to chat to 'Jason', the Big Issue seller and gave him a bit of money. Jason is so polite and most times that I'm down he's there. Hardly anyone else ever stops and he said that Londoners weren't that friendly and especially to, "someone in my game". I said that he should move further 'North' as people were much friendlier. He said, "Is that just after Watford?"

Inside the station a woman lost her suitcase as she was coming down the escalator and it bounced all the way down on its own and then righted itself at the end. She caught up with it and nonchalantly grabbed the handle and walked off as if nothing had happened. A guy at the bottom of the escalator gave her a round of applause.

I have been travelling a lot just recently which zaps my energy and always results in me putting on weight (because I eat and drink too much) and buying more lottery tickets (because Alexandra and I really need our ski chalet). Whilst I was on a break yesterday afternoon I logged into my lottery account and decided to buy a Euromillions ticket (and I ticked 'continuously by direct debit for every week'). I'll just have to dock Mr H's pocket money a bit more to pay for them. I'm sure he won't mind if we win and he gets his tractor though.

Whilst I have been writing my book Mr H has headed outside to chainsaw some of the fallen down trees on the new bit of land that we have just bought. As he was putting on his chainsaw protective clothing (heaven forbid he chop off a limb) he thought that his boots felt funny. As he turned them upside down a load of peanut shells fell out. "I think the mice have been living in my boots in the shed." I was quite surprised. His feet smell quite bad. I did expect to see a dead mouse also come out of the boot but maybe the mice here have very low standards.

As he headed off I remembered our friend Bobby had named the mound on the land 'Mount Graham' and said, "Are you off to Mount Graham?" I quickly realised that this joke only really works if it's me that's going out.

Whilst Mr H was happily chain-sawing away I decided to do poo-picking on the front garden. You might remember that Mr H and I have very defined jobs in life. Mr H makes all the cups of tea in our house because I struggle to make a nice cup. In the same way I pick up all the dog poo off the lawn as he struggles not to gag. It really doesn't bother me at all. But I do find this strange. I don't understand how men can:

1. pick their own noses and then eat the bogies,
2. scratch their balls, not wash their hands afterwards and proceed to chew on their finger nails,
3. not wipe their bums properly after doing a poo and have skid mark pants (obviously this doesn't apply to Mr H)

...but can't pick up a bit of dog poo when their hands don't actually touch the poo. And they say that us women are the complicated ones! Although thinking about it I did have a 'fingernail through the poo bag' incident once, so maybe it's the fear of touching the poo that means they can't pick it up. But then I refer you back to the list above - man-logic at its best again.

My friend Jade came over today and I told her about the poached egg incident and the merkin. Jade hadn't heard of the word merkin before so I told her that it was an artificial wig for your fru-fru. We then hypothesised about how merkins would attach to one's nether regions. Jade thought that they be on some type of string pants that you pulled up and wore like normal pants. I thought that they would be more likely to attach with tit tape. We didn't ask Siri as in all honesty the conversation was creeping us out a bit. We did wonder who would actually buy one. Jade does a lot of reviewing for products on

Amazon. I bet she's now added one to her list of things to try, just out of curiosity of course.

Sunday 17th April

Missions for today:

- *Get rid of headache*
- *Try not to have any unusual interactions with dogs and the furry pom-pom*
- *Check out the visitor book in the first class lounge*

I woke up this morning with a splitting headache. My friend, Bobby, helpfully said, "Do you think it's a brain tumour?" In all honesty, I did wonder that myself. But I soon forgot about it when opening my parcels that had come from Roxy.

I seemed to have a red mark and pain in my shoulder this morning so I said to Mr H, "Can you see anything on my shoulder?" He said, "There's what looks like a bruise, or it could be a handprint. What have you been up to in London then?" Personally, I thought it was more likely that it was his handprint, as apparently I had been snoring badly last night and he had gone to sleep on the settee at 2am. I expect that he had tried to smother me at some point and his hand had actually left the red mark.

Mr H went out to do more chain sawing of trees on the new land in readiness for the Alpacas arrival. Being the good wife that I am I made sure that he didn't befall to some accident. Rather than going out to check on him periodically I just listened to the noise of the chain saw. If he had accidentally cut off a limb then the chainsaw would stop. Occasionally when I heard it stop I just checked Facebook. If he was posting on there then I knew that he was safe. I congratulated myself on being so attentive and caring.

I had forgotten that I hadn't told Mr H about all of my Roxy purchases and put on my new fleece. Unfortunately, when I put my iPhone in the front pocket I nearly injured myself. The fleece was quite long and as I bent down to pick something up my iPhone turned at a right angle and jabbed me in the right side of my stomach. It felt like it pushed one of my ovaries through to the back and I winced in pain. But I like to look on the bright side - at least it wasn't my liver that had been damaged. I didn't need my ovaries but I don't think that I could live without my liver. Mr H would say that this was karma for 'buying another top that you really didn't need'. Mr H immediately noticed the new top. He does not notice if Lucy has been sick on her bed for two days when I'm away in London, but he's all eagle-eyed when I've bought something new. I think that they must give men a special lesson in school about this.

After Mr H had finished chain sawing for the day (I must admit that after a while I did forget to listen out for it and when it stopped for 30 minutes I hadn't noticed. But again, looking on the positive side, he was ok so I didn't need to tell him that I'd forgotten to check on him) he said that he was going to cut the front lawn again on his new sit on lawn mower.

"So can you do poo picking while I'm getting the mower ready?"

"Only if you make me a cup of tea first."

We are such a good team.

Part way through cutting the front lawn he stopped to adjust the mower. He said, "I wonder if I'm supposed to adjust this bit when I'm cutting the lawn?" What is it with men and not reading instruction manuals? I said, "I don't know - what does the instruction manual say?" I knew that the next steps in his man logic would be to continue messing with it for five more minutes before admitting defeat and going to read the instructions. This is exactly what happened. Two more minutes (after the obligatory five minutes) later he came up to me and said, "Do you know where the instruction manual is?" Having directed him to where he had left it I said, "Is it supposed to have that burning smell coming from the back of it?"

I was travelling back down to smelly London tonight so I made it my mission to avoid any incidents with dogs and the furry pom-pom. I was also determined to have a flick through the visitor book in the first class lounge for any funny stories. I managed the pom-pom mission but failed with the visitor book. I had forgotten that the first class lounge shut at 6pm on a Sunday.

Before we headed off to the station we popped down the road to see Chester, Cyril and George the Alpacas. They seem to be getting on well, so fingers crossed we will be having them when the land is fenced. Mr H looked wistfully at William in the field and mumbled, "I really did like him." I thought that I should handle this like the pillow situation, delicately and carefully so as to not hurt his feelings. However, as I have been travelling a lot and I have no patience, what actually came out of my mouth was, "He's not coming – get over it." Mr H went into a state of shock at this outburst and he hasn't mentioned him since. I think I might use this tactic in the future. Maybe now is the time to tell him about the pillow...

Tales from travelling to London...

At Wolverhampton train station a guy was waiting on the platform and leaning against the wall. He was rubbing the soles of his shoes up and down the wall. Wise guy, I thought. Wipe your feet on the way out...

First class on the train on a Sunday is really disappointing though. Because it's only £10 to upgrade from standard class you only get a snack box and there's no free alcohol but only tea and coffee. The service manager asked if I wanted milk in my tea and I said, "Only a little bit please, I like builder's tea". She said, "Oh I know what you mean. I don't like to milk the cow." I thought this reply was a bit odd. Did Sir Richard actually keep a cow in carriage K that the staff had to milk? I made a mental note to catch her on the way back and tell her that I'm sure this would offend her human rights and that she couldn't be forced to milk the cow under Employment Law.

I'm also pretty sure that the Virgin Trains bin would be full to the brim of the red pepper spread that no one had put on their crackers. If you happen to be reading this Sir Richard, can I suggest that you swap it for something else? Maybe pretzels or peanuts or a miniature of whisky – whatever you fancy.

I can understand why there's no free alcohol on a weekend. Everyone on the train was really depressed with it being Monday tomorrow. The demand would be far outweighed by the supply. Even 'Hilda' the 70-something sitting across from me didn't look happy. She took a flask out of her bag and poured something into her tea. I'm pretty sure it wasn't milk... She went to sleep shortly afterwards and didn't wake up for the rest of the journey. I really want some of what she had in that flask.

To try and shut out the depressing air of the carriage I decided to listen to some of my music. Dido 'Here with me' came on. This made me chuckle for a while as my sister always calls her 'Dildo', as the first time she saw it written down, she mis-read it. I was chuckling again when another of her songs came on as the train went through Bushey.

Back to my journey then. Having had two mugs of tea, I really needed a wee but I really didn't want to go as the carriage was busy and the toilet might not have been as clean as usual. I took my handbag with me in case I needed tissues and wet wipes. I really should stop using the toilet when the train is going at 125mph.

On the plus side the train toilet talks to you. It helpfully reminds you to lock the door (note for thickies, I always think) and tells you not to flush your goldfish down the toilet. Luckily on this occasion I did not have a goldfish with me. I can imagine some idiot trying to flush their Chihuahua down the toilet and then suing Virgin Trains because they didn't tell them not to. I swear that the announcement used tell you not to flush your Pterodactyl down the toilet but that has now gone. I'm now thinking that I can bring one and flush it down with no consequences. Maybe I will bring one of the Alpacas with me and take a picture of them in the toilet (not actually down the toilet) and tweet Virgin. Sir Richard seems to have a good sense of humour.

There wasn't much loo paper in the toilet (obviously due to the busy carriage) and I did my random act of kindness (RAOK) and told the girl queuing after me. Good job I hadn't needed a number two. Mum (when I lived at home) and Mr H (who I obviously live with now) despair over the amount of loo paper I use. I can't help it. It comes from growing up in a family of five where you can always guarantee that you would be mid-poo and look across to see an empty loo roll.

I now have toilet issues as an adult and in our house, although there is only the two of us, we have three toilets and at least three toilet rolls in each loo at any one time (there's actually around ten spare in the main bathroom). The amount of loo paper I use is one of the factors as to why we didn't have children. We couldn't afford it with the loo roll expenditure being nearly as much as the mortgage. And if my loo roll fetish was genetic and my children inherited it, we would be screwed.

I also need to tell you about my toilet issues as a child. I think there is when my toilet roll fetish started... I'll do this in a bit.

Hilda woke up as we trundled into Euston and looked quite refreshed from her sleep. I wished I had asked her what was in the flask. The girl and boy sitting opposite her were taking a selfie as they arrived into London (I have no idea why) and Hilda offered to take their picture for them. They thanked her but said it had to be a selfie. I swear I heard Hilda mumble, "My George used to like a selfie when I had a headache." Obviously, it didn't mean the same thing back in her day... (It took Mum a while to get this. Bless her!)

London was its usual bonkers self on a Sunday night at 8:45pm. A woman at the bus stop was eating an ice cream and further down Southampton Row a guy was wearing flip flops and Bermuda shorts. Luckily my furry pom-pom did not attract any dogs. Weirdly, I did kind of miss having a dog hump my case though as I was walking along the pavement...

Coming back to the loo roll issue. I weirdly, frequently, dream of toilets.

Tales from toilets...

Ok this is a weird one. But apparently not that weird if you are my Facebook friend or a female relative of mine... Me and my sister often dream of toilets. They are toilets that aren't really toilets, so you need to go but can't. Often they are really dirty so that you don't want to go or are open to the elements so that everyone can see you go. I made this small confession on Facebook once thinking that I would get some ribbing but was surprised at how many other people also dream of toilets. I'm sure that psychologists would have a field day with this one!

Signs in toilets also make me chuckle. The sign on one toilet I used once said, 'Please flush toilet after use.' It makes you wonder what sort of people don't realise that you need to flush it? Someone had written (I suspect a bit sarcastically) underneath, 'No shit Sherlock!' I resisted the urge to add, 'Especially if you shit, Sherlock!' But I don't condone criminal damage, so I wrote it in pencil.

I mentioned that I have toilet roll issues and have to use loads and I think this started when I was little. Apparently at the age of four, I wouldn't go to the toilet. I had to go into hospital to have someone look up my bum to see if I had any medical issues. I remember wearing a gown that didn't fully close at the back and lying on a cold metal table when they carried out the procedure. I'm glad the NHS has improved since then. When I was in hospital they force fed me prunes to make me go to the toilet. I have not been able to eat any since. Personally, in my mind, the only reason why I didn't go to the toilet was the lack of loo paper. Being so young though, no one actually bothered to ask me. I'm sure the NHS could have been saved thousands if someone had just asked me why I didn't go then I would have told them. They could simply have sent me home with my own special supply of loo paper and all would have been well in the world. There are more tales on toilets in a bit...

Monday 18th April

Missions for today:

- *Get rid of headache (and Google symptoms for 'brain tumour')*
- *Buy a comb from Boots*

I have woken up again with a headache so have decided not to have as one of my missions today: 'Smile at Londoners'. Quite frankly it's exhausting.

Today I was providing training on 'mentoring' and the location of choice was the beautiful Kensington. I had to firmly lock my credit cards away in the hotel safe lest I spent £350 on a scarf. Obviously I'm kidding! The hotel I stay in is too basic to have a safe.

I nearly jumped out of my skin this morning on the way to work though. I thought I was about to be mugged as I heard a guy shouting behind me (grabbing the first thing to hand to defend myself was my Oyster card. I'm not convinced that I made a sensible choice of weapon).

Turns out that he wasn't about to mug me (I knew that) but was shouting and swearing at the cyclist that had nearly mown him down on the pedestrian crossing. The cyclist obviously did not appreciate being shouted at (even though he had gone through a red light) and gave the pedestrian 'the bird'. The pedestrian shouted, "Don't think you'll get away with it. I'll get you!" I think this was a bit of optimism on his part. He was at least 23 stone in weight and struggled to catch his breath after the altercation. I couldn't imagine him catching the guy on the bike. I did give him a sympathetic, 'Cyclists!!' look and shrug of the shoulders though.

The training was taking place in a nice hotel today and as I had left early I had time to grab a latte and some crumpets in Costa which was conveniently situated nearby. There were a lot of depressed looking Londoners in here, as well as lots of happy Londoners. You could see that the depressed ones were putting off the inevitable of going into work on a Monday morning. One guy ordered three espressos (which I thought was nice of him to buy for two of his colleagues as well) but had drunk two of them by the time I was sitting in there. The happy ones looked like WAGs of famous footballers or the like who would be spending their days having fun and shopping.

Something I do notice in London is that they are eternally fearful of being sued. There are signs up for everything here. One of the signs in the ladies loos in the hotel was, 'only use the sanitary bins for proper purposes.' Honestly! Do we really need to spell out such obvious things? But then again, I did think that the sign wasn't actually that explicit and did skirt around the houses.

As my attendees were doing some mock interviews with each other, I was pondering what my sign would say. I thought it would be much more obvious if it said, 'only sanitary towels or tampons along with the blood that has been wrenched from the wall of your womb' are to be disposed of in the bins. I congratulated myself on how catchy this was and thought about putting a banana skin in one of the bins with half of it hanging out, just to show that I didn't understand their sign. I didn't of course. I don't tend to eat fruit so didn't have a banana to hand.

I could see Caffé Nero from the window of the room that I was in and there was a homeless guy sitting outside it wrapped up in a duvet. I felt sorry for him as no one was stopping to give him money but then I couldn't see a hat or other receptacle for them to put money in. It was as if at this point he had read my mind. He wandered off (leaving his duvet behind) and promptly came back with an empty cup. Unfortunately, in the ten minutes I was watching not one person put any money in his cup. I put this down to it being posh Kensington.

At this point he got up and wandered off with his duvet, leaving the cup behind. I hoped that I had just missed someone giving him some money and maybe he was heading off to get some food. I got worried when I saw a guy smoking in his place and using the cup as an ash tray. I had visions of the homeless guy coming back to see his cup being used for this and a massive fight breaking out. He didn't come back though. I hope he had moved on to a more lucrative spot. As I left for the day the cup was still there lying on its side.

Tales from Boots…

At lunchtime I went to Boots to get a 'meal deal'. When I was in Birmingham last week and had popped to 'Little Waitrose' I had spent £11 on prawns, edamame beans and mango pieces. I was determined not to spend that much again. I could have gone to Wetherspoons for the same amount and at least had a pie, chips and beer (and not felt hungry and scoffed a Twirl an hour later).

The Boots was really busy but I got my comb (mission 2 complete) and my meal deal. I started to get in a panic though as I accidentally ended up in the self-service till queue. I swear that they conspire against me. Mr H will buy a whole trolley of shopping at Sainsbury's and proceed to take it through the self-service till.

I still can't work out where I'm supposed to put my basket, when I'm supposed to put my own bag on the scales thing and where exactly the packing area is. I think the sales assistant noticed the 'rabbit caught in a headlights' look in my eyes as he gently led me to the next free till. I thought that I had been quite successful in my scanning as he only had to come over to me three times. Once was to correct the fact that I had put my own bag into the bagging area too quickly. The second time was to override my double blipping of my creme egg and the third time was to show me which way round my Advantage card went into the reader.

In all honesty if all the customers are like me then these self-service tills will end up costing more. I still needed a member of staff and must have used more electricity than they would have at a normal till. However, in my eyes this was a successful visit. The till didn't blare out, 'unexpected item in the bagging area' and I left with my dignity intact. Well I thought I had until I overheard a girl in the queue behind say, "Flipping heck some people really shouldn't be allowed out." I should have been offended at this. Let's be clear - I should. But I wasn't – I kind of agree with her...

On the evening I was eating with my work wife, Alexandra. We were going to a curry house in Covent Garden. I was meeting her outside Oxford Street Tube station but completely forgot about her appalling sense of direction. I should have realised that we'd be in trouble when she announced, "I know where that is." 45 minutes later, after she's headed off in the wrong direction twice, we finally met up and headed to dinner.

I happily announced to Alexandra that tomorrow was my last day in London. I'm sure I saw the look of, 'No one likes a show off' cross her face. Either that or she was plotting to kill me – it was one or the other. Although she did smile when I said, "So I'm going to have it off for the rest of the week." Alexandra said, "Too much information."

We reminisced about when we used to stay in the Tavistock hotel. Reception there seemed to be under the misapprehension that I was a travel writer (I honestly have no idea why they thought that). But in all honesty it was great. They always gave me a twin room instead of a single (Alexandra always got a single) and I always got one on the front where you didn't have to listen to the rumble of the air con system or the recycling bins being emptied at 3am (Alexandra always had a room here) and I always had a hair dryer in my room (Alexandra had to give a £10 deposit for one at Reception). I never actually used the hairdryer either but I haven't told her this.

It also used to make us chuckle that the hotel staff thought that Alexandra and I were a lesbian couple. (In all honesty I think that Alexandra could do better and would be aiming low if I was her partner) but as she is ten years older than me then maybe the hotel thought she just wanted a younger play-thing.

After leaving the curry house, my bus APP told me that the next bus wasn't due for five minutes so Alexandra and

I decided to walk back to the hotel. This probably wasn't a good idea as we are normally so engrossed in our conversation that we forget to look when crossing the road and nearly get mown down by a cyclist. Once on our way to the hotel on the bus we were chatting so much that we missed our bus stop and had to walk back on ourselves for ten minutes.

We were getting close to the hotel and I think both of us were congratulating ourselves on our uneventful journey. Unfortunately at that point something fell out of a tree and bounced off my head. (I think it was something like a conker – if they're around at this time of year – it definitely wasn't a squirrel – it wasn't that big and it was really hard. Mr H would have definitely cried. He has no pain threshold. I, however, have a head as hard as nails. I think it's to do with having a stone lobbed at me at the age of five.) And just after that happened Alexandra tripped over the pavement and did a comedy slip forwards. I'm sure that London is trying to kill us. I couldn't blame this one on Mr H (unless it was him in the tree throwing something at me).

In the bar tonight Alexandra got some awful news about a friend of hers that had died at the weekend. He was only in his mid-40s and had a wife and children. This reminded us that life is precious and that you should follow your dreams. Sadly it still meant that we needed to work tomorrow. Until a Euromillions win happens we have accepted that we have to have dreams with a touch of reality.

Tuesday 19th April

Missions for today:

- *Stop reminding Alexandra it's my last day in London as it's only her first (and she's getting a bit tetchy about it)*
- *Don't die today (I have this weird thing about dying in London and thinking what a waste that would be)*

I failed in my first mission but was grateful to succeed in my second.

At breakfast today we decided that after last night's awful news we were determined to live life to the fullest and enjoy every minute. With this in mind I had five sausages for breakfast. I told Alexandra that a random mobile number had called me yesterday but as I didn't know who it was I hadn't answered it and they hadn't left a message. Alexandra chastised me and said, "It could have been heir hunters. You've probably just missed out on some big inheritance now. We could have had our ski chalet".

I pointed out to her that given that both of my parents were alive then the chances are that they would be telephoned before me. Although this reminded me that as a child I, apparently, use to routinely tell people that I

246

was adopted and that I was really a princess. I think this comes back to the loo roll issue. A princess would never be caught mid-poo without any paper. Or at least if she did then she would have a bell to ring to get the servants to bring her some. If ours ran out it meant that there wasn't any more and screaming for Mum wouldn't make a difference. I'm not sure what we did when that happened... I must have blocked this traumatic experience from my mind. By the end of breakfast I had reminded Alexandra at least three times that this was my last day in London. I think she is now considering divorcing me...

We went to eat lunch together at EAT, as I was training in some offices close by to where she was working. We were finishing off our salad and sandwich and about to head back to our respective jobs when Alexandra started clearing the table. "What are you doing?" I said. She said, "I'm clearing up. It's polite for the next people." "This is why we've just paid VAT on our food – it's because we're paying them to clear up after us."

The topic of VAT came up again later with Helga taking her UK purchases back to Japan and claiming the VAT back. A few friends had had a conversation on Facebook about tax avoidance/evasion and planning. This because of David Cameron's trust fund overseas whatever blah blah blah and the Panama papers scandal that's been in the news recently. (As I mentioned in the intro, I don't do politics and don't generally keep abreast of boring news. When someone said 'Panama' to me, I thought they were talking about cigars.)

In our conversation on Facebook I said, 'Well of course I buy my trainers in the children's section. Luckily for me I'm a size five so there's no VAT on them.' Of course I'm kidding. I don't exercise. Why would I need trainers?

Tales from dinner...

After work Alexandra and I had chance for a quick dinner before I headed to Euston for 7:23pm. We had one of our usual hilarious conversations. It was to do with weird presents that we've received in the past. I think Alexandra won. She has been bought an ash tray (she doesn't smoke) and size 16 Bridget Jones's knickers (she is a size ten when she's overweight).

As I was chuckling about the presents I managed to drop my iPhone in my curry. As I was scraping off chicken makhani, lamb Rogan Josh, mango chutney and mint yogurt dressing I thought, 'Well there goes my warranty.' I think Alexandra thought it was karma for my constant bragging about my last day in London. (I'm really surprised that when Mum did her read through she didn't say, "Are you sure it wasn't korma and not karma?" She's slipping...)

Whilst we were on the subject of Bridget Jones's knickers, this reminded me that I had my fru-fru test at the doctors the next day. Alexandra helpfully reminded me to make sure that my lady garden was tidy. I was thinking that maybe for a bit of fun I should Google some vajazzle ideas and perhaps go in with glitter stuck to it. A serious point again readers. Get your fru-fru checked regularly. You never know when the big C is going to hit.

I received a Facebook message when I was on the train from a friend who was trying to provide some helpful advice about my headache issue. She helpfully said, 'If you're over 45 then cutting out caffeine will probably help.' As I said in the intro, I'm 42. I replied with, 'Living with Mr H just makes me look old.'

The sun was glaring through the train window while it was setting so I put my sunglasses on. I think that the serving staff in first class mistook this for some 'weird celebrity trying to be inconspicuous whilst being conspicuous' thing. But it got me some extra Uglies* chocolates so who was I to complain. This reminded me once when I was travelling first class and a group of women had been nudging each other and smiling at me for a lot of the journey. Apparently they though that I was Hannah Waterman. A lot of people say that they can see it (I can't – she has a lovely nose whilst mine is both big and long and she doesn't have my awful double chin).

* You really need to try these — they are moreish though and you will get fat and possibly diabetes.

I think Virgin are trying to save money. My lager was served in a plastic glass tonight. I did tweet them with a photo and with the hash tag #imaladyyouknow. They have a good sense of humour as they liked my tweet (and let's face it — I'm no lady). When the food trolley came round I said to 'Alan' the server, "I'll have a pastrami sandwich, some plain crisps and some cake." Alan said to me, "Do you want some fruit as well?" I responded with, "No thanks — I'm watching my calorie intake."

Wednesday 20th April

Missions for today:

- *Have a very long shower and 'tidy up' down there as it's fru-fru checking day*
- *Spend the day writing my book*

It's been a beautifully sunny day today. Mr H chuckled when he saw me sitting inside at lunchtime with a fleece on. This is the problem with an old house. It's always cold inside no matter what the season or weather. I had no clue how warm it was outside. At 3pm I did finally go and lie on the swing seat, although many of my friends berated me for posting a picture of me still wearing said fleece outside. I suspect that they were all in bikinis today. I wore my new £2 Primarni sunglasses and was really pleased with how comfortable they were. I 'accidentally' fell asleep on the swing seat. I woke up when Bonnie jumped on top of me and noticed that I'd been drooling (to clarify I noticed the drooling, I don't think she noticed). I also had sunburn on my cheeks and nose.

Thankfully the nurse for my fru-fru check did not get to see me like this. She had phoned me this morning to say that there had been a mix up in my medical records and I wasn't actually due for a fru-fru check. (She obviously did not call it this.) In some ways I was a bit disappointed. After all I had spent longer than usual in the shower tidying up the bush and using my new strawberry shower gel. I did think that maybe the new shower gel was not the best choice when I noticed it had lumps of real strawberries in there and seemed to look a bit glittery. Oh-oh I thought… my vajazzle joke is actually going to become a reality. But as luck would have it even if there is a bit of glitter left it should have disappeared by February 2018 which is actually when my next test is due.

Mr H has been down the new paddock chain sawing wood again. He has had Tim helping him today. Tim is deaf and I asked him if he used sign language. I was hoping that I might be able to practise. He cheerily announced that he lip reads and doesn't use sign language but he does know swear words in sign language. I'm not sure our tutor will be very impressed if my five minute presentation for my assessment is full of swear words…

Tales from the new land…

After Mr H had finished chain-sawing for the day we took a walk down the paddock with the dogs. I had taken my contact lenses out when I fell asleep on the swing seat but did notice that my left eye didn't seem to focus very well on the walk down the paddock. I took my sunglasses off and realised that there was still a sticker on the left lens that said that the sunglasses had some super-dooper UV light reduction or something or other feature. Once I took the sticker off my vision improved immeasurably. Given that the sunglasses were £2 I'm quite surprised they went to the expense of putting a sticker on them.

Mr H said, "Oh! New sunglasses then?" I said, "You know I bought two pairs when I was down in London with Helga." What then followed was a totally pointless discussion of, 'Did you really need some new sunglasses?' Sometimes I swear that men are put on this earth just to annoy us. I had spent £4 on sunglasses. <I should pause for a really long time now if I were you, to let this sink in>.

I definitely won't tell him about my £11 Waitrose lunch last week, I thought to myself. To try and put things in perspective, I said, "Well Alexandra is buying a new bike this weekend, I think that's around £1,500." (Sorry Alexandra – I used you in my argument. But I think you'll understand.) So Mr H says, "Well the amount of sunglasses you've got I bet you've spent £1,500 in total." I do find that when men are acting like total nobs then the best thing is just to ignore them, or whack them over the head with a sledgehammer and bury their body where no one will find it. Luckily for him as I wasn't travelling for a bit I was in a generous mood and chose the former.

Now that my travels are technically over I'm back on my diet and have logged back into My Fitness Pal (MFP)*. Having logged my breakfast and lunch I was left with only

500 calories for dinner. I knew that today I would need alcohol. This headache has severely restricted my alcohol intake over the last week. I opened a can of Carlsberg and poured it into a glass. The can said it contained 440ml but the glass said that it was nearly a pint. Sometimes I have glimpses of genius and said to Mr H, "This can't be right. I'm sure a pint is 568ml." So we did the 'ask Siri' and she happily pronounced that it was 470-something. I thought that Siri was lying so went back onto the internet. Turns out it's different in America and the UK. I was (for once) correct. Now you are probably thinking, 'This is really dull...' but it was critical to my logging of calories. Thankfully I was only drinking 141 calories and not 183. On the downside I still only had 359 calories left for dinner. 'Maybe I'll just have two or three more lagers', I thought. I messaged Alexandra to say that I missed her at dinner tonight. Conversations with Mr H are just not of the same calibre. Although tonight they were, I ate dinner on my own because he was out at a meeting.

* I'll explain more about MFP. In order to try and keep my weight down (apart from when I'm travelling) I use the APP 'My Fitness Pal'. I did lose over a stone and a half using it, and then put back on a stone and a half by stopping using it. MFP has an activity area where you can log your exercise. Once I logged 40 minutes of driving, 15 minutes of 'cleaning, light to moderate' and 45 minutes

of 'sitting, talking' just so that I could have a Wispa. And then I wonder when I don't lose weight...

My love of Costa Coffee is probably another reason as to why I don't lose weight. I realised that I bought a lot of coffees in London when I added up the receipts one month and had spent £100. Mum tutted when I told her and I said, "You should be grateful it wasn't spent on alcohol!" I obviously did not tell her how much I had spent on alcohol that month, it's really not the point of the story.

This 'Ask Siri' is not an unusual occurrence in our house. When we went skiing to Austria in January we had to rely on the wisdom of Siri. This is not the first time that we have been to Austria but I turned around to Mr H and said, "Are Austria using the Euro?" Usually I rely on Mr H's general knowledge to answer my questions (which he normally does by saying, "You really are thick aren't you?") but he faltered and said, "I can't remember" so he decided to ask the Siri version on his windows phone. I think she's called Cortina or something like that.

Mr H: "Are Austria using the Euro?"

Windows Siri: "Are Austria winning the Europa."

Mr H: "Do Austria use the Euro?"

Windows Siri: "Did Austria lose the Europa."

Getting frustrated with the modern technology we deferred to our Facebook friends to answer our question. After much ridiculing from our friends we determined that they did use Euros. Obviously last year's holiday to Austria had been completely forgotten by us.

We also struggle with the modern technology at home. Mr H spent about 30 minutes trying to remember his password to get into the parental controls on Talk Talk on the telly. He finally remembered his password and was able to pick up the free Sky channels. Given that there are no children in this house I have no idea as to why he had set a password in the first place. This is one of the mysteries of the male mind that I will never understand.

We were watching a football match a few months ago and Mr H likes to think that he is really funny - it's a Hughes male family trait (as in, they all think they're funny but none of them are). Mr H pipes up, "Oh look Honey - Chesney is in goal."

I said, "Who?"

"Chesney - you know - wasn't he in Corrie?"

Me, "I don't think it's that Chesney."

"Chesney Hawkes then?"

"I don't think it's that Chesney either."

Suddenly there is a big pause from him and I pipe up, "You're out of Chesney's now aren't you?"

Begrudgingly he says, "Pretty much..."

We do sometimes have intellectual conversations in our house. One of which is what would we do if the apocalypse came. We decided that we would be able to live off the land for quite a while but if food ran out then we both concluded that we would have to eat Casper first. Don't get me wrong, we adore the little fella but he is the biggest baby in the world and we wouldn't be able to stand his whinging if there was no food to eat.

We have had four cats in total before Casper and only one of them was a boy. He was deaf though so didn't act the same as a hearing boy cat. Our other cats have all been girls and I think that next time we will definitely get a girl. Boy cats are the biggest cry-babies in the world. Casper will give out this most pathetic meowling sound when he wants feeding or wants fuss.

Our all ginger female cat - the Minxster- by contrast was as hard as nails. When we moved into the farmhouse 11 years ago she immediately decided that this was her territory and stood up to Duke, the German shepherd, on the farm. I remember coming home one day to find Duke shaking like a leaf but rooted to the spot. As I rounded the corner I could see the Minxster sitting all fluffed up on the steps staring into his eyes. I could tell that Duke was thinking, 'What do I do?! You're supposed to run away. Why aren't you running away?! I don't know what to do... but I daren't break eye contact with you!' Luckily for him I was there to take over. "Come on Duke off you go home now", I said. His look was one of, 'Thank goodness! A human to get me away from this creature.' He happily bounded off back home and the Minxster gave me the look of, 'He will think twice before coming back again.'

Miranda saw Mr H a few days later and said, "Oh that reminds me, I've got something of yours in my pocket" and promptly brought out a cat's claw. "It was in Rhea's nose." Rhea was her German Shepherd and another victim to the Minxster.

Casper, in total contrast, is totally dim and does not show the farm dogs the door. Twice he has fallen in the moat after being chased by them and he still doesn't learn to keep out of their way. He does chase other cats off though and costs us around a tenner a month in cat collars. I say 'us' but given that Mr H wanted him then it's only fair that it comes out of his pocket money.

Thursday 21st April

Missions for today:

- *Go to the hairdressers to get hair colour changed back to blonde for the summer*
- *Go to the nail salon to get nails done*

I think you can tell that today I have decided not to work. I find that work generally interferes with fun and happiness and I try not to do it too much. It's one of the perks of being self-employed. The downside is, if I don't work then I don't earn any money either...

I remember last time that I was at the hairdressers there were some funny tales.

Tales from the hairdressers...

I was sitting with my hair wrapped in foils when a bouquet of flowers arrived for one of the hairdressers. Her response was, "OMG - they're from my boyfriend and he hasn't even cheated on me this time, how lucky am I?" 'Oh yes - he's definitely a keeper', I thought. I obviously didn't say this out loud but like everyone else I made the right oo-ing and aah-ing noises at how beautiful they were.

Whilst I was in there a woman looking well into her 90's came in and asked if anyone could squeeze her in. She was telling the receptionist that she had been asked out by a younger man and he was taking her out for dinner. My ears perked up at this imagining her dating some strapping 20 year old. It turned out he was in his 70's but to her that was much younger. This made me smile for the rest of the day. I hope that if I ever get to that age then I will be the same. I relayed this tale to Mr H when I got home and his little face fell as he said, "Oh so you want to be dating a younger man when you're 90 - what about me?"

"Well given that you are 13 years older than me, then as statistics go, you're likely to be dead." He didn't seem best pleased at this but maths does not lie.

Today's trip to the hairdressers and nail salon has once again provided me with many tales. After trying out a new bleach on my hair, I am now blonde* again. It only took two lots of application and four hours in the salon but all is well with the world again as I once again look like my passport picture. Hopefully, I can now go abroad without any dramas.

* I am most definitely blonde. I am not ginger as five of my Facebook friends cheerily announced on the picture that I posted. Dan (who is ginger) told me not to fight it. I

said that I would fight him if he continued with this. He then pointed out, 'That's the ginger temper talking.'

To be fair it's a surprise to both me and my hairdresser as to what my colour will turn out like. My hair has been coloured so many times that it often doesn't behave as it's supposed to. But in the time that I have been going there I have never disliked any of the colours. I get bored really easily, which is a paradox of my personality as I haven't changed Mr H in 25 years but change my hair colour virtually every six weeks. I should remind him about this and that he should therefore count himself lucky.

Before I went to the hairdressers I put on my decent make up (sitting in the chair staring at yourself in a mirror with sludge-y stuff on your hair and foils that make you look like an alien is not attractive and looks even worse if you're as pale as the snow with dark circles under your eyes.) I forgot to mention that I did inherit one feature from Mum's side of the family... dark circles under the eyes. So with Dad's double chin and Mum's dark circles genetics were truly poking fun at me when I was born.

As I was putting on my make-up this morning I noticed a really long hair sprouting from my chin. I kid you not it was at least two inches long. I'm seriously hoping it grew that big in the night and hasn't been there for the last month or so. If so, I can't believe I haven't noticed it. I also can't believe that if it has been there a while that no one has told me. It looked like a worm trying to crawl out from its hole.

I didn't bother actually straightening my hair this morning. Luckily having washed it yesterday and having straightened it properly I hadn't woken up looking like Tiffany (of 'I think we're alone now' fame) but it was a bit curly around the neck area where I had obviously overheated in the night. Knowing that I was off to the hairdressers it seemed daft to eat into my, 'not a morning person' sleeping time, to get up early to make it look presentable.

I must admit though that when I wandered into the hairdressers it did give me flashbacks to the vets with Brandy and Precious when I hadn't brushed Bonnie. Three women turned to face me and gave me looks of, 'Well we can see why you're here.' It's like people who have a cleaner for their house and then clean it before they come because they don't want them to see it dirty. It just doesn't make sense to me. But the stares this morning have made me re-think this…

In the hairdressers I was earwigging on others' conversations (of course). One lady had very dry curly hair like mine and the hairdresser said that she really needed an intensive treatment on it. The lady announced that she liked her hair as it was and actually had loads of the treatments at home but didn't bother to use them. This perplexed me. Why spend the money on going to have your hair done if it is going to come out looking the same as when you went in. I do anything to get rid of my mad dry frizzy hair. And I definitely did not want to be leaving the hairdressers today looking how I arrived (with grey hairs showing through my roots and gingery/reddy bits over my natural mud brown dull hair).

Another lady was chatting away with her hairdresser.

Hairdresser: "Was it that your mum died last time you were in – or was she just ill, I can't remember now?"

"Oh yeh she died", said the customer.

I'm glad that her mum had died (well – not glad as that's awful but it would have been even more awful to have killed the woman off if she wasn't actually dead). The customer then went on to say that she had died of a broken heart as her husband of 35 years had left her for his secretary and disappeared abroad. She then cheered up no end when she said, "But he's now got some incurable disease so it serves him right really." I kept my mouth shut and busied myself in 'Hello!' magazine reading about preparations for the Queen's 90th birthday.

Another customer, Sandra, piped up, "Oh look! It's the Queen's 90th birthday today – do you think I should put a card in the post to her?" 'I'm pretty sure the Queen wouldn't be crying into her G&T that Sandra had missed her birthday', I thought. I imagined Sandra ordering one from Moonpig with some catchy joke inside it of, 'At your age there's only one thing to look forward to' with the answer inside: 'being able to pick up your knickers when they fall to the floor.' Somehow though I think the Queen probably doesn't pick up her own knickers...

This also made me think that maybe this is why the Queen and Prince Philip have stayed together all these years. She won't have had to deal with his dirty underpants lying on the floor each morning and have to tidy up after him when he left his crap everywhere. There is something to be said for having servants. Maybe I'll do the maths later and see if I can afford one. I'll probably have to let Mr H go... and ironically he's the reason that I need one.

What then followed was a hilarious conversation about whether the Queen and Prince Philip still 'did it' at their age. This seemed to create a bonding session amongst everyone in there. Everyone had an opinion. One person (it wasn't me.... well it might have been) proffered the idea that maybe she hired some high class male prostitute to see to her needs 'down there'. There were a few 'eeewwww's' from people at the thought. I wasn't sure whether it was the thought of some poor 20 something having to service the Queen that made them 'eeewwww' or whether it was the thought of 90 year olds having sex. I will spare you the discussion of what 'position' everyone thought she would prefer. (I apologise Ma'am – and really hope that you've had a nice birthday.)

In the nail salon the Queen came up as a topic of conversation again. We hypothesised as to whether she would resign. (I think the technical term is abdicate – but for some reason that always makes me think of beheadings so I don't really like to use it.) Someone said, "Well she's 90, so let's face it she's only got a couple more years in her at best."

But given that her mum lived well into her hundreds a lot of us weren't so sure. "One thing is certain" piped up Sam. "Prince Charles won't live as long as her. He's had too much stress to deal with in his life." We all thoughtfully nodded at this. We also discussed how totes hilaires it would be for Harry to be King. Although Gemma said, "He shouldn't be King as he's really the son of that soldier guy – Major Hewlett, or something like that." "I think you mean Hewitt" I said. "Oh yeh!" said Gemma. "Why did I say that? Oh - maybe I was getting mixed up with the make of my printer..."

We also had a comical discussion about one of the nail technicians that was going on a date tonight with a guy that she had met a month ago. She was convinced that he was actually gay. She based this on the fact that he spoke with a posh accent and it made him sound a bit camp. We all tried to help out by asking her if he had made a move on her since meeting a month ago.

This didn't really help the situation as she was totally drunk when she met him a month ago and had been messaging him since but this was going to be the first time she had met up with him. We recommended that she wear some killer heels and a low cut top and if he didn't even try to look down her cleavage then she was probably right.

It also didn't help that she said that he wore a wedding ring on the opposite hand. I helpfully piped up, "Oh I know a lot of gay people that do that. It's when they haven't gone through the civil ceremony but want to show commitment." Apparently, this didn't help matters.

She also though that he might be gay as he had lied about his name on meeting and had given a very elaborate name. It was something like 'Sebastian' when his name was really Steve. She said that she had been very drunk when she had first met him and maybe Sebastian was his alter ego. Either that or it was the name that he gave his 'thing', I thought. We quizzed her on how drunk she had been. Had he introduced her to 'Sebastian' and she had thought that she was shaking his hand...?

One customer helpfully said, "You know what men are like. They are complicated creatures. If you are too keen and want them, then they don't want you. And if you play it cool then they immediately want you as they think they can't have you." (Or alternatively, he was playing it cool because he was gay.) None of us said this last bit out loud as she was stressing enough as it was.

We did helpfully joke that maybe he wasn't actually a 'he' after all. She had been so drunk when she met him that she couldn't really remember what he looked like. Maybe Steve was actually Stevie and after a lesbian lover.

Changing my hair colour reminded me about one of my trips to Belfast.

Tales from Belfast...

As I change the colour of my hair all the time this results in eternal confusion by passport control. I once waited over five minutes boarding a flight to Belfast whilst the security woman kept exclaiming, "You look nothing like your passport picture, have you got any other ID?" Unfortunately, being the lazy person that I am, when I renewed my driving licence it asked if I wanted to link it to my passport picture, to which I said, "Yes" as it would avoid the need to get another picture done. She looked at my driving licence and said, "It still doesn't look like you". I resisted the urge to say, "No shit Sherlock - it's the same picture" but I didn't fancy being whisked off to some room and having some strip down procedure being applied to me. After all, I wasn't sure whether I was wearing matching underwear. I made a mental note to always put on good underwear when flying just in case it happened again.

To make matters worse I forgot to take my kindle out of my bag and as it went through the x-ray machine it got spotted. This resulted in a burly 40-something border guy asking me if it was alright if he went through the contents of my handbag. Seriously - who makes up these rules? I knew if I said, "No! Get your dirty mitts off my feminine stuff" then I would risk the full cavity search, so what is the point of the question? He made a point of putting on blue gloves and proceeded to take everything out of my bag. He also swabbed the bag - which at the time I thought was for drugs - and hoped my plentiful supply of Nurofen wouldn't cause any problems, but later I learned from a friend 'in the know' that he was swabbing for explosives.

He fished out the three cable ties that I had in there and said, "You can't take these on the plane madam." I feel the need to clarify with you as to why I had cable ties in my bag. When I travel to Belfast I use my Roxy bag and the zips don't link together to padlock. If I padlock the zips there is still a gap and I have visions of my undies escaping at the other end and happily circling round the carousel while I pretend that they are nothing to do with me. I use the cable ties to hold the zips on my case together tightly. I was trying to explain this to the guy with the blue gloves, all the while very aware that my face was getting more crimson by the second. His response was, "Hey, I'm not one to judge sexual preferences, but you can't take them on the flight." I scuttled off highly embarrassed, glancing up at every security camera, convinced that I would now be on some 'watch' list and would never be allowed back in the country again. It's a good job that I have relatives in Belfast.

My travel traumas did not end there as when the flight landed in Belfast the Flybe cabin crew announced, "If anyone has been on a farm in the last month could they please report to the appropriate area in the arrivals hall." Given that I live on a farm, this was not what I wanted at the end of an already stressful trip to get out of the country. But being the good law abiding citizen that I am I duly reported to the 'disease control' area. I don't think it was called that - it had some long unnecessary name like 'parasitic intervention security screening'. Maybe not, that would be 'PISS' for short. But anyway, there were two guys there who looked completely bored out of their brains and seemed confused to see me rock up. When I explained the Flybe announcement they said, "So you've been on a farm in the last month?"

"Yes - I live on a farm."

"Are you going to be visiting any farms during your visit?"

"No - I will be in the city centre only."

"Oh well that's fine then - just don't visit any farms and that's ok."

Unfortunately the delay cost me a decent place in the taxi rank and I had to wait in the cold. Belfast weather is very changeable - it generally changes from wet and windy to very wet and windy to horrendously wet and windy in the space of a few minutes. Luckily I finally got a taxi and a nice driver called Declan. Declan insisted on doing the usual Belfast patter on the journey to the hotel, pointing out the famous landmarks:

"This is the pub where the stabbing took place of Robert McCartney."

"This is the hotel that's the most bombed in Europe."

"This is where the IRA...." I started to tune out at this point.

They really work hard to sell the place. I shouldn't complain though as the taxi drivers in London are generally miserable b*****ds and mute apart from the occasional grunt. But I do wonder whether the taxi drivers here could point out happier places, such as, "Here is Castle Court shopping centre which houses a big Primark."

They could make them more relevant to the passenger. Unless he was trying to tell me that I looked like a terrorist and maybe that's why I had the bombing and stabbing talk? Maybe Security at Birmingham had already warned him about me...?

Once I was settled into the hotel I went to the bar and bought myself an expensive Stella and small tube of Pringles to get over the traumatic journey. My mobile rang with a number that I didn't recognise and a woman with an Irish accent asked if this was Joanne Hughes. For the love of God, 'What now?!' I wondered. It turned out that they had a bag left on the carousel at the airport that had been checked in under my name and she was wondering when I was going to come and collect it as the airport was shortly due to close for the night. I looked at my Roxy bag about three times before assuring her that I had all my luggage and had only checked in one bag. Apparently Birmingham check in had cocked up and logged the next passenger's bag under my name. I assume this happened because of the dodgy passport photo incident. I nearly went down to the bar to get another Stella but resisted.

The journey back from Belfast was just as bad - I'm convinced that there is now some sort of alert on my passport as the woman at security at Belfast airport took away my liquids saying that she would have to take samples of them all. She also chastised me on my clear plastic bag as it apparently wasn't the right dimensions and should not have said 'Sainsbury's' on it. She swapped it for an appropriate one and gave me back my makeup. I hoped that this was the end of my mad journey to Belfast and back.

Never tempt fate. I think that Belfast and I are destined not to be together. When the ash cloud descended a few years ago, I was due to be working in Belfast. Ironically I was giving a presentation on 'Coping with stress at work.' The ash cloud stopped flights on a Wednesday (I think) and I was due to fly out the following Monday. I said to Mr H, "Do you think that I should look into alternative arrangements for getting there?" Mr H said, "Don't be stupid! It will all be over by then." Well this time 'Stupid' was right.

I ended up on a ferry from Birkenhead at 10pm on a Sunday night, which would arrive at 6am the following morning. I'm pretty sure that the ferry could have done the journey in about 30 minutes if the driver had taken it out of first gear. I thought about heading to the cockpit (or whatever it's called) to tell him. Quite clearly, he didn't understand how gears worked. It went about two miles an hour. I could have sworn that I could see the Belfast harbour from Birkenhead and even thought that I could have swum it faster, although maybe not with my suitcase...

Unluckily for me as this was one of the few ways to get to Belfast, the world and his brother were also on the ferry with me. I had to sleep in a chair in the small cinema as all of the cabins were booked. If I had been going for pleasure purposes then I would have stayed up all night drinking at the bar, like a lot of the passengers did. But sadly I needed to be bright eyed and bushy tailed for work.

When I got off the ferry I think I was suffering that 'white finger' that people used to get after using industrial pneumatic drills for long periods of time. But this was a shaking that went through my entire body. How anyone can make that journey on a regular basis, I will never know. I don't think my body stopped shaking for another six hours. Unluckily I was staying in the Europa hotel, the most bombed hotel in Europe. But at that point I really didn't care. I just needed a bed to crawl into and quite frankly if it had have been bombed whilst I was sleeping then I'm not sure that I would have woken up.

On the plus side I had lots of material for my presentation...

I was panicking that I would have to get the ferry back again to come home (although this time they did thankfully have a cabin available). As luck would have it though, I was on the first flight back out from Belfast. I had geared up for some mad carnage at the airport being this was the first flight back out and thought there might be fights near the check in desks as passengers scrabbled to grab a seat. I couldn't have been more wrong. The airport was eerily quiet and there were only 25 people on my flight. They made us all move seats on the aircraft so that they could 'balance it out'. I was quite offended when they said to me, "Madam can you move to the other side to provide a more even weight distribution, please?" I originally was on the left hand side with mostly men who were easily heavier than me. I was moved to the side that mostly had petite women. I did make a mental note to start dieting again when I got back home though. Luckily there were no more dramas. It was the most serene flight I have ever been on and it landed 20 minutes early at Birmingham. Mr H was still on the M42 as I was out at the arrivals hall.

Tales from bedtime… (No – it's not what you think)

Mr H decided to put *Question Time* on tonight. I forgot to tell you that he has a really annoying habit of talking to me whilst I am trying to concentrate on something else but if I try and do the same to him woe betide me as he will have a massive hissy fit. He was wittering on about Paddy Pantsdown (I don't think that's his real name – but not doing politics, I have no idea) and how stupid he was coming across, whilst I was struggling to get past level 1,617 on Candy Crush. Being a man he couldn't understand the importance of what I was doing. He really should know by now that I hate politics and do not want to chat about it just before going to sleep. In fact, I don't ever want to chat about it.

Friday 22nd April

Missions for today:

- *Pop to the fruit farm to stock up on meat*
- *Go to sign language class*

Since hitting 40 I decided that there was more to life than work and now try and take every Friday off. It doesn't always work like that but it's amazing how much more relaxed I feel from working fewer hours. This is a win-win situation as it means that I am more able to tolerate Mr H's nonsense and don't fly off the handle so quickly.

Last night we met up with some of our sign language buddies to practise for our forthcoming exams in June and July. We always have funny tales to tell from this.

Tales from sign language...

When we are practising our sign language we will often forget the sign for a word and the four of us will have a slight variation on what the sign should be. We then resort to using the internet to see what the correct sign should be.

On one of the Sign Language websites they have videos showing the signs. Occasionally there is more than one sign for a word so you will have a few different videos to look through. It is generally the same four people that do the different variations and we have affectionately come up with nicknames for them.

1. The first one is the 'boy next door'. This is what I call him but Mr H and I had a totally pointless ten minute argument as he calls him the 'nice man'. I said that that was a rubbish nickname. He looks like the 'boy next door' as he would be your best friend but someone that you definitely didn't want to sleep with (although he would be gagging for it with you). Calling him the 'nice man' wasn't that accurate a description.

2. The second guy is known as the 'paedophile'. You can guess what he looks like... and I don't think that I need to elaborate further on this. Although I'm always a bit perturbed when he finishes his sign as his hands rapidly disappear out of view.

3. We also have the 'serial killer'. He has very sinister eyes and tends not to smile and when he signs you are convinced that he is looking into your soul and wants to kill you.

4. The final one is the 'token woman'. Obviously they realised that they needed to be politically correct, so this is where she comes in.

Generally the 'boy next door' is the one that we trust and his signs are nice and slow and precise. I think numbers 2. and 3. have other things on their mind which is why their signing is a bit sinister and quick.

We were also at sign language class tonight and Mr H and I are generally split up because we are a bit naughty. Tonight this did not work. We were learning signs for 'work' and 'jobs' and Mr H was struggling with the sign for 'policeman'. Our teacher said, "Have you never been arrested?" Mr H being the good citizen that he is has never been arrested. (Just to clarify, neither have I. Although I did get handcuffs put on my wrists as a joke when we went to the Olympics and had a selfie with two policemen). But I'm going off track... Back to the sign for 'policeman'.

The sign is basically your dominant hand making the action of putting handcuffs on your secondary hand. Mr H struggled with this concept. He said that he had never been arrested, so our teacher asked him whether he had ever worn handcuffs at all. He had to call across to me from the other side of the room, "What were those handcuffs we had? Were they pink and fluffy?" Good job I had coloured my hair yesterday – I don't think that a lot of the class thought that it was me sitting there with the blonde hair (and the bright crimson face).

One of the members of the class asked me at one point if the blonde was really my own hair. I was a bit perplexed by this. Whose hair would it be, if it wasn't mine?

During the day today I went to Essington Fruit Farm to stock up on meat for the freezer. We like to support local businesses and as they rear most of their own livestock or buy in from local reputable farmers we also feel that we are doing our bit for animal welfare. This trip also provided me with some tales.

Tales from the fruit farm...

Heading up to Essington someone has graffiti-ed on the road a little happy message. It says, 'Have a nice day' then a little bit further up it says, 'To You.' You can tell that this is Staffordshire and not Wolverhampton as the graffiti is polite and respectful. Nothing like what you see in Wolverhampton on the train journey to Bham. That normally says things like, 'I shagged Shaneese right here.' This is normally followed with further graffiti of, 'Who hasn't?' I thought this road graffiti was quite a cheery, pleasant start to the day. Although I did wonder who Shaneese was...

At the fruit farm I spent a while buying lots of meat. As I was in the queue my new blonde hair caused confusion with the butcher. He has served me regularly in the past but I could see that the look on his face was, 'Do I know you? Do you have a twin with dark hair?' As soon as I told him how Mr H likes his pork chop scoring around the edges and how fussy he is about the cut of his bacon, it all came flooding back and he realised who I was and that I had dyed my hair.

There was an elderly couple buying some meat from another butcher and Donald had accidentally wandered off with the basket.

'Olive' called over to him, "Donald! Come back over here – I need you to choose which sausages you want."

As Donald obediently came back Olive said, "Do you want the big fat sausages or the skinny lean ones?"

Donald turned to me and said, "Which ones would you have?" (I swear that he winked as he said this.)

I said, "Oh definitely the big sausage, always go for the big sausage."

Olive then got a fit of the giggles and said, "I've just realised what she meant! I've been a lucky lady to have had a big sausage in my life."

She turned to Donald and looked at him with a really loving smile and grabbed his hand. I should have been creeped out by this but in all honesty it was a really touching moment. I hope that Mr H and I are like this at that age, although I will be choosing the lean small sausages…

I did a typical girly thing on the way out and asked if there was a fit strapping man to carry my sack of potatoes to the car. I didn't want to chip my nails, having only had them done yesterday. The girl on the till said, "They're never around when you need them. I'll get a trolley and bring them out." I was a bit disappointed. I had fancied watching a big strapping young farmhand carry my sack of potatoes out on one hand and putting them in the car like they weighed as much as a loaf of bread. I didn't fancy the girl on the till one bit. Although she did admire my nails so I forgave her for not radioing one of the lads.

When I got back from the fruit farm I decided to cook Mr H some bacon, egg, sausages (lean and small), chips, mushrooms and beans for lunch. His suspicious nature kicked in as he said, "What have you bought now?"

"Honestly! Can't a wife do something nice for her husband?" (Secretly, I thought, 'Rats! He knows about my latest online purchases.')

Although I did get annoyed with him when the first thing he said when he saw his dinner was, "Oh?! I thought that I was having a pork chop." Lucky for him I was in a good mood today and he is not currently sitting in A&E with a sausage rammed up his bum. It made me think that next time I really should buy the big fat ones, just in case.

Whilst I was cooking, Mum sent me a message on Messenger to say that she had been out for a cycle ride and had swallowed a fly. This reminded me of the song we used to sing as children, 'There once was a woman who swallowed a fly....' It made me think that we really did used to learn some stupid songs as kids. I'm sure it involved her swallowing a mouse and a cat at one point in the song. No wonder children grow up confused! When I re-counted this story to one of my friends they very rudely said, "So the woman ate pussy did she?" I should be shocked at this... I should...

I happily told Mum that I have been good the last two days as I have stuck to my 1,200 calories on MFP. Then I showed her a picture of today's fried lunch... She sent me a picture of her healthy pasta/bean lunch and I am starting to wonder if I am actually a princess and not her child. After Mum sent me the picture of her lunch she then sent me another picture of the empty plates. They looked like they had been licked by a dog but beautiful Callum, the golden retriever had gone over the rainbow bridge, so I knew that a dog hadn't licked them. Mum happily replied, 'No they weren't licked by a dog - we just fingered them.' Wrong... just wrong... Today is turning out to be 'double entendre' day.

Mr H left his phone at home when he went back to work after lunch. I did think about spending some time updating his Facebook status with things like, 'I love my wife so much' or as my ruder friends would do, 'I have now taken the opportunity to come out. I have realised that I like big cock.' I didn't though. I couldn't work out how to use his Windows phone.

I remembered that Mr H had to get his doctor's report sent off to the police for the renewal of his shotgun licence. I think that maybe his poisoning of me is taking too long, or maybe I am resistant to the poisons, so I am now thinking that I might fall foul to an accidental shooting at some point in the near future. I asked him if the doctors had done the report and he said, "Yes. They told the police that I am mentally sound." After I had finished chuckling (which was a while) I said, "The NHS really is going to pot..."

Saturday 23rd April

Missions for today:

- *Try and finish the book*
- *Google whether 'St George's Day' is always on 23rd April*

I started with my second mission first. I like to be a rebel. This was to check whether St George's Day is always on the same day every year. I told you that I'm dim. But they move Easter each year so I felt the need to check. This made me think that Jesus would not be happy about this constant moving of Easter. He wouldn't know whether he was coming or going.

Siri was no help with my dilemma though. I asked her, "What day is St George's Day" and her answer was, "St George's Day is today." And I swear that she said it sarcastically. Even my phone mocks me. Google was also no help as it said that it was on the 23rd April, the 6th May and the 23rd of November. 'Blimey!' I thought. 'St George is a greedy so-and-so having three dates.' (I originally used a naughty word beginning with 'B' to describe St George but as I could hear Mum tutting in my head I replaced it with so-and-so. Although, as we have now established that I am a princess and not her child then she can wash her hands of me if she wants.)

I was interrupted writing up today's and yesterday's tales as I could hear Bonnie barking outside. This was because Carrie and Miranda were at the gate, so I went out to have a chat. The Farmer passed us as he was coming back from his Saturday morning catch up with his friends and said, "Oo! Look at these ladies of leisure and their fancy new hair dos." I said, "We're not being leisurely." But Miranda quite rightly also pointed out, "And we're not ladies!" (She speaks the truth...)

She told us that she woke her husband up this morning by poking him. The last few days have been full of constant innuendos. I blame the nice weather. Everyone seems to be getting a little frisky. I suspect Olive and Donald have been at it today with his big sausage...

Tales from book writing...

The rest of my missions have been going well. I have gone through the book and checked that my friends are happy with their tales being in there (Remember none of their real names feature. This is to do with decency and also I don't want any of them getting above their station and demanding to come on Graham Norton with me when the book is a hit). It is funny as to the responses that have been coming back... These are some of them:

285

1. "As long as you pay me some royalties" (this came up at least three times). I have concluded that these friends must really hate Mr H as they obviously don't care about eating into his tractor fund.

2. "Can I have my name changed to 'Hugh Janus'" (You might need to think about this one. I didn't get it straight away either. And another one was, "Can I be called 'Philomena Engleberger'". (I'm not sure if this one is a euphemism... I still haven't worked it out.)

3. "As long as I don't come across as a nob" (Quite a few of the men said this. I have assured them that apart from my constant ribbing of Mr H no one else looks like a nob ... It is funny how none of the woman asked whether they would come across as idiots...)

4. "Can I come on chat shows with you when you're famous?" I liked the optimism of this one but also refer you back to my point above...

5. This is my absolute favourite though! "Didn't realise you were serious about publishing a book. What for? Who do you expect to buy it?" Needless

to say this wasn't from a close friend and the bit that they were in has now been deleted! Another friend said "That one smacks of jealousy methinks…"

On a philosophical note, I like to think that life is about building each other up. Yes, my book might not end up selling and Mr H will fall into a fit of depression and not get his tractor, but I do know that (and will have to let him go… or have him sectioned). I don't need 'friends' pointing it out. We really should spread positivity and encourage each other and stop putting others down.

Seriously though. I am really touched by the number of friends that have promised to buy the book and have said complimentary things like, "I love your stories." and "You're a good storyteller". I love you all for being so supportive. (I have decided that this will be my speech at the Oscars.)

Now tractor-ites, it is down to you. The tales are on hold for the time being (well, I am still writing but these will go in the sequel). Mr H's tractor is now in your hands. Obviously if you have got this far then you have read all of the tales and bought the book. But if you would recommend these tales to someone else then I would be eternally grateful. 'And don't lend them your copy! Make them buy a new one.' (To clarify, this was Mr H saying this last sentence. He really, really, really does want that tractor...)

And most of all I hope that you have chuckled and not been offended and buy the sequel too!

OK... I lied... I want you to feel like you're getting your money's worth. Being the inherently tight person that I am, I always like to feel like I'm getting value for money. So, I've decided to put some of the tales from the sequel, into this book. Turn over and I'll continue the tales...

Sunday 24th April

Missions for today:

- *Hope that the friends that are doing a read through of #tractor4graham enjoy it (this isn't really a mission as such)*
- *Vacuum and clean the cars out (and don't swear at the vacuum cleaner whilst doing it)*
- *Do the ironing (I can combine this with watching Shemar Moore in Criminal Minds and drinking beer. Female multi-tasking at its best)*
- *Stop getting spooked every time I pass a mirror wondering who the blonde girl is that's looking back at me*

Tales from home...

I emailed the first draft of the book #tractor4graham to a few of my friends that have volunteered to read it through. I hope that they chuckle and enjoy it. Mummykins has been reading it as I've written it and chuckled but she is my mum and it's 'Mum Law' that she has to enjoy it. My friends will be honest and tell me the brutal truth (and when I start to cry they will ply me with alcohol). I do love them for this.

Lucy is still sleeping badly. Last night she was up at 2:30am and I swear that she has doggy Alzheimer's. The vet agrees with me but Mr H thinks it's tosh. Given that she went out for a wee at 2:30am and then proceeded to lie on the lawn watching the world go by, I think it's safe to say that this is not normal behaviour. Although on the subject of normal behaviour, I have realised that I have quirky bedroom antics (not of the variety that you're currently thinking). I have no idea why but I can't sleep in socks. I don't know where this comes from but even if my feet are freezing I just cannot sleep in socks. If anyone has the answer to this weird behaviour then please tweet me. Maybe it's not only Lucy that has Alzheimer's....

I have woken up with a pain in my head that feels like it's been crushed in a vice. (I can hear Bobby's, "Are you sure it's not a brain tumour?" question ringing in my ears). I asked Mr H whether he had put my head in a vice whilst I was sleeping. He answered, "Do you really think I did that?" I noticed that he gave a politician's answer and didn't actually answer the question. I think I need to check under the bed for any weird devices that shouldn't be there. He had received a delivery from Amazon in the week so maybe that's what he had ordered. If I start to receive some of those 'Amazon thinks you might like this...' emails which include various S&M torture devices then my suspicions will be confirmed. I think he's moved on from the ideas of poisoning or shooting me...

I have tried to be a really good wife for the last few days since I've been back from London. I made Mr H a bacon sandwich for lunch yesterday. Instead of saying, "Thank you, Honey. What a lovely treat", he proceeded to put a picture of it on Facebook as 'apparently' one piece of the bloomer bread was cut thinly and the other was disproportionately thick. He knows that I'm no good at Physics, so in all honesty I don't know why he was surprised that I can't cut a bloomer loaf straight. And we have been together for 25 years. For 25 years I have never cut a loaf straight. Of course I'm joking! It's 22 years. For the first three years we couldn't afford fancy bread.

I'm thinking of stopping making him nice things now. I've put a joint of lamb in the Rayburn this morning and he will get a shock tonight when I'm tucking into a roast lamb dinner and he has a plate with lettuce on it. I'm kidding of course! He can make his own lettuce dinner.

Whilst we are on the subject of Physics, I actually managed to use it in a correct way yesterday. During the afternoon, Mr H and I were taking a break (I didn't tell him that I had already been resting for an hour whilst he had been clearing bracken from the new bit of land) and Mr H said, "Where do you want to sit outside?" I said, "Well, the swing seat will be the warmest as it has cushions, so the material will be warmer on your bum." He looked at me like I was a mad thing. I said, "It's Physics – D'uh!"

If you sit on a wooden seat with no cover then it is cold on your bum and you might get piles. (I'm not sure whether this is true or not but we used to be told it as kids and I don't like to take the chance that it's true.) Also, the covers were black so would have soaked up the heat from the sun. I was really chuffed at my excellent knowledge of Physics but Mr H just kept shaking his head at me. I'm now starting to doubt his knowledge of Physics.

Our friend Bobby sent me a message yesterday. Apparently, he bought us a present a while ago and is now getting round to posting it. He asked me to give him our address and he is going to write WOLVERHAMPTON in big shouty capital letters on the envelope just to annoy Mr H. He is a good friend.

As you can see from my missions it is 'cleaning' day. I really need to do the ironing as Mr H hasn't got many clothes left and he has no colour coordination and will put the worst combinations of clothes together. I remember when my step-son was 15 and Mr H took him and his friends ten pin bowling. Mr H was wearing jeans with some awful shiny green shirt from the 70s (that I had thought that I had taken to the charity shop years earlier) and when he got home I said, "OMG! What on earth are you wearing? You will have just totally embarrassed a 15 year old!"

About a minute later I had a text from my step-son saying, 'What on earth was Dad wearing tonight? I was totally embarrassed'. I apologised to him that I had been at work and not got back before he went out to put out decent clothes for him. The green shirt went off to charity shop heaven the next day. Mr H is still looking for it to this day. "Do you have any idea where my nice shiny green shirt is?" "No honey! No idea. It must be around here somewhere." It's a bit like Pillowgate. Sometimes he can't handle the truth and being a good wife means protecting him from potentially upsetting situations. I must make sure that I use charity shops further afield in the future though. We were shopping in Wolverhampton once when Mr H piped up, "That tramp has got a green shiny shirt on just like mine." I muttered something like "Well, it was a popular design. Oo-look! There's a tractor in that shop window!"

He also had to dress himself on another occasion that he went out with his son. I texted my step-son in advance to apologise for what he was wearing. He said, 'He looks like a German tourist.' He was wearing a beige shirt, beige trousers and beige trainers. When Mr H got back I said, "What on earth are you wearing?" He said, "Well you always say that I can't colour coordinate, so I thought that I couldn't go wrong if everything was the same colour." Between his knowledge of Physics and my knowledge of colours we do actually make a good team. It's another of the reasons as to why we have to live together.

I do the ironing in our house. It is too traumatic to watch Mr H do it. I remember one day a few years ago I had been at work in Birmingham all day and got back to see the ironing board still up and ironed clothes hanging on the back of the lounge door. Mr H looked like a two year old that had just been congratulated on using the potty for the first time (or a 54 year old that's just been told that he can have a tractor) and I asked him why he was grinning. He said, "I've done the ironing today." "Oh that's great – what else did you do?" "I did the ironing! It took me seven hours."

I could see that his little face was starting to fall and there was a tell-tale wobble of the lip. In order to avoid:

a) a crying episode b) a sulky strop c) a temper tantrum or d) all of these things, I took evasive action. "Well done! That's great!" Secretly I thought, 'Jeez. I'd have done that in an hour.' It reminded me of one of those e-cards on Facebook, 'They call it 'man hours' because a woman would have done that shit in 20 minutes.' Mr H has been banned from doing the ironing since this incident.

It's 12:30pm now and I am still in my jarmies (remember this means pjs). This is one of the reasons that I love not having kids. Not being a morning person, there is no way that I could cope with hyper-active little people jumping on me at 6am. I would have to lock them in their room until at least 10am and I think that this is 'frowned upon'. Of course I'm kidding! It would be 11am...

So many people ask me whether I miss not having had kids. I think they miss the point that I do have a kid. Having a husband is just like having children (apart from the fact that kids can look cute in clothes). There are too many similarities between them...

1. Children like routine and **hate it** when you upset it. They will have an irrational paddy if their dinner is served in the 'green' bowl when they wanted the 'blue' bowl. Mr H has the same outburst if I put his cup of tea in anything other than his favourite mug (and don't get me started on the pillow thing again...) Of course I'm joking - we've established that I don't make tea in this house.

2. You have to pack kid's school bags to make sure that they have everything for the day. If we go away on holiday, I have to pack for Mr H and woe betide if I forget his mint humbugs for the journey. He doesn't seem to be so bothered if I forget to pack his toothbrush though (man logic).

3. Children will have irrational outbursts when you're shopping. "Mummy! I want the shiny

yellow tractor and I want it now!" I don't need to say anything more about this...

4. Children cry when they break their toys. Mr H is currently in the kitchen huffing and puffing because his chainsaw has stopped working. It is in pieces on the kitchen table and I have decided to avoid the kitchen for the next few hours. Because of this I have just made myself four lattes and scuttled off to hide in the lounge.

5. Kids cry at anything. "Mummy! My hand has dirt on it." "Mummy! I don't like the colour purple anymore. Make it go away!" Men are exactly the same. I swear I can hear tears from the kitchen at the broken chainsaw (along with a few swear words). Mr H also cried when I chipped his favourite cup.

The only time that I miss having a child is being able to go and watch a kid's film at the cinema. If you go without a kid then people will stare at you wondering where your child is. I now go prepared for this. I go with sick down the front of my top, carry a child's rucksack, wear no make-up and look really stressed out. This tends to work as I get sympathetic looks and people think that my child is in the toilet. I can therefore sit in the cinema without feeling guilty that I should have a child with me.

Obviously if I go with Mr H I don't need to do any of this as he acts like a child. He runs to the pick 'n' mix, goes to the toilet at least four times before the film starts and laughs louder than the kids in there. If someone gives me a quizzical look, I just mouth, "He's got special needs." They tend to nod empathically and walk away.

Living with Mr H is challenging. I remember the first time that I met one of Mr H's colleagues and before she even said, "Hello", she shook my hand and said, "You deserve a medal." I think that I have a really high tolerance threshold living with him full-time. But I am thinking that with going to London for fewer days this year I might need to loan him out, as I won't be able to cope with him on my own.

There is a big campaign at the moment for the 'Borrowmydoggy' idea. I'm wondering whether I can do the same with 'Borrowmyhusband'? The only thing is doggies are furry, cuddly, give unconditional love and are fun to be with. I'm not sure how I'm going to sell Mr H to other people... I might have to actually pay them...

I totally failed in my second mission today. To be honest, I haven't vacuumed the cars out in months. I keep putting it on my job's list but keep failing to do it. I think I need an incentive. Maybe I will ask Mr H to hide some chocolate bars in the cars and that might incite me to clean them? Who am I kidding! He will need to hide at least three bottles of wine as well...

I also failed in my last mission too. I still can't remember that I'm blonde and screaming, "Arghh!" every time I walk past a mirror really needs to stop. It's getting embarrassing. Mr H just keeps shaking his head and sighing every time I do it. Even the dogs are giving me the, 'Really Mummy? You are stupid!' looks as well.

I really should have been born blonde (*ducks for cover as my natural blonde female friends bristle at this comment.*) It has been a common theme in my life though. People will often say on meeting me face to face for the first time, "Oh! We thought you would be blonde?!"

To be honest I'm not bothered when men* call me 'Sweetheart' or 'Darling' or offer to carry my bags or open doors for me. I think it's sweet and I'm sure when I'm decrepit and wrinkly I'm going to miss it.

* Just to clarify this point. I don't mean all men. I mean fitties and if they're in uniform then all the better. Unfortunately even in my 20s I was always a man magnet for the over 50s. And not the George Clooney/Brad Pitt over 50s but the balding, beer bellied and smelly breathed

men in their 50s. I have never seemed to attract the fitties of the world – oh! except Mr H of course (nice save Jo-Jo).

Monday 25th April

Missions for today:

- *Get my summer's job list sorted, so that I (more importantly) can plan my free time*
- *Seriously - stop screaming when I glance in a mirror as I pass it*
- *Buy more wine*
- *Obviously do a day's work (I really should put this as my first mission as it's non-negotiable)*

Tales from working from home...

Today I am back to working from home after my recent travels. This is the time of year for my job that I really love because the weather is normally better in the summer than the winter and I get to work in the garden a fair amount (D'uh! It's Physics... or maybe it's something else... Meteorology... or is that to do with asteroids? I need to Google this and check).

Last night Lucy slept like a log. Sadly I was wide awake at 3am and accidentally woke Mr H up as well. He swears that I deliberately woke him up. I actually didn't and was surprised that it was a happy accident and that I didn't need to deliberately wake him up. I went downstairs to play some Candy Crush on the settee and see if anyone on Facebook was up for a chat. Just my luck this was the one night that everyone slept well. When I heard the telly go on in the bedroom I knew that Mr H was awake and went back upstairs. It's bizarre the programmes that are on telly at that time of the morning. We watched *Come Dine with Me* until Mr H went all boring and put *BBC News 24* on.

Whilst we were still awake at 4am Mr H said, "Oh my goodness! It looks like BHS are going into Administration." Unfortunately, I mis-heard him and thought that he said the 'NHS'. "Cripes!" I replied. Do you think we need to tell our friends that work there that their jobs might be going? (I listed out at least three friends that worked for the NHS for him). He looked at me with a puzzled expression and said, "They don't work for BHS?" "Oh! BHS... I thought you said the NHS". I'm sure I saw him re-adjust the pillow behind his head. I wonder if he was contemplating smothering me for the sake of mankind?

I did think afterwards that the NHS going into Administration would have been strange. But in my defence it was early in the morning and I am blonde*. (This is my failsafe reason for any future dim comments that I make.)

* When I put this snippet on Facebook, one of my friends said, 'You're ginger'. I AM BLONDE!

Happily though after Mr H put the news on it did make me drift back off to sleep at 5am. I think he thought that I had woken him up deliberately though as he put the hairdryer on at 9am whilst I was still in bye-bye land. He turned around and said, "Oh you're awake then?" Never mess with a tired grumpy woman, I thought. I was plotting my revenge as I was sipping my morning latte.

My third mission is extremely important. While we were tucking into our lamb dinner last night (I know... I relented on the lettuce) Mr H said those eight words that no wife ever wants to hear... "I think we are out of white wine..." (And I bet you have just counted that there are eight words there... I did – just to check that I wasn't going to look dim again with my maths letting me down...) Luckily he was wrong though as I found a bottle in the pantry. But I have made a note to take a trip to Sainsbo's soon. Running out of wine is worse than running out of loo paper. At least you can use other things to wipe your bottie: kitchen roll, newspaper, one of Mr H's shirts, a cat... whatever really. There is no substitute for running out of alcohol.

Due to the bad night's sleep, I once again felt like my head had been crushed in a vice and that the rest of my body had been run over by a bus. Whatever these torture implements are that Mr H is using they are really successful. I hope that he gives them a good review on

Amazon. The day continued to go from bad to worse as one of my friends asked on Facebook was I feeling rough because I knew that Shemar Moore was leaving after this season of *Criminal Minds*. I'm not sure that I could have had worse news on a Monday morning. I didn't know this and I am now thinking of un-friending her on Facebook. There really was no need for that.

On a positive note, I found the jeans this morning that I lost over a month and a half ago. They had gone in with Mr H's jeans. I'm sure that I had looked there. He said, "You obviously didn't look properly" and glimpses of his 'liar' face appeared for a fleeting moment. I think he knows about the pillow and has been hiding my jeans deliberately. But then again, this doesn't make sense. Pillowgate only happened a couple of weeks ago and my jeans have been missing for longer. Even worse! Maybe he knows about his green shiny shirt?

Last night my sister messaged me with some old photos that she had found. There was one of the four cats that we used to have (so cute) and some passport booth ones of her and mum (not so cute). After I stopped laughing I said, "If ever either of you become serial killers - these are the pictures I will give to the news channels to put up." I'm sure Mum and my sister would prefer the ones that we had taken at our make-up – photoshoot - Mother and Daughter's day but they will be the ones that I use if ever they go missing and fall foul to a serial killer. Getting the right serial kill-er/serial kill-ee picture is an important thing in life and not one to be taken lightly. When people go missing on *Criminal Minds* the pictures they put up of the victims look like they've been standing in front of a wind machine, fully made-up with perfectly coiffed hair. I think it must be some 'serial kill-ee' law that you look your best. It's a shame when they actually find them that they look nothing like their pictures.

One of the old photos my sister found shows me with really long curly hair (remember it is naturally curly and naturally the colour of dried dog poo) and I said to Mr H, "Look! I can't believe how long my hair was!" He said, "Yes... that's when it was nice" and then sighed with an, 'I long for those days again' kind of a sigh. (I think it's the same sigh that he will make when he finally learns the truth about his pillow.) I refer you back to the point about his colour coordination though. My natural hair colour and natural unruly dry curls can never in any way, shape or form be described as 'nice'.

I don't know why but this has just reminded me of something that came up on Facebook a few years ago. It was, 'A recent study asked women about their arses. Some said their arses were too small, others said their arses were too big and the rest said that their arse wasn't perfect but they loved him anyway.' I'm still working out which category Mr H falls into. I'm kidding! I know exactly which category he falls into... it's none of them.

Mr H was late back from work at lunchtime today as he had to take the chainsaw to the chainsaw hospital. Unfortunately, it has died. Even more unfortunately, if we want to be warm in the winter then we need to buy a new one. I do wonder whether he breaks his toys deliberately so that he can have new ones. I think I need to keep a closer eye on him. If I hear weird banging noises coming from the container in the future, I better investigate them. (Normally I just ignore them thinking that maybe something has fallen on him and an hour or so later I go to check and see whether I can claim on the life insurance.)

I phoned him (after he was due to be home an hour earlier) and he said, "I'm just finishing up at the chainsaw place, I'll be home in ten minutes. Don't forget I'll want a cup of tea with my bacon sandwich". This, once again, is man-logic. He knows that I can't make a nice cup of tea. He also knows that I won't use his favourite mug either. I also know that he will most definitely moan when he sees it and screw up his face when he drinks it. Why do we go through this unnecessary hassle...?

Although, in actuality, by some freak of nature I managed to make a nice cup of tea for him. I should have taken a picture and put it on Facebook. People moan when I put pictures of food and drink up. But in my defence, my friends that are parents put pics of theirs kids up when they do well in dance class, win some football trophy or are released from prison on bail. I don't see why my achievements shouldn't be lauded.

Whilst I am writing my book Mr H is out on his new lawnmower cutting the paddock. He always looks like a toddler riding his bike (with stabilisers) for the very first time. He will have this inane fixed grin on his face. Whatever keeps him happy. People normally say, 'Happy wife... happy life'. In this household it's, 'Happy husband... wife won't kill him with a sledgehammer'. It's not very catchy but it's true.

Tuesday 26th April

Missions for today:

- *Do a day's work (notice that I put this first today... got to get your priorities right...)*
- *Book the Snowdome for tomorrow night*
- *Go and fetch a cream cake from Miranda (this has become a last minute addition as Miranda just texted to say she had bought one for me and Mr H)*
- *Keep poking Lucy awake so she will sleep through the night (wonder if my friends do this to their babies...?)*

Tales from working from home...*

* I really need to get out more as my tales are going to become really boring if I don't go out and meet any bonkers people (other than Mr H). But I will be off to Sainsbo's later in the week and also have a trip to Aldi lined up. I will wear my stab vest for my visit to Aldi. This is for two reasons:

1. It's in Wolverhampton and people have been stabbed over a Subway 12 inch sandwich, for taking the last Xmas jumper in Primark and for hogging 'hot and spicy' Peri Peri sauce on their table in Nando's, before now. You can't be too careful.

2. It will be Thursday and this is the day that new products are released into the shop. I've also been doing some stretches and lunges as I will need to be flexible and fast as soon as the doors open to bag my picnic hampers. I've also been lifting some weights in case I need to pick up some old people and move them out of my way.

Being the consummate professional that I am, I completed my days' worth of work first (gold star for me). Mr H has also been at work today, apart from an hour when he came back for lunch. This means that I have been very relaxed for most of the day as I haven't had to deal with his man nonsense and as the weather has been bad he would have been stuck inside to annoy me all the more. When he is gone from the house I always think, 'He's not that bad' and miss him. But then within half an hour of him getting back, I start to remember why he annoys me. I'm kidding! It's ten minutes... I suspect that a lot of my friends that are parents have similar thoughts about their (devil) children.

One of the ways in which Mr H annoys me is that he just don't listen. Fact. (I'm sure I can feel some virtual nodding of heads from my female readers.)

Today I said to him, "I'm doing a sausage sandwich for lunch," (lean and skinny) and he said "There's only four minutes left according to the oven clock and you haven't even put the kettle on yet!" He does get irrationally worked up at the smallest of things. I replied, "They're taking longer to cook so there's probably actually about seven minutes left so you've got plenty of time to make a cup of tea." A minute or so later he looks up and says, "How come the clock now says six minutes? It said four minutes just a minute ago. The tea will go cold now!" I just gave him 'the look'.

For all the women reading this book, you'll have a similar look that you give to your menfolk. I told him that I had just that second said to him that they might take longer and had therefore re-set the timer. We then had a totally pointless discussion about how I hadn't at all and I must have told him while he was outside emptying the compost tin. He was only back for one hour at lunchtime. It felt like three hours. After he left I glugged some white wine from the bottle in the cooler. I'm now thinking that his new tactic for killing me is to turn me into an alcoholic. He won't need to crush my head in a vice or shoot me after all. I will do the deed myself.

This has reminded me to tell you about my alcoholic family. It's mostly Mum's side of the family that are alcoholics. They come from Suffolk, whereas Dad's family come from Duddeston, which was (ok - is) a rough area of Birmingham. You would think that it would be the other way round and that Dad's family would be the alcoholics. But maybe Mum's family could afford to drink and Dad's couldn't (I'm surprised they didn't just steal it though). I think Mum is the only one that isn't an alcoholic in her family.

I don't know why Mum's side of the family drink so much. When we went to visit Suffolk it was really pretty and mostly rural. I found it a very relaxing place to be and wasn't that bothered about drinking whilst I was there (well until a lot of the family showed up and then I definitely needed a few drinks*).

* bottles

I remember when my Uncle came to stay with us once for a couple of days. We had a lot of family staying over with us as we had a family wedding taking place. My Uncle pretends that he doesn't drink. We all know that he does drink. But we all pretend that we don't know that he drinks. He pretends that he doesn't know that we know that he drinks. It's one of those lies that keeps families together. (This reminds me of the scene in *Friends* when Monica and Chandler are dating and Rachel and Phoebe try and catch them out, "They don't know that we know that they know that..." I can't actually remember how the sentence ends. Go and YouTube it, it's funny.)

But given that we are naughty we do like to wind him up. He will hide his alcohol in a Fanta bottle and claim that he just drinks fizzy Orange all day long (and throughout the night). Once he couldn't remember where he had left his bottle and was getting really agitated. I said that I had given it to one of the kids* to have as they fancied some fizzy Orange but couldn't remember which one. He spent the rest of the afternoon going up to each of the kids trying to find his Fanta or trying to work out which of them was drunk. It's hard to tell in my family. A lot of the kids have ADHD, so having had a drink wouldn't necessarily be that noticeable. I know it was mean (but it was funny though).

* Obviously I hadn't given it to one of the kids. I wouldn't waste alcohol on a child. They all had water whilst staying here.

Talking of family has reminded me of the time that we were in the car on the way to sign language once. We were chatting about growing up with brothers and sisters and sibling tales then followed. I told the tale of when my sister stabbed me with a fountain pen once and it bled everywhere and stained her beige bedroom carpet. (Apparently when I posted this tale on Facebook her husband was horrified as she hadn't told him this story.) I think he was horrified about the stabbing and not the stain that it left on the carpet. Tina then told us about when she trapped her sister's fingers in the car door and two of them turned black. Mr H then told us of the time that his brother once shot him. Tina and I exchanged a look of, 'No one likes a show off'. Although when I put this tale on Facebook most comments were, 'We're not surprised that your brother shot you,' 'I'm surprised that Jo hasn't shot you yet.' I'm surprised too in all honesty. But it's only because I don't have a key to the gun cabinet.

Miranda bought Mr H and me a cream cake today. She is a good friend. Whilst I was collecting the cakes she told me that a girl had crashed into her car last night, on a roundabout, as she was heading home around 8pm. The girl was wearing pyjamas. As the girl was young she called her mum and dad to come out and apparently they arrived also wearing pyjamas.

Now, you already know that I am not a morning person and am often in my pjs until 10am. But even I manage to get out of them at some point (although I've just scrolled back to Sunday and realised that it was in the afternoon that I got dressed. But to be clear, I have never left the house in my pyjamas. Well, ok, apart from the one time that I forgot to put the grey bin out and was tearing after the bin men with it bouncing behind me trying to stop my dressing gown from flapping open – but honestly that's the only time... I think.)

In all honesty though this is not an unusual sight in Wolverhampton. I have been to Sainsbo's before and seen customers wearing rollers in their hair and walking around in their dressing gowns and my work wife Alexandra says it's a common sight in Liverpool too.

But back to Miranda's story...

Miranda said that the Dad gave her a hug goodbye as a thank you as she was really calm in dealing with his daughter and after all it was the daughter's fault. I had visions of the mouse peeping out the house as this happened. Thankfully Miranda didn't see anything and only felt a slight grazing of her leg. She likes to think that it was his car keys in his pocket. Being as she had just bought me a cream cake I nodded vigorously in agreement.

Being the good wife that I am I once again cooked dinner for us tonight and as we ate 19 roast potatoes each yesterday with the leftover lamb I thought it best to have a lighter dinner. (I am wondering whether this might be some Guinness World Record – I must remember to check this out). I cooked a lighter dinner because otherwise MFP will start exploding with the calories and I'll never lose weight. I cooked chicken and we had it with salad and a few onion rings. As I was dishing up Mr H put on his, 'toddler not happy' face and said, "Where are the chips? We always have chips with chicken. They go so well together." I swear I saw his lip quiver. I carefully explained to him (as I took a large sip of my wine) that we needed a healthy dinner and he said, "Don't get me wrong. I wanted the salad. I just would have had it with the chips."

Sometimes men need to hear home truths. I said to him, "You're starting to get a bit* annoying. I've lovingly cooked meals for you all week and you've not thanked me once." He then said, "And I've been lovingly clearing the new land ready for you to have your Alpacas." We both paused for a minute and said, "Let's call it a draw then."

* He wasn't ready for the harsh truth

Whilst we were eating dinner, I told him that I needed a name for the sequel to #tractor4graham. He said, "#mercedesforgraham?" I had to give him 'the look' for the second time today. He then said, "Well. It will have to still be called #tractor4graham as the first one won't have sold, or maybe #tractor4grahamasthefirstbookdidntsell." He actually chuckled whilst he said this. I said, "Maybe it needs to be called #newwife4graham." Unfortunately, this backfired as he said, "I wonder if Anna Friel is single?"

He said this because we were watching Marcella whilst eating dinner. Initially I hadn't recognised her. Mr H said, "You know her! She was the young lesbian in Brookside." It took me a while and then the penny dropped. I said, "She's looking a lot older now." "Well she was probably quite old when she did Brookside. She was probably a 30-something playing an 18 year old. If it was 27 years ago then she's 57 and I think she looks really good for 57." I still didn't think that she was going to take him off my hands, even if she was that age.

In usual fashion we had to resort to Wiki to settle the question. I didn't bother to ask Siri. I think she's getting a bit cheeky and I can hear sarcasm dripping in her tone when she replies to my questions. Even Siri thinks I'm dim. Wiki pronounced that she was 40. "See! She's quite old," said Mr H. Coming from a 54 year old, I thought his comment quite cheeky. And, in all fairness, it didn't help his cause as she would be even less likely to take him off my hands if she was only 40.

As we were watching it, we were playing 'Spot the famous actor.' There were some big names in it and I commented that it must have cost them a fortune to make with all these big names. I got excited when Jamie Bamber made an appearance. Mr H said, "Oh look! It's him from Criminal Minds UK". For the third time today I had to give him 'the look'. "I think you mean *Law & Order UK* and that's Jamie Bamber – he's on my laminated list you know." "Oh is he now?" So Anna, if you are willing to take Mr H off my hands, will you please ask Jamie if he is willing to take me on? You can tweet me and let me know...

Whilst we are on the subject of the laminated list, Mum messaged me to ask whether Matt Damon was on my list. I replied, 'No – he's not,' but forgot to ask her why she was asking. I'm assuming that he wasn't sitting in her kitchen and that's why she was asking me. I do hope she's not back to her kidnapping ways...

It's been like four seasons in one day today. We've had hail, sunshine, rain and now we were encountering thunder and lightning. Mr H said, "Oh no! I need to get the fence down so Ron the Digger man can get in to move the mound tomorrow. He's coming at 8am" (Mount Graham will be no more. Sorry Bobby, we will no longer be able to say, "Is Jo off to Mount Graham?")

I said, "Well you can just do it in the morning before he comes. Lucy will be up at 6am so you'll have plenty of time." I made a mental note to stop poking Lucy awake. It will be just my luck that she doesn't wake up at 6am and Mr H will be all, See! I should have done it the night before.' He said, "Well of course you're going to get wet doing the fence" as he looked at me with that, 'This is what happens if I don't get chips with my chicken' face. I swiftly responded with, "Erm No! I think you'll find that's man's work. I'll continue to cook nice meals for you." Honestly! Once again he really doesn't listen. We had only just had the conversation an hour ago that he dealt with the land and I dealt with dinner. D'uh...

Tomorrow night we are off to the Snowdome. Now it's out of season they have cheap slope passes (because I am inherently tight) and I need to keep up the practise on my snowboard, otherwise I will be back to square one come the next skiing holiday. I am hoping that there will be some funny tales to tell, but hopefully not of the A&E variety...

Wednesday 27th April

Missions for today:

- *Do not break anything at the Snowdome tonight (including Mr H – I really need him alive – at least until the land is sorted for the Alpacas)*
- *Try and make good cups of tea for the workers that are here today (this will be my hardest mission)*

Tales from preparing the land...

Today, Ron the digger man has been here to move the soil on the new land so that we can get fenced for the arrival of George, Chester and Cyril the Alpacas. Mr H was humming and whistling first thing this morning and said, "Morning Honey – what a beautiful day it is and you are looking lovely this morning." Given that:

1. I still had sleep in my eyes,
2. looked like a drag queen because I hadn't been bothered to take off last night's make-up before bed and the mascara had run down my face,
3. had the breath of a dog that's eaten fox poo (where does that come from?),
4. had a stain down my pyjama top from where I had dribbled last night's cup of tea in bed and
5. had hair like a poodle that's been electrocuted...

...then I am wondering whether his gammy eye is back.

But then I realised that it was digger day and that in the next 30 minutes or so the digger would be arriving and Mr H would stare at it with his mouth agog like a child seeing Father Christmas for the first time. The digger obviously put him in a very good mood.

I did nearly think of buying him a tractor at this point. Let's face it, if he called me 'lovely looking', when I looked like this, then the money that I saved on make-up and crap for my dry frizzy hair could in all likelihood pay for a tractor for him. I might take a sneaky peek at Tractor's Weekly (if there is such a thing) and see how much they are.

I also nearly told him about his pillow and his green shiny shirt. But I bit my lip as I remembered that Mr H, just like a toddler, can turn from happy and content to irrational psychopath in a matter of minutes. I was pleased that I didn't tell him about either of these things because when I accidentally gave Ron the Digger man a cup of tea in Mr H's favourite cup, I could see that his happiness was indeed fragile. He's not ready to be told about the pillow or the green shiny shirt. (I don't think he ever will be.)

Ron the digger man called me 'young lady' so I did the 'cutesy head flop to the side' and giggled. At my age I'll take any compliment. At least I knew that his was genuine as I had by this point made myself presentable and no longer had awful breath. (I did have a bit of spilled latte down my body warmer but I don't think that he noticed that.)

I put a photo of the digger on Facebook and said, 'Mr H is excited as he gets to ride in a digger. I'm kidding! He's not allowed in there without adult supervision.' One of our friends commented, 'Ha! The only way that he should be allowed in there is with a straight jacket, a gag and shackled feet.' I think she knew how I was going to interpret this as she commented immediately afterwards, 'As long as it's made clear that it's not a sexual reference to see Graham in said get up.' I told her that this would be going in my book but with the second comment in there. She really doesn't want people thinking that she thinks of Mr H in these S&M ways... even if it's true...

Trying to get organised for tonight I decided to get our skiing/boarding gear ready so that we wouldn't have a last minute panic trying to find everything. After spending an hour searching all the places where things could be I heard Mr H coming into the kitchen and I called out, "You haven't seen where my crash pants*, elbow guards, wrist guards and knee protectors have gone have you? Oh! And I also can't find our gloves." He cheerily called back up, "I think they're all still in the washing basket."

* These are shorts that have built in coccyx protection (yes I needed autocorrect to spell that for me... cock-sick

was (funnily enough) not the right way to spell it) along with padded bits here and there to protect your bones/hips/fru-fru etc if you fall – which you do on a snowboard – all the friggin' time.

Now, being a woman, I can remember in detail every conversation that Mr H and I have ever had. Mr H does the washing in our house. Basically it's an easy job for him to do as the washing machine does the hard bit, but it makes him feel like he's contributing to the housework. I distinctly remember him saying two weeks ago on Sunday at 8:03pm, "I've just done all of the washing, why did you change the bedding?" Obviously he was telling lies as there were still items in the washing basket. It's down to me to point out his lies.

However, he wasn't sitting in the kitchen alone so I am going to have to bring this up at another time. He said, "You'll just have to wear them as they are." So I had to get my crash pants out of the washing basket and I gave them the 'sniff test'. I'm sure you've all done it before. Luckily, the fact that they'd been in the basket for five weeks since we came back from holiday meant that the air had dispersed some of their ponginess. However, to be certain that I wouldn't smell 'down there' tonight, I have sprayed some deodorant onto the fru-fru area.

I'm now a little worried that I have sprayed too much and that they'll be a bit itchy. Oh well! My snowboarding isn't that great anyway so I doubt anyone will notice if I make some odd manoeuvres. I must just remember not to scratch myself (while anyone is looking at any rate). This is one of the things that does annoy me a bit though about men/women. Apparently it's man law that a man can scratch his balls, bum, pick his nose etc in public with no consequences at all. But if a woman tries to scratch her fru-fru or twirl her nipples in public (I have never done this) then all hell breaks loose.

Whilst I was working at my desk today Lucy came in to sit with me. She is virtually deaf now (although can still hear a Dentastix wrapper being opened two rooms away) and because of this she likes to sit with you. She did the most disgusting loud fart at one point. She looked up accusingly at me (the cheek of it) to begin with and then looked at her own bottom and wrinkled up her nose with a, 'What on earth was that?' look. She promptly got up and left the room. Charming! I thought — leave me alone with the smell.

I blame Mr H for this. He hadn't eaten two out of his 21 roast potatoes the previous night (light weight) and gave them to Bonnie and Lucy along with a bit of veg and gravy. My, "It will only disagree with her digestive system," comment was obviously totally ignored and now I'm suffering the consequences.

On a positive note, today, I have not screamed once at my reflection in the mirror. The dogs appear to be relieved at this.

I also had a 'genius' moment when I realised that I did not need to brave Aldi tomorrow. (It was a good job really as I couldn't find my stab vest and thought that I would have to go dressed as a horse rider wearing my body protector instead.) In all honesty no one in Wolverhampton would have given me a second glance if I had and it would have resulted in at least two kids and one adult asking if my pony was tied up outside and whether they could stroke it. Even though 'stroke the pony' is a fantastic phrase to retort back with some innuendo, I don't use innuendo with shoppers in Wolverhampton. They don't get it and I don't want to have to buy a new body protector because some Aldi shopper has gone mental and stabbed me with some metal fork from a £2.99 barbeque tools set.

Tales from the Snowdome...

The Snowdome was a success. Mr H, Shane and I suffered no injuries (well apart from Mr H bending back his finger carrying two pints in the bar when we had a break). Shane did forget to bring his helmet, base layer, salopettes and ski socks though. I asked him what he did actually remember to bring. "My gloves and me" was his answer. To be fair I don't think the people of Tamworth noticed him skiing in his work suit. He was definitely the best dressed on the slope...

I was on the travellator* with a 20-something lad ahead of me at one point. He was wearing skis and far too much aftershave. I had to bring my coat up over my nose because I was afraid of passing out. I concluded that he didn't have a girlfriend. The aftershave was one hint but so was him breaking wind and then turning round to me winking and saying, "Oh you ski on one plank do you?"

* If you have watched *Gladiators* (to clarify, the gameshow with Wolf and not the film with Russell Crowe. Incidentally I just had to Google, 'Who starred in the film Gladiator?' as I couldn't remember his name. Sorry Russell – but you're not on my laminated list so it doesn't really matter if I have offended you) then you will know that this is basically a conveyor belt that slopes upwards.

I resisted the urge to say that it was a snowboard and in order to avoid any conversation I just did sign language to say, 'I'm deaf. I don't understand.' Our teacher would have been proud at my practise (especially as I was balancing a snowboard at the same time). It seemed to work and he left me alone. I do feel a bit guilty. (Not towards him. I used sign language for naughty purposes and I really shouldn't have done. Although our teacher has a fantastic sense of humour so I don't think she will mind. It was an emergency situation after all.) I can still smell his aftershave now. I think I'm going to have to wash the bedding at home as well as all of my ski clothes. His smell seems to have come home with us.

Whilst I was putting my snowboard on at the top of the slope and waiting for Shane and Mr H to come back up (they did two runs for my every one), Messenger beeped. Mum was messaging me to say that she had emailed my book to a friend that was going to read it through and that as it would be easier for her to print out my book she had sent it to a work email address.

Unfortunately, her friend's IT department had quarantined it for 'inappropriate or offensive' language. Mum and I were hypothesising as to which word(s) were offensive. My money was on fru-fru...

Mr H videoed me snowboarding. It got much better after I had drunk a pint of beer in the bar. Thankfully he didn't video me falling off the rope pull and only managing to get half way up as the muscles in my arms couldn't take any more. He put the videos up on Facebook and most of my friends were complimentary and supportive. Bobby, however, said, "I think that Graham is the unsung hero in all of these video exploits. He deftly skis backwards managing to capture expertly all of the show-off antics of the ginger* haired nutter on the surfboard." I shouldn't have laughed at this but I confess that I did.

* I'm not ginger

I must admit that I think Bobby hasn't put enough stamps on our present though. Despite telling me a few days ago that he was sending it, it hasn't come. I wonder whether the capital letters WOLVERHAMPTON have meant that it has gone to some sort of terrorist sorting centre? I don't mean that this a place that they sort terrorists but maybe they think his package contains something dodgy. Once Bobby posted me some Nando's peri peri sauce. It could have been mistaken for some liquid to set off a bomb. (Don't laugh at this – *MacGyver* on CBS once made a bomb out of some sort of pasta sauce).

This has also made me think why an IT department would have quarantined my book. I'm pretty sure that I used the word 'terrorist' and 'bomb' in there at some point. I hope that my mum's friend is not now going to be on some covert watch operation at her job. My book will really have to sell if she loses her job over it!

Thursday 28th April

Missions for today:

- *Pop to Sainsbo's to pick up wine (and other essential shopping like chocolate and crisps and totally ignore Mr H reminding me to check the use by dates on fresh stuff)*
- *Wash and straighten my hair*

Lucy woke up early so I got up to let her out. I noticed that Mr H had left his ski boots outside on the front doorstep last night. Good job it hadn't rained. I remember once when we lived in Rugeley, he had left the boot of his car open and driver's door wide open. I'm surprised it didn't get stolen but I expect that the local thieves thought that it was some sort of Police sting operation. Our neighbour kindly shut it for us at 3am when he came back from work. I am thinking that I should re-write my will. I clearly need to think about leaving a carer for Mr H for when I'm gone. He's not going to survive on his own.

I woke up this morning looking like Liz McDonald from Coronation Street (or 'Bev' as Mr H likes to call her.) She is on his laminated list (I think he aims quite realistically with his list. Although he quite clearly hasn't understood the idea of the list. But then again, Pixie Lott is also on there, so maybe he has? He might just be really clever and maybe is covering all bases and age ranges...)

This was due to sweating under my helmet last night whilst snowboarding and this morning my natural dry curly hair was back with a vengeance. I won't go shopping at Sainsbo's until my hair is decent. You can guarantee that the one time that I pop to the shops, wearing rags for clothes, no make-up and my hair tied back to tame the curls that I hadn't straightened the shit out of that day, will be the one time that I bump into all of my ex school friends.

I can't cope with the sympathetic, 'Life hasn't treated you well, since leaving' looks. Obviously if I leave the house with nice clothes, immaculate hair and make-up then I bump into no one that I know. It's the law apparently.

Tales about fru-frus...

I also woke up this morning and got a shock when I went to have a shower and pulled down my pj bottoms. A load of 'dandruff' seemed to fall away from my fru-fru. "What the frig?!" I said. To begin with I couldn't work out whether this was an age thing that they didn't tell you about in school. (This reminds me that I should write to whoever is in charge of schools these days and tell them that they need to add certain essential life experiences onto the curriculum. I am constantly shocked at things that happen in life that I really could have done with a 'heads up' about.) They should also have 'Man-classes' on the curriculum to explain the oddities of the male mind. For example, they really need to tell us girls at a young age that:

1. Men don't listen.
2. Men can't multi task.
3. Men are totally irrational hypocritical human beings.
4. If you don't want children then don't get married (as in your husband is like a child, not that you have to be married to have children).
5. There is a concept of 'Man-logic'. (I think there would need to be a whole term on this, or maybe a whole school year?)

I could easily go on with the list...

But I've digressed. Back to the flaky fru-fru... It took me a while (and Google was no help) to realise where it had come from. I had forgotten that I had sprayed lots of deodorant onto my crash pants last night for the Snowdome and it must have rubbed into my knickers as I was boarding. I must admit that I was relieved when I realised what it was. There were some awful stories on

Google as to what it might have been. This took me back to the merkin conversation with Jade. Maybe the dandruff was a sign of going bald and that's why people ordered fake fru-fru hair.

Mr H had been in work this morning. Sadly he had chosen his own clothes and I was too tired to get him to change them. He came back from work saying, "The photographer complimented me that I was the best dressed there for the picture day." 'Oh no!' I thought to myself. His awful dress sense is now going to be in print. I suspect that the photographer's wife also dresses the photographer and that Mr H's get-up would be right up his street. On a positive note Mr H said that the photographer didn't seem to know how to operate the camera, so I'm hoping they will all turn out blurry and will have to be taken again. I will be better prepared for next time.

When Mr H got back at lunchtime he said that he had phoned Dad to see when he was going to come back next week to help with the spare rooms. Apparently, Dad was in the bath when he phoned. I jokingly said, "I bet my step mum took the phone to him!" He replied, "Yes she did actually but came back and said 'He's still in the water, so as he isn't decent he will call you back later.'" This made us chuckle as I had visions of Mr H facetiming Dad in the bath. To be clear Mr H was phoning on his mobile without video so he could have spoken to Dad while he was naked. No one would have known... apart from the fact that I've just written about it in my book (but given that no one will buy it then I stand firm that no one will know).

Within ten minutes of being home Mr H was doing my head in so I decided to pop out to Sainsbo's and stock up on Sauvignon Blanc. Normally I can be guaranteed that there will be some bonkers person there to tell a tale about. You might remember that the last time that I went there, there was an old guy staring at me funny as I was choosing Mr H's bio-yogurty drinks for his dicky-tummy. I swear that the same guy was following me again today.

As I was choosing my £1 basics loo roll brush I thought that I might need to use it as a weapon to defend myself. (Although a more useful weapon would have been the dirty one that I was replacing at home. No one would want to be touched by that.) I then saw the guy touch his right ear and walk away. I am now thinking that he is an undercover security guard. I'm actually quite offended by this. Today I was wearing nice clothes, my hair had been straightened and I had make-up on. Believe me, I was probably the most normal looking person in the store. Obviously in his mind this made me a thief! And why would I steal a £1 loo brush? If I was going to steal then I would at least choose something more expensive... I would at least go for the premium range loo brush at £5.99.

Because of the nice hair/clothes/make-up combo, the law dictated that I did not bump into anyone that I knew either. Rats! It would have been fabulous to do some 'lardy-dah' 'Oh yah! I live on a farm and will be getting some Alpacas soon,' to an old school chum whilst they were trying to stop 'Pretentious' their child (I don't think anyone actually names their child this) from having a strop in the toy section. That will have to be for another day...

I do like going to Sainsbo's as it makes me feel reassuringly normal. I went to pick up my chicken hotpot from the gluten free range and a customer said, "Oo! Are they nice?" I replied with, "Yes they are. And they are actually for me and not my husband. He's the one that gets the trots if he eats too much wheat." OK, so I didn't say that last bit. What I did say was, "They are for me and I'm not gluten free. But they are really tasty." She replied, "Really? So are you allowed to eat it then? Because if you're not gluten free – wouldn't it cause some weird reaction?" I decided to stick close to this lady as she was clearly going to make me look like a frickin' genius! Obviously I didn't Google, 'Can you eat gluten free products if you're not allergic to gluten' when I got home. Oh no! That wasn't me...

Mum sent me a message whilst I was shopping. Since my patience ran out at the age of 41 I did the decent thing and parked up my trolley at the end of the fruit aisle out of the way of everyone else, so that I could answer her. I knew that no one in Wolverhampton would be buying fruit so this was the best place to be out of everyone's way. I am a considerate customer like that. It annoys me when people abandon their trolleys in the way of other customers. This tends to happen in the alcohol aisle where fights break out when Sainsbury's basic white wine is on offer for £1.99 a bottle.

The rest of my shopping trip was quite boring. Maybe next time I need to shout, "Bomb!" in order to create some exciting tales for my book. But I don't fancy being whisked off to Guantanamo Bay and suffer water boarding or whatever they do. Snowboarding has been hard enough to learn, I don't think I'd be any good on water skis.

When I was paying for my shopping I was reminded once again that my patience ran out last year. A lady in front of me had her three year old child standing in the food bit of the trolley. I had to bite my lip from saying something (after all I wasn't wearing my stab vest) as I think it's totally unhygienic to have your child stand in the bit that other shoppers will have their food in.

I tried not to look closely to see whether the daughter had dog poo on her shoes, as she jumped up and down in the trolley. It made me think that today more people seem to be inconsiderate to others than would have been the case years ago. (Oh-Oh! I've turned into my Nan... 'back in my day...') Although back in my Mum's day she would never have done something like that with us. But then again she didn't drive so we actually never saw a supermarket as children. We only saw the local food shop which didn't have trolleys and we were needed to pull her 'old lady' shopping trolley around that anyway.

The lady on the checkout asked me if I wanted the 'fitness for fat kids' vouchers. I told her to give them to someone else. She asked the woman behind me in the queue if she had children. The woman seemed to take offence to this as she said, "Oh good gracious. Yuk. No!" and vigorously shook her head.

As predicted when I got home, Mr H and I had one of our totally pointless conversations. This time it was, "Did we really need a new loo brush?" I'm tired of sighing now. Even though he spent a few hundred pounds on a new chainsaw earlier in the week, the world is about to end when I buy a £1 loo brush. I had to hide the new £6 long handled dustpan and brush. I'm pretty sure that that would have tipped him over the edge. I refer you back to my earlier discussion that schools need to have lessons on men, for girls. If we knew about this nonsense at an earlier age then I think we would prepare better for it. Maybe through experimenting with lesbianism or celibacy instead.

I can't remember who it is in the government that is in charge of education. I'm thinking it might be Michael Hunt or Jeremy Gove... or maybe I have got them the wrong way round. 'Mike Hunt' would be a hysterical name for a politician! (Say it fast... and with, 'Has anyone seen...' at the start of it). Sorry Mummykins – I can hear you tutting as you're doing your read through. If it helps then I think my sense of humour comes from your side of the family. (I am still chuckling at writing this.)

Friday 29th April

Missions for today:

- *Confirm that my hair hasn't started turning ginger*
- *Catch up on home admin*
- *Vacuum the cars out*
- *Tell Bobby that his package still hasn't arrived*

Lucy started barking at 6am this morning. I have been up to let her out most mornings this week so today I decided to let Mr H get up. (When I say this, what I mean is that I pretended to be sound asleep until I heard him swear with what sounded like 'bloody dog' and stomp around the bedroom before going downstairs to let her out.) I went back to sleep and didn't wake up again until 8am.

Remember, since turning 40, I realised that there was more to life than working all the hours under the sun and try to take every Friday off. I love setting up an 'Out of Office' telling people that I will reply to them on Tuesday.

I did actually do a few other bits and pieces of work this morning. This is the beauty of being self-employed. Provided I have my work done by my deadlines then when I work is up to me. This is good as I'm not a morning person. (This has just reminded me to add this into the introduction, as I had forgotten this crucial bit of information.) Being self-employed is also good when there is a Bank Holiday. Being England it usually pisses it down on a Bank Holiday weekend. I will often work instead of going out somewhere with the world and his brother - listening to everyone moan about the shitty weather is so paseé (yes I had to Google how to spell it...)

My first mission of the day is quite important. I washed my hair yesterday and it seems to have gone ginger since I straightened it. I'm sure Bobby has been putting pins in a voodoo doll to turn it ginger. I was a bit distressed about this (it is after all supposed to be blonde) but when Bobby posted on my Facebook timeline that ginger haired people look much younger than other people I was instantly cheered up. (I know I'm shallow – but at least I don't fight it.)

My arms are absolutely killing me today. It's a delayed reaction from holding onto the rope pull at the Snowdome. I was starting to panic when I struggled to make my morning latte and pick it up. I'll have to knock vacuuming out the cars on the head. Oh what a shame...

Mr H outfoxed me today. We have a board in my office where we write where we are going to be for each day of the week. We have to do this as he has weird working hours and being a man always forgets to tell me if he's going out. According to the board he wasn't going to be back until 2pm but he arrived back just after 1pm. I don't like it when he doesn't stick to what it says on the board. I mentally have to prepare myself for his return (and sometimes hide my glass of wine) and I hadn't done so.

He did redeem himself a bit though. This morning, as he was leaving for work, he showed me a creme egg that he had found at the bottom of his rucksack. I said, "Oh – is that for me?" Apparently, it wasn't and he took it with him. I started to think of renaming the book '#newshoesforjo' and putting all money into a shoes and handbag fund instead. However, since arriving back he has offered me the 'squashed on one side' creme egg (it looks like it has melted flat having been next to his mobile phone). And they say that love is dead... Of course, there is the possibility that he is worried that microwaves from the phone have gone into the egg and he's worried about getting some sort of brain cancer if he eats it. He won't care if I get brain cancer. He will get the life insurance and I'm sure a tractor will be his first purchase.

Tales about HMRC...

I had an email from HMRC today saying that I had a message from them and that I needed to log into my account. Being the sensible person that I am, I did not click on any links in the email, just in case it was some baddy trying to steal all of my money (which I don't have – otherwise Mr H would have his tractor by now – d'uh!)

I tried to log into their system. I nearly gave up with the amount of information they wanted. First of all I had to put in my user ID. This took me five minutes to find. Then they asked for my password. This took another five minutes to remember. Then they sent me a security code to my mobile. This took me another five minutes as I couldn't find my phone. Then they wanted me to confirm some information on my P60. This took me another five minutes to find. I was about to give up as I wasn't really that bothered about retrieving the message. I was (being the consummate professional that I am) up-to-date with all of my tax affairs after all. But given that I had got this far, I didn't want to give up. It was becoming a challenge now.

Their system told me that the information I had given on my P60 didn't match their records so they couldn't let me access the system. There was a button to say 'click here to try again' and after pressing that it took me to my personal page. 'Great security there,' I thought! Maybe I didn't need my password or security code at all either to get in?

The message, as predicted, wasn't essential. It was asking me to file my 15/16 tax return. Given that the filing date is next January, I really don't think they needed to remind me now. There was a short survey to complete at the end that asked me whether the information they held on me was correct. I checked 'Don't know' (as I hadn't accessed my return). They asked me to explain and give further details.

It then asked whether I found the service easy or difficult to use. I checked 'difficult' (due to the excess information for logging in that didn't seem to work but then did). It asked me to explain further, which I did. It finally asked me whether I was satisfied with the service. When I clicked dissatisfied, it obviously did not want to know why as no box popped up so that I could provide further information! Although I lost around 25 minutes of my life to this, the chuckling about it since then has been well worth it. I also contemplated that one of my friends had written this piece of technology. I have a few friends that work for HMRC (or the 'dark side' as my accountant friends call it) and some of them are approaching retirement. I could see one of them writing it and chuckling to themselves.

We are off to sign language again tonight. Last night we met up with two friends to get in some more practise. Unfortunately, when practising 'jobs' Mr H said that he didn't like his job because he died there. He was supposed to say that he didn't like it because he couldn't have his dog there.

We chuckled when Jayne asked, "How do I say that I go to other people's houses to work?" This reminded us of Mr

H mixing up the sign for 'prostitutes' with 'hallelujah'. Mel's sign name is vomit as when she went to church and was trying to sign 'Praise the Lord' she 'vomited on the Lord' instead. Personally, I think that Jesus has a sense of humour and I think he would have chuckled at this. The fluffy handcuffs came up again as Mr H once again struggled to sign 'Policeman'. We went back on to the Sign Language website that we use to check some of our signs and they now have another woman doing videos. We need to come up with a slang name for her now.

It was a bit unfortunate when we were trying to look at the sign for 'sometimes'. We clicked on the video done by the paedophile and he signed something that looked more like the universal used sign for 'wanker'. We laughed for a while about this. Our catch ups are always hysterical. I do wonder what the pub think we are doing though. We get some interesting looks from other customers in there.

Saturday 30th April

Missions for today:

- *Get rid of headache/brain tumour*
- *Catch up on home admin (I failed in this mission yesterday)*
- *Stop obsessing over hair turning ginger*

Today looks like being 'one of those days'. It didn't start out well for two reasons.

1. I woke up with a headache (or maybe Bobby has been voodoo-ing a doll and it is a brain tumour), and

2. I had an incident when I went to put the joint of pork in the Rayburn. (Seriously though, I should be up for some award for 'Wife of the Year'. Considering how annoying Mr H is, he has the life of Riley here. Unfortunately when I wrote the word 'Riley', autocrapet (remember this is my name for autocorrect) changed it to 'Rikers'. From watching Law & Order, I know that this is a harsh men's prison in America. Autocrapet does at least have a sense of humour at times.)

But back to the joint of pork. It was wrapped up in one of those tight shrink wrapped thick plastic bags that mean that you can have it in the freezer for about five years without it going off. The plastic was proving problematic to get into, so I had to get the scissors on it. Unfortunately, as I cut into it Physics decided to play a cruel joke on me and the blood in the packaging spurted all down the front of my dressing gown. I didn't tell Mr H that I had only just put this dressing gown on last night and that it would now need to go straight into the wash. He moans at the amount of washing that I put in the basket each day as it is.

Because I knew that he would have some mini seizure at seeing two dressing gowns in the basket at once (I actually own four dressing gowns and five onesies – I think I have a bit of a fetish in this clothing area, although I don't know why...) I continued to wear my blood soaked dressing gown whilst I ate my breakfast and vowed to wash out the blood in the sink, after I had had my morning bath.

Unfortunately, a courier arrived with my Aldi order (gold star to them for quick delivery, although upon opening the box and finding a broken plate in the picnic hamper, I have downgraded their gold star to bronze) whilst I was drinking my morning latte and I had forgotten about the blood stains.

343

I opened the door to the courier (who was from Hermes*) and saw him do a double take with a look of, 'Woah! What's gone on here then?' Even though I'm not a morning person - the naughty side of my personality (my evil inner twin) quite clearly is. I said, "Oh! Don't worry about this," as I pointed to the blood, "That's just my husband's. Where do you want me to sign?"

* I chuckle at 'Hermes' as I call them 'Herpes'. I don't know why... I blame my genetics for my naughty side.

He looked rather flummoxed and said, "Just here thanks. OK, have a nice day." The even naughtier side of my personality decided to come out at this point, as I said, "Oh! Aren't you going to help me get the parcel into the house? My husband, is... indisposed... at the moment." As I said this, I looked down at the blood and delicately stroked it. He mumbled something like, "Erm... health and safety... I can't bring it in in case I trip over and injure myself... I'll be going then now..."

OK... I'll confess. There is a possibility that I have embellished this story and I apologise. It was a onesie, not a dressing gown. As tempting as it was to continue wearing the blood stained onesie, I did get dressed shortly afterwards.

At least my 'home admin' has been going well. Although it once again makes me chuckle at Mr H and his irrational and hypocritical nature. I mentioned what he said when I bought the £1 loo brush two days ago. Going through the bank statements and credit cards today has blatantly shown that he spends the most in this house. His new lawnmower and chain saw trump my £1 loo brush and £6 dustpan and brush. Even bringing in my Roxy skiing/snowboarding purchases (which of course were all necessary) doesn't come close to his spending this month.

Even yesterday he was still going on about my Sainsbo's shopping.

Him: "Why did you buy biscuits?"

Me: "You don't have to eat them."

Him: "Of course I have to eat them! I love them!"

Me: "Then why are you moaning that I bought them?"

Him: "Because I shouldn't eat them – they're not good for me."

Me: "So, don't eat them!"

I do wonder how many women go through these same totally pointless conversations with their menfolk... sadly I suspect it's lots. Just to annoy him I'm going to hide the biscuits somewhere that he won't be able to find them* and wait until he says, "Where have all the biscuits gone? I was just going to have one with my cup of tea."

I will look at him and say, "I've eaten them all — you know — woman time of the month." I will also give him a pained expression and rub my tummy to emphasise the monthly wrenching of blood from my womb. Men can't cope with 'women's problems', so it's a safe bet that he won't pursue this.

* There are numerous places I could choose: the ironing basket, the cleaning cupboard, in the pot where he keeps his toothbrush… the list goes on.

Apart from successfully completing my 'home admin' today, I do seem to have a case of the 'dropsies'. First it was the pork blood incident. The second one was dropping one of my sausages on the floor when I got it out of the oven to have for my lunch in a sandwich. Luckily, Bonnie wasn't within a one metre range when I did it otherwise said sausage would have been gulped and in her tummy within three seconds flat. I picked it up and plucked off the dog hairs and popped it back into my sandwich. I know — it sounds disgusting and of course I'm joking. There was more than a few dog hairs on it…

I'm sure Mr H has been having a word with the universe about me becoming a bit porky (excuse the pun) as when the rest of the sausages were happily defrosting on the side, I heard something fall to the floor in the kitchen and as I walked in I saw that Casper had knocked the plastic lid off the dish that they were in. He was happily sitting there licking the sausages. I shooed him off and noted which ones he had been licking. Mr H could have those for his lunch tomorrow.

We are off to the theatre tonight to watch *Dial 'M' for Murder*. Mr H booked it. I'm wondering whether he is hoping to get some inspiration for how to kill me without anyone knowing...? I'm hoping that my dropsies don't continue there. I don't think the theatre will be pleased if my Revels* decide to roll down the floor from the back of the stalls to the front.

* Mr H always buys a bag of Revels for him and a bag of Minstrels for me. I eat all of my Minstrels in the bar before we go in and then proceed to 'share' his Revels. It drives him insane. I do it every time. He knows I will do it every time. Why he doesn't buy two packs of Revels is anyone's guess! I know we will go through the same palaver again tonight.

The theatre didn't go to plan. My tummy was feeling weird in the afternoon and it was the sort of 'weird' that it feels before I chuck up a week's worth of undigested food with food poisoning. I said to Mr H, "Should I have cooked the sausages from frozen that I had for lunch?" "No! Are you an idiot! That's how you get food poisoning." I started to get a bit worried so did some Googling. But according to 'Mumsnet', Mr H is totally wrong and the majority of posts said that you can cook sausages from frozen.

But then I had a feeling that Mumsnet was for stressed out Mums, so maybe they're the ones that are trying to kill their kids. Fairymum83 from Basingstoke (I've changed her name to protect her identity, although I don't think she used her real name either...) said, 'I always cook mine for my five kids from frozen.' I'm thinking that she's been trying for years to kill off her kids (obviously without success). The number of posts she has made on Mumsnet suggests that her kids are evil devil children and she is regretting not having used contraception. I was starting to feel a bit sorry for her... but then she really should have learned after the first one, or at the very latest after the second one arrived. I concluded that she would have to take a good proportion of the blame for her predicament and started to lose sympathy for her.

Mr H ended up going to the theatre on his own as I fell asleep after dinner at 6:15pm and didn't wake up until 7:23pm. (It's important to be precise.) I had asked him before I fell asleep if he wanted to see if Jade was free to go with him but he said he was happy to go on his own. I suspect this has something to do with the Revels. Jade likes Revels too and I think Mr H was wanting to have the bag to himself. Again I call this 'man-logic'. He could simply buy two bags and avoid the problem... but being a man he won't be told.

I texted him, after I had woken up, to say, 'Have a nice night' and finished it with, 'Have you bought me some Revels?' His response was, 'I will. And no.' He did redeem himself at the interval though as he texted me to ask if I was feeling better and said, 'I have bought you some Revels... if I don't eat them all that is.' He is such a sweetie...

It has been a bit handy that Mr H has gone to the theatre on his own as it has been bed changing day and I haven't wanted him to see the new pillow. I changed the bedding while he was out to avoid him noticing. Even when I'm ill I have to remember to pander to his man nonsense and I couldn't cope with the 'Is that a different pillow?' conversation tonight...

So tractor-ites…

All is well in the Hughes' household at the moment.

1. Mr H thinks that he is still sleeping with his mouldy pillow

2. He has two new toys to play with at the moment to distract him from his yearning for a tractor (the yellow lawnmower and the new chainsaw)

3. The Alpacas will hopefully be arriving soon, once the land is finished and their shelter is up

4. Mr H hasn't killed me yet (I think I have a good tolerance for poisons)

5. Wolverhampton is its usual bonkers self (which is why I love it)

6. I'm working from home for most of the summer, so will be more relaxed and able to put up with Mr H's man nonsense (a win-win situation all–round)

7. The sequel is nearing completion as well, so you won't have long to wait for #tractor4graham2 (May-June), if you need your daily fix of 'bonkers' tales'.

Don't forget to follow the Facebook page 'tractor4graham' for snippets from the books

And huge thanks if you took the time to buy and read this book. (And shame on you if you borrowed it from a friend!) Just kidding... it just means that I will have to put up with Mr H's moaning for longer, as all money from the books are going into the tractor fund...

ACKNOWLEDGEMENTS

Big thanks to the 11 people that encouraged me to write this book:

Angela Buckley for being my first time through reader (any mistakes are totally her fault...)

Nick White who has been a proof reader and made excellent suggestions to make the first draft much better

Stephanie Ogunjimi, Lynn Rowe and Jane Blair who offered to do a read through

Ellie Banks

Nicki Sanders

Debbie Tandy

Dave Halford

Sam Bate

Janice Shaw

Jane Garner*

*I told you that maths wasn't my strong point (I think that's twelve friends – but then again, one of them is mum and it's 'mum's law' that she has to like me.)

The friends in these tales were my friends before I started writing my book. I'm not sure that they still will be now! Maybe the sequel will be #newfriendsforjo

Oh and before I forget, thanks to Robin Wiggs for actively discouraging me from writing the book, "For the love of Thor, please stop writing" has motivated me to finish it.

Printed in Great Britain
by Amazon